# Terrorism in Paradise

# Terrorism in Paradise

## A Grant Kingsley novel

Bill Fernandez

Photographs and sketches by Judith Fernandez

This is a work of fiction based on historical events and imagined ones. Conversations are the product of the author's imagination. The following are historical figures: Pablo Manlapit, Sun Yat Sen, Syngman Rhee.


ISBN: 9780999032688

Makani Kai Media Publisher
Printed in the United States of America
www.kauaibillfernandez.com
fcb: Bill Fernandez Hawaiian Author
An Approved Kauai Made Product

Typeset by Amnet Systems

# DEDICATION

*I lovingly dedicate this book to*

*my wife,*
***Judith Fernandez,***

*and to the*

*Kauai Filipino Community*

# ACKNOWLEDGMENT

The Hawaiian ethic of family, *ohana*, means no one accomplishes alone. We are who we are today because of who came before us and who are with us along our path of life.

I particularly want to say *mahalo*, thank you, to my teachers, especially those at Kamehameha Schools who turned this barefoot boy into a serious student. Vernon Trimble, my sophomore class advisor, stands out in my memories as a strong influence on me urging me to attend college.

My editor and friend, Bill Bernhardt, taught me about commas and tries to mold me into a good writer.

Many others have helped me in many ways encouraging me to continue writing. Mahalo to the Kauai Historical Society, Kauai Museum, and Kauai libraries and local stores for honoring me by including my books in their publication sales and collections, and inviting me to give book talks. Bill Buley of the *Garden Island Newspaper*, and his wife, Marianne, encourage me in many ways. Thank you to Ed Justus of the Hanapepe Bookstore for invaluable advice, carrying my books, and inviting me to do book signings. To all of the readers of my books, I give a loud *mahalo!* for your keen interest in my writings and your comments.

My fellow Kauai Historical Society board member, Stewart Burley, wrote a college term paper, *Hanapepe Massacre: 9 September 1924*, dated December 2006. He was generous enough to give it to me for this book. He passed on in 2018. I am deeply grateful for his kindness.

Without the encouragement, support, and hard work of editing, design, photography and sketches, publication, and promotion of my writings and book talks by my loving and devoted wife, Judith, I could not have written my books. All the credit for what I have written goes to her.

## Other Works

### NON-FICTION – MEMOIRS

*Rainbows Over Kapaa*
*Kauai Kids in Peace and WW Two*
*Hawaii in War and Peace*

### FICTION

*Splintered Paddle, a novel of Kamehameha the Great*
*Conquest*

### The Grant Kingsley Series:

*Cult of Ku, A Hawaiian Murder Mystery*
*Crime & Punishment in Hawaii*
*Terrorism in Paradise*

### The John Tana Trilogy

*John Tana, An Adventure Novel of Old Hawaii*
*Gods, Ghosts and Kahuna on Kauai*
*Hawaiian Rebellions*

• • •

## *KIRKUS REVIEWS*

NOVELS:

### *Splintered Paddle, a novel of Kamehameha the Great*

"A **historical novel** set during the period of **Kamehameha the Great's battles** to consolidate the Hawaiian Islands stars a **fierce yet tender-hearted young warrior** determined to bring security to his family.

...**1790**, and **17-year-old Kalani** Moku Tana...sent by his mother... to attend **Kamehameha's Pa lua, a military training academy**. He faces **daunting challenges**...His mother warned him: *"...you cannot show ancestry to the gods...will be tested, humiliated. Be Strong*. ***You must become a koa (warrior)*****."** Kalani's father, captured during a battle, was sacrificed to the War god Ku. Gruesome **human** sacrifice...brought to Hawaii by the Tahitians...end of the first millennium A.D. On his first day, Kalani makes one fast **friend, Moki**, and **one very dangerous enemy, Hauna**. Kalani becomes skilled in the use of the Hawaiians' primitive weaponry...also...a **risky romantic liaison** that will cost him dearly...capture of the Western schooner...a new opportunity...**muskets and cannons**. In this **rip-roaring** tale, **Bill Fernandez...has done his research**...narrative is **rich in small details of island life before the impact of Western civilization**... numerous **battle scenes are graphic, bloody** and **riveting...endless intrigue**...**An action-packed adventure, a wealth of historical and cultural minutiae, and an engaging protagonist**." **(Emphasis added.)**

• • •

## The *John Tana* Trilogy

*John Tana: An Adventure Novel of Old Hawaii*
(Book One of *John Tana* novel trilogy)

"…**19th-century Hawaii, historical novel… handsome young hero… hatefully racist time and place…Fernandez *(Cult of Ku, a Hawaiian Murder Mystery…)*** a **native Hawaiian…authentic voice** for John and the Pacific archipelago's **turbulent history. Plot twists** come thick and fast…seductive undercurrent of John's **love** for Leinani…**vivid and intriguing details of Hawaiian daily life in the 19th century ring true**… the striking ending is not tidy, a plus…For the setting and era alone, this **ripping adventure yarn**…" (Emphasis added.)

• • •

*Gods, Ghosts and Kahuna on Kauai*
(Book Two of *John Tana* trilogy)

"…**resourceful Hawaiian John Tana is back**…Hawaii…**political tipping point**…beginning of the end for the Kingdom of Hawaii…**racial tensions…gods and superstition**…festering wound on the marriage…As a Hawaiian, **he wants the respect that he feels he deserves…Hawaiian history and culture…mysteries and terrors of…"old religion"… sketches by Judith Fernandez**…effectively **primitive charm** to the story and bring to mind Antoine de Saint-Exupéry's sketches for ***The Little Prince***." (Emphasis added.)

• • •

### *Hawaiian Rebellions*

(Book Three of the *John Tana* trilogy)

"...wrap-up of a **historical fiction series...19$^{th}$-century Hawaiian freedom fighter**...old loves...familiar hatreds flare**...threats...native religion...danger...kidnapped... sugar baron Robert Grant**...**over-throw...**Hawaiian monarchy...**annexation...by the United States... raped... leper**...**no safety** in this Eden**...save the Kingdom of Hawaii... well-rounded character...Action scenes are Fernandez's forte...**tensions...John's **Christianity and the native religion...trapped...two worlds...hard choice...the realm...born into**...**always be pulling at him...the whole trilogy—is worth a read."** (Emphasis added.)

• • •

## The *GRANT KINGSLEY* Novels

### *Cult of Ku, a Hawaiian Murder Mystery*

(A *Grant Kingsley* novel)

"**Hawaiian history, folklore, and labor struggles...a 1920-set mystery packed with violence and murder**...Grant Kingsley...his **status in his wealthy family...is in question**...**A deathbed confession by his mother**...grandmother...wants to **disinherit** him...found dead...**charges Grant with the murder**...Four more...The **depth** of the author's **historical knowledge** is evident...many **fascinating insights** into the era... explores **cultural conflicts in Hawaii**..."

(Emphasis added.)

• • •

*Crime & Punishment in Hawaii*

(A *Grant Kingsley* novel)

"**An attorney finds trouble in paradise...novel set in Hawaii...skin diving** with his friend...come under fire. Keoki is killed, and Kingsley is left with an **enemy** who vows to **harm his family**...local news...**a different case...the Massie Affair...racial unrest**...story **combines the factual and the fictional** and seasons them with...**gunfire and Hawaiian history**...a **vivid** picture of discord..." (Emphasis added.)

• • •

**MEMOIRS**

*KIRKUS REVIEWS:*

*Kauai Kids in Peace and WW Two,*

*a memoir*

"**1930s and 40s Hawaii...childhood...Kauai** isolated...**multiracial**... poor families share...large **Japanese** population...gives **marine life glorious** coverage...does his best to avoid **sharks...Part II: War...Pearl Harbor and its aftermath**...overt **racism**...engaging **tales of innocence and worldly wisdom**...father opens the **Roxy Theater**..." (Emphasis added.)

• • •

*Hawaii in War and Peace,*

*a memoir*

"...**military school in Honolulu...1944...war...** ...the war was over, **Hawaii remained at unrest...worker's strike, tsunami...toured the**

**mainland** U.S. with his family...a **nation with unbridled prejudices**... **riveting** account of...a world in disarray...the **grandest impression is the more personal side**...mistake him for a **Mexican**, mistreating him... which of the **segregated restrooms** he could use...**Engrossing** and identifiable." (Emphasis added.)

• • •

## Other Reviews

### *Rainbows Over Kapaa*, a memoir

"...spent his **childhood barefoot**, cutting **sugar**, **diving**...**surfing**... **Stanford University**...the **history** of the Hawaiian Islands from a Kauaian perspective...**people from all over the world**... **Fernandez family, Kapaa and its Roxy Theater**...popular movie house...**World War II troops**... **on Kauai**...**story of the theater...intertwined with...the Fernandez family**...Hawaiian words...mingled with English...**Aloha feeling**,...**remarkable collection of pictures...**Kapaa through the years...**a diverse community can live in harmony**..."

*San Jose [CA] Mercury News Review* (Emphasis added.)

# TERRORISM IN PARADISE

Manila, 1924

Miguel smoothed his fingers over the oiled-sleek surface of his Mosin-Nagant. He loved this weapon that he won as first prize in marksmanship at the CHEKA School of terrorism in Moscow. An infantry man's rifle, if you added a scope, turned into a long-range sniper's gun. Tonight, it is a grenade launcher.

For many hours, he had practiced hurling the metal-covered TNT at targets as far away as two hundred yards. Miguel knew the dynamics of spin for accuracy, trajectory to compensate for the effects of gravity, and speed. All three are vital, but velocity is the key. Once fired, the grenade must reach its target in less than eight seconds, or it would explode without killing.

He watched the lackeys of imperialistic America. They felt secure in the grand room of their precinct outpost. *Why wouldn't they*? A concrete wall protected the military structure. Trees and shrubs had been cleared up to a hundred-fifty yards from the building. A searchlight panned over the empty ground, its brightness dissipating as it reached the heavy jungle foliage.

Miguel intended to drop his explosive through one of the open windows of the grand room where the soldiers were playing at cards, dice, or simply reading. They would feel the pain that he had carried since he was nine years old when the American General Smith had ordered that all Filipinos beyond the age of ten were to be killed. He had watched his mother and father shot and hacked to death as he and his brother hid in the jungle.

Somehow, the two of them had managed to survive, thanks to Christian missionaries that had taken pity on them. Because Miguel had proved to be very bright, he had been well schooled and graduated from the university at nineteen. But he was not satisfied to be just a clerk in an office of the corrupt Philippine Government. Russia had undergone a revolution. Lenin had decreed a new Soviet state dedicated to ending imperialism. Miguel fled Manila for Canton, China, and the Communist Third International in 1920.

By stealth and fighting, he worked his way into the meetings that denounced colonialism and pledged war against capitalism. His genius and revolutionary fervor shone, and he was recruited to be trained as a terrorist.

As Miguel sighted his rifle, he thought: *"I'm not a terrorist, but a freedom fighter. A warrior against America for the hundreds of thousands of Filipinos they have killed."* Tonight, he would strike his first blow for freedom.

With great care Miguel judged the distance from a spot one-hundred-and-seventy-five yards from his target window. He attached the launching mechanism and grenade to the front of his rifle. He tossed dried leaves into the air to check the wind and its velocity. What he threw fluttered slowly to the earth. Perfect conditions.

He placed the butt of his Mosin-Nagant onto the ground and adjusted its angle. He didn't like its position. With a sigh he raised the rifle and rested it against his shoulder. It was difficult to shoot this way, because the gun's powerful recoil could knock him to the ground. But to have the best result he must plant his feet firmly into the soil and aim through the scope.

Laughter from the grand room flowed out the windows. Lights revealed at least a dozen soldiers. Miguel aimed just above the top sill of a window. He slowly squeezed the trigger. The cartridge ignited, spinning the bullet through the rifle and grenade. The exploding gasses shot the projectile toward its target.

Miguel fell backward into a tree. He heard an explosion. Screams burst from the grand room. A direct hit. He hoped many of the imperialists had died. He shouldered his weapon and melted into the forest.

As he worked his way through the brush, he wondered how his brother fared in a plantation in Hawaii. Life there is harsh, controlled by the overlords like a feudal kingdom. *The workers needed to be freed of their shackles by a revolution.*

# CHAPTER 1

Honolulu, 1924

Grant Kingsley fought to control his temper. His brother David ranted how his "coddling" of the Japanese had cost the family plantations thousands of dollars.

"The sugar people have been calling you a 'Mikado lover.' That you have sold out to the yellow peril," David shouted.

Grant glanced at his father seated in the armchair to his left. The older man's fingers touched together in the universal sign of prayer. His face mirrored distress, his brow furrowed like a plowed field.

Without waiting for a response from his Dad, Grant launched into his answer. "The plantation elite have no one to blame for their troubles than themselves. Instead of treating workers with decency all they want to do is squeeze the last ounce of labor from them, all in the name of profits. Instead of negotiation, they hire strike breakers. They bring in new races to divide the work force, Koreans, Filipinos. When the Filipinos turned militant the Big Five asked Congress to repeal the Chinese Exclusion Act to cause more trouble for the Japanese and further unrest."

"There you go again, siding with the agitators. We are called to a meeting today by a committee of the Hawaiian Sugar Planters Association, the HSPA. All because of your liberal attitudes and how it has affected our plantation operations." David turned to his father. "Dad, if we don't correct our business plan, the HSPA will shut us down. We will lose everything!"

James Kingsley sighed and gripped his fingers together. "Your grandfather, who established much of what we own, was a hard man. He believed in profits above all no matter the cost to the working man. But as he lay dying in the hospital, he confided to me that he wished he had lived more like your mother. She was an angel, always did good things for others, especially the poor. For years, bless her heart, she worked at the hospital without compensation. Whenever people could not afford care, she paid for it. I think your grandfather realized at the end, that greed is not the key to heaven."

"Dad, what does that have to do with our present situation where we are faced with the wrath of the HSPA for our liberal attitude toward the workers?"

"It explains why I have sided with your brother in the great strike of 1920 when twelve thousand Japanese were kicked out of their homes by the plantations. Many died from privation and the Spanish flu that killed your mother. It is why I sided with him in the recent strike where Filipino workers sought pay the same as other plantation laborers and a forty-hour work week."

"Then we have no hope of saving our plantations if we remain adamant in being benevolent to the Asian races," David said in a sarcastic tone.

"Don't be pessimistic. Let's hear what the HSPA committee has to say. It may be that you are wrong. It is possible we could persuade those in power to be kinder to their workers.

"I agree with what Dad has said. Treating men like slaves will not bring labor peace. I think there is a new era dawning in the world where the working man cannot be considered merely a tool to produce wealth."

"All I can say is that these high-sounding words are a bunch of claptrap. We're going to lose if we don't knuckle under to what the power brokers want. Okay, let's go and face our doom."

# CHAPTER 2

The three Kingsley men entered the Honolulu offices of the Hawaii Sugar Planters Association. One of the secretaries behind a curved counter rose from her desk. Grant noted the sparse surroundings of the reception room. There were no pictures on the walls. The office furniture was utilitarian, not ostentatious.

"What can I do for you gentlemen?"

"We have an appointment with Mr. Patterson," James Kingsley answered.

"Who should I say is calling?"

"David, Grant, and I, James Kingsley."

"Be seated, you are expected."

He watched the woman go through a door into an inner area. She seemed too formal, Grant thought. But maybe he was being edgy about this meeting. What the HSPA wanted was not important to him. He had a thriving law practice and did not need the money that their two plantations produced. His brother concerned him, and made him uncomfortable. After college, David had put his entire working life into the family business. *It's the stress of losing what they have that makes him angry and willing to do whatever the HSPA demanded.*

The receptionist returned. "The committee is waiting for you. Enter this door, down the hallway, turn right into the main conference room."

As they stood, Grant whispered to his father, "Not very friendly, Patterson didn't come out to greet us and show us in."

"Don't be pessimistic."

"I am," David interrupted. "I feel like I'm about to face a den of lions."

"If they growl at you growl back." Grant laughed.

"Let's hope we find a friend in this room," James sighed as they walked in.

Large picture windows faced out to the street. Grant could see the harbor of Honolulu on the left. Across the roadway a three-story building bordered the avenue. Pictures of plantation life filled the walls: mills smoking burnt cane waste; molasses cooking; trains chugging through forests; men working in the fields loading cane onto wagons.

Two dark brown tables set in T fashion lay centered in the room with a couch along a back wall. At the top end of the T sat three men. They looked like a triumvirate at a court martial. Along the stem of the T were several dark brown wooden chairs with the seat backs and bottoms cushioned in black.

Grant saw the man in the center of the group stand. Without smiling he said, "Welcome, Mr. Kingsley. I gather these are your sons. I am Earl Patterson. Let me introduce John Doolittle on my right and on the left, Abraham Marston."

"Thank you for your welcome, my sons Grant and David Kingsley."

"Gentlemen, be seated, please."

James Kingsley took a seat closest to the picture windows. David sat at the foot of the T and Grant placed himself next to his brother. He watched the three HSPA men, noting that Marston and Doolittle did not welcome them. From reports he had received these two men wanted to continue the divide and rule technique of the plantations and suppress any strikes with force. It was rumored that Patterson had armed with rifles the forty strike breakers involved in the Hanapepe massacre.

Patterson folded his hands, looked down at the table and abruptly looked up. "Thank you for coming to this meeting. I trust that you understand why this HSPA committee has asked you here. You have broken ranks with your fellow sugar planters. In the Japanese strike of 1920, you would not turn them out of their homes like the rest of us did. That indiscretion we overlooked at the time. In the dynamiting trial of the fifteen Japanese labor leaders you gave them financial aid."

"I did not," David interrupted. "To my knowledge, neither did my father. My brother Grant did it. He favors the Japanese."

"I'll admit I helped some of the accused dynamiters fight the prosecution," Grant said.

"It is my understanding that you also paid for the appeal of those convicted," Patterson answered.

"I was approached to help finance the effort, but I did not contribute."

"All right, you have corrected me, but didn't you and your family assist the Filipinos in this latest strike that has now been concluded successfully by the HSPA?"

Grant could not control his anger. "This 1924 labor strike ended in blood by the use of deadly force. Outside the Hanapepe schoolhouse, sixteen Visayan men were gunned down, several shot in the back as they ran away from the confrontation. You caused the governor to send two machine gun squads of the National Guard to Kauai. They threatened the strikers in Hanapepe and Kapaa town with their .30 caliber rapid fire weapons. At least a hundred Filipinos have been arrested and are on trial for criminal acts. I think all of this could have been avoided if the HSPA had used some compassion in considering their pleas for democracy, equal treatment, and fair play. Instead of negotiation with the union you dealt with the strike like a revolution."

"Are you accusing us of instigating this massacre?" Marston blustered. "You very well know that a special mediator appointed by the governor of the Philippines found that these malcontents were unstable, preferring to be gamblers and con men instead of performing good work. He reported that the plantations provided wholesome working conditions and decent wages."

"If that were all true, why are there so many deaths among Filipino laborers?" Grant responded.

"Just a minute," David interrupted. "My brother and I do not agree on the issue of labor strife in the plantations. I take the side of the HSPA and will do what you want us to do."

"I will not," Grant answered. "I do not accept unfair treatment of the working man."

"You don't understand our problem. There are over a hundred thousand Japanese and Filipinos in Hawaii. If we are not careful, they will take over the government," Marston cautioned.

"And your answer has been to lobby Congress to end the Chinese Exclusion Act so you can dilute our population with other Asians. All you succeeded in doing is cause the passage of the Alien Exclusion Act barring all Japanese from entering American soil. This has led to a threat of war from Japan."

"Mister Kingsley, you do not understand the fragility of the Hawaiian economy. We are dependent on sugar to keep these islands moving forward in an extremely competitive world," Patterson said, pounding his table furiously. "We are barely able to hold our own with Cuba that produces a pound of sugar for five cents, the same as we do. How do we do this? By keeping our labor costs at rock bottom. With restive Japanese and now the Filipinos wanting more money we needed to get the Chinese back into Hawaii who will work for less than those brown people."

"Well, there you have it!" Grant shouted. "You prefer to exploit poor Asians for the sake of profits! That's the easy solution. Why don't you use science to enhance your production? My wife, who is an expert in botany, has shown my family how to increase sugar cane yield per acre. Why don't you follow this approach to making profits instead of refusing to be fair to the working man!"

"Damnation," Patterson swore. "You sound like one of those yellow-bellied union agitators."

"I am—"

"Gentlemen," James Kingsley interrupted. "I'm sorry to see this meeting descending into turmoil. Let me excuse my sons and continue our conversation without them. You two, wait in the reception room."

As Grant left, he saw his father stand and move closer to the picture window. He felt frustrated. His outbursts had sidetracked the HSPA committee away from their intended goal. He knew what they wanted, "conform with the rest of us or be destroyed."

When they entered the reception room David backed away from Grant and said, "You did a great job messing things up in there. I don't think Dad can patch—"

*The sound of shattering glass followed by a blast that shook the building, screams, shouts, and acrid smoke filled the hallway through the broken door blasted off its hinges. Grant's ears rang from the concussion of the blast as he and his brother dashed into the smoky room and saw only two men. They stepped over the broken chairs as they made their way to their father, face down on the floor by the shattered windows, a pool of blood expanding around him. He was silent. Glass crunched under their shoes as they rushed to their father.*

The two brothers rushed to his side. Grant turned his father over and saw the front of his suit shredded and saturated with blood. Grant checked his pulse. He leaned over listening at his bloody nose. Tears welled in his eyes. "David, Father is dead."

From the end table Patterson raised himself. Blood covered his face from a gash in his brow. "It's those damn Japanese dynamiters who did this."

# CHAPTER 3

Grant waited for a report from the Queen's Hospital Emergency Room doctors. He knew there was nothing medicine could do to save him. Dad died at the scene.

By his side, his older brother kept repeating, "It's those damned Japanese dynamiters who killed him."

"I don't know who did it, but I swear to you, I will find the killers and see them hanged."

Marston, laying on a stretcher nearby, with his beard shaved off and a nasty facial cut being stitched, said loudly, "You need look no further than the fifteen convicted Japanese dynamiters. They have a big grudge against the HSPA. They are the ones who did it."

"Aha," a soft voice from just inside the emergency room interrupted. "You have identified the bombers. Did you see who did it?"

"And who the hell are you, a Chinese devil?" Marston bellowed.

"You owe the man an apology," Grant answered. "This is Detective Asing of the Honolulu Police, an excellent officer. He and I have worked together in the past."

"I should have known the department would send us an Oriental. They don't have any white men working there," Patterson complained.

"In that, you are wrong," Grant answered. "The higher command is white. Don't be put off by the color of his skin. Asing is the best investigator the Honolulu police have."

"Thank you for clearing the air about my capabilities. Let me ask where each of you were when the bombing occurred?"

"My brother and I were outside in the reception area. My father, Mr. Marston, being stitched, Mr. Patterson, on the gurney, and Mr. Doolittle were in the conference room," Grant answered.

"Mr. Marston, you said 'Japanese dynamiters' are the culprits. Did you see anyone throw explosives into the room?"

"Everything happened so fast. I'm still in shock. My memory is hazy. It must have been the Japanese. They have a grudge against us. It has to be them."

"But did you see anyone throw an object into the room?"

"I saw no one," Patterson interrupted. "There were no pedestrians on the street. No one opened the door to throw dynamite in."

Marston nodded. "I'll think about it more when I feel better, but for now I'm forced to agree with Earl."

"And where is Mr. Doolittle?"

"I think he's upstairs getting patched up. He got hit hard by the explosion. I'm told he will live," Patterson said.

"And your father?" Asing looked at Grant.

"He's upstairs too." Tears welled in Grant's eyes. "I- I-think he is dead."

"I'm sorry I caused you pain. Mr. Marston, Mr. Patterson, can you tell me what happened?"

"Mr. Kingsley stood near the windows. We three were seated at the long table. Suddenly glass shattered. Within seconds something flew in. All three of us dove to the floor. An explosion rocked the room. The table saved us, but Mr. Kingsley took the brunt of the blast."

"Can you describe what came in?"

"Everything happened fast. I closed my eyes because of the breaking glass. I don't know."

"Mr. Marston?"

"I concur with what Earl said. Things happened quickly."

"And you two Kingsleys were in the reception area when the blast occurred. What did you do and see?"

"We rushed down the hall and entered the conference room," Dave answered. "Smoke filled it. I thought the smell was like rotten bananas. My head ached. Dad lay on the floor. Tables and chairs were thrown by the explosion. The three HSPA men were trying to stand."

"We went to Dad first, to check his condition," Grant interrupted. "Once I knew the truth Dave and I helped the three men. The windows were broken. I looked outside and saw no one on the street."

"Did any of you receive death warnings before the explosion?"

All four agreed there had been none. Nor threats of any kind.

"Then we go upstairs and check on Mr. Doolittle and Kingsley."

"We were told to remain downstairs," Grant said.

"This is a police matter. Time is of the essence."

"My brother and I are going with you."

On the second floor of the hospital medical staff barred them from visiting the two injured men. Asing showed his badge, told of the bombing, and stated his need to investigate. His demands got him through security, but Grant and David could not go beyond the reception desk.

David huddled in a chair, occasionally wiping tears from his eyes. Grant tried to comfort him, but he wanted to be left alone, and burst out, "You caused Dad's death."

Grant moved away from him, stifling an angry retort, and found a quiet place to sit and wait. He grieved. He loved his Dad. He recalled the time his mother's death bed letter suggested another man was his father. James Kingsley had refused to reject him even though there were doubts. David looked like Dad Kingsley, but Grant did not. His features were like his mother and everyone said she was an extraordinary beauty. His hair dark and wavy, his eyes brown, and with too much sun, his skin darkened rapidly.

He was born when David turned eighteen. His sister was fifteen. At the time James Kingsley boasted about his virility. But grandfather's wife, Sheila, doubted his ability. "I think someone else is the father," she claimed.

Everyone knew she hated Grant's mother, Leinani, because she was one-half Hawaiian. "Trollops," she called all native women. Her views were suppressed by the family only to be resurrected again by the death bed letter.

Asing walked back into the reception room. For several moments he stood silent, then said, "Doolittle has nothing to add to what we already know."

"What about our father?" David asked, his voice shaking with emotion.

Asing grimaced, "You already know the answer. He is gone forever."

"No, no it can't be," David shouted, his outburst startling several nurses.

"Please be quiet you will frighten sick people," a hospital aide said.

"Get ahold of yourself, 'bro." Grant reached out to comfort his distraught brother.

"Stay away from me. You killed Dad. Let me grieve on my own." David stalked out of the reception room.

Grant dropped his arms. His chin sunk to his chest. He felt lost. He suffered as much as his brother, maybe more.

Asing, silent while the emotions stirred the room, stepped over to Grant. "I have one more puzzling piece of information to add to this calamity. From your father's side doctors removed this lump of metal. It isn't a bullet. I have not seen anything similar to this before."

Grant held the object in his hand studying it. "It's not a rock and certainly not a piece of dynamite. Let me take it to one of my military friends to identify what it is."

"Yes, keep it safe. It may be an important clue to unravel this murder."

# CHAPTER 4

Exhausted, bewildered by his brother's anger, Grant arrived home. His four-year old son, playing with blocks in the hallway, spied him, leaped up, whooped, and ran to him.

Grant scooped up little Dan, hugged and kissed him. The child did the same, wrapping his tiny arms around his father's neck and giving him a squeeze. "Whoa, whoa, big guy, not so hard."

"Happy see you."

"Me too," Grant answered, his pain easing as the love of his son comforted him. He set the boy down on the floor. Dan turned and ran toward the kitchen hollering, "Daddy's home."

Grant hung his coat in the hall closet and placed his hat on a hook. His wife, Selena, entered the hallway, an apron wrapped around her slender body. She came to him, a happy smile on her face. "Hi, Handsome." Grant took her in his arms, kissing her passionately.

As she pulled away from his embrace, Selena whispered, "Darling, let's save the love for later. Not now in front of Daniel."

"I'm sorry to squeeze so hard. It's been a difficult day. Dad is dead, murdered, and my brother blames me for it."

"Oh, oh! That's horrible! My poor darling, what happened?"

Grant sighed, stepped back from Selena, taking her hands in his. "It's hard to begin, but Dad and I have been lenient toward the Japanese and Filipino workers at our two plantations. The HSPA believes in tough treatment. Dave supports them. Today we were called into the business office of the association. You need to be aware that twenty-one

Japanese were indicted for dynamiting property at the Olaa Plantation after the 1920 strike. Fifteen Japanese union leaders were convicted and imprisoned.

"Dad, David, and I went into an HSPA conference room. Three of their leaders were sitting there. I'm sure they were ready to skin us alive. I got into a heated discussion with one of the men about fair treatment for workers. David took the side of the HSPA. Dad ordered us out of the room. After we left, there was an explosion. We rushed back in. Dad was on the floor, covered in blood. Patterson, an HSPA guy, yelled 'The Japanese dynamiters did this'. Though I believed Dad was gone we took him to the hospital."

Grant paused, took a deep breath, tears welled in his eyes. "Asing went to talk to the doctors. When he came back and confirmed my father was dead, David lost it. That's when he accused me of killing Dad. You can't possibly know how much—" Selena came to Grant and folded him into her bosom. His body shook in her arms as he sobbed. "David's wrong. You would never harm your father."

Grant raised his head from her shoulder. "David believes Patterson said it right, and my helping the Japanese caused them to attack today."

"Whoa, he put one and one together and came up with murder by the Japanese!"

"I'm not sure of your meaning, but yes, David is twisting facts and is blaming me for the end result."

Daniel came up to the couple and tugged on Selena's apron, "Me hungry."

"Baby, the right way to say it is, 'Mom, I am hungry'. Okay, scoot to your chair at the table and I'll get you some food. Grant, wash up, we will talk more later."

Grant couldn't eat, his mind in turmoil. He felt sick and thought he would lose whatever he ate. He watched Daniel shoveling in his food. *At least my boy is not aware of the trouble, he thought. Let's hope we can keep it that way.* After dinner Grant supervised his bath and helped Dan into his pajamas. They said prayers and the little boy slipped into bed. Grant kissed him and turned the lights out.

He joined Selena on a settee in the living room. For many minutes he sat silent, his only action the gentle rubbing of her back and shoulders.

"What is troubling you?" she asked.

"I have to find the murderers of my father and somehow win back my brother's love."

"It's the job of the police to solve crime, not you."

"I promised my brother I would find who did it and see them hanged. Maybe if I do so he will soften, apologize, and we can be a family again."

"But your brother is so wrong for blaming you for what happened."

"Like everything in families, it goes deeper than what happened today. I never grew up with David. When I was born, he left for college. As I got older, he remained away on the mainland. When he finally came back, he went off to Maui to run our plantation there. I hardly knew him. Matters got a little sticky during the 1920 strike. Dad sided with me as to what to do with the workers. David felt I was being coddled. In an argument he said I had been Mom's favorite child and got everything I wanted. Now Dad was treating me in the same way in our dealings with the strike."

"You're suggesting that there is sibling rivalry that made him accuse you of the murder of your father?"

"I know he's upset about Dad's death, but to blame me for it? His anger must have been smoldering long before the explosion today."

"Assuming that is true, my darling, together we will win back his love. But why do you have to find the killers?"

"Don't you see? Maybe it wasn't the Japanese or even the Filipinos that caused the attack. Maybe it was someone else. I have to find out the truth."

Selena kissed him with a passion that overwhelmed him. After some moments she whispered, "I will help you in any way that I can."

# CHAPTER 5

Grant walked into his King Street office and found his law partner Joshua Kanakoa waiting for him. The elderly man said, "I'm very saddened by your father's death, my deepest sympathy to you and your family. Despite the turmoil you must be in, I would like you to sit in on this meeting I am involved in this morning."

"Is it that important?"

"Can't say for sure, but it could shed some light on the labor strife we are having, and possibly why the attack on the HSPA office occurred. I also need your wisdom. Ah, look who is coming through the door. Aloha, Charles. This is my law partner, Grant Kingsley. Grant, meet Charles Robinson, editor of the Japanese newspaper, the *Hinode Times.*"

As the men shook hands the office door opened, and a tall Hawaiian entered the reception room. "*Aloha ou kou,* Solomon," Joshua said. "Gentlemen, meet *Alii* Solomon Kama of the Royal Society of Chiefs of Hawaii. Sol, my partner, Grant Kingsley, and this is Charles Robinson of the *Hinode Times.* Gentlemen, come to our all-purpose room. The secretary will take your orders for coffee, tea, water, and she will serve some sushi."

Once everyone settled into their chairs set along a narrow rectangular table, Joshua said, "Let me explain why we are here. Recently, Sol came to me regarding an article in the *Hinode Times.* It was critical of our late Congressman, Prince Kuhio. It called him a "toady" of the sugar plantations and a legislator who failed to represent the Japanese in Hawaii during the recent Congressional hearings on the Exclusion Act. The article went on to say that Hawaiians must support the labor unions in their efforts to secure fairness for the working man. The *Times* called on the Royal Society to take a leadership role in ensuring equal rights for all races in Hawaii.

"Since I knew the owner of the *Hinode Times*, Sol prevailed upon me to set up this meeting with him. I'm just a facilitator, not an advocate for any cause. Mr. Publisher, the floor is yours."

Robinson glanced at Grant. "I heard of the death of your father. Let me express my deepest sympathy. Rumor has it that Japanese dynamiters did the attack. Let me assure you that is not true."

"Thanks for your kind words. Unfortunately, the HSPA considers the Japanese responsible for what happened," Grant said.

"That is one of the reasons I agreed to this meeting. Alii Kama, or may I just call you Sol?" Robinson asked.

"Eh, you guys can call me Sol. No need formalities. We *kukakuka* the Hawaiian way."

"He means we conference like family solving a problem," Joshua interrupted.

"I'm for that, but what I may say could be disagreeable. Let me get to the point of our meeting. The Japanese community needs the help of the Hawaiians in these troublesome times," Robinson said.

"Why come to us? We're a society established during the Hawaiian monarchy to honor the high chiefs, the man who united all the islands into one kingdom, Kamehameha, and to preserve our culture. We are not a political organization," Sol protested.

"But you are an organization of the last surviving chiefs. In ancient times these men were obeyed."

"No way, not anymore. Hawaiians don't want to make waves. They want to be left alone. Just complain about the plantations taking the land, but take no action."

"And that is the problem. For half a century you have allowed the few who dominate the islands to make laws and rules that inflict upon the native people a disease of inferiority, inequality, and powerlessness. This illness has become entrenched in Hawaiian minds, so they become accommodating to haole control and give up their political power to them. Instead of speaking out against this dominance Hawaiians find comfort in a sub-culture of complaints against western ways that has only resulted in low social and economic status and educational under-achievement."

"Whoa there, that is a powerful condemnation of my people," Joshua interjected.

"You can't ignore the truth," Robinson answered. "Not too long ago, Hawaiians were twenty percent of the population. European-Americans, twenty-three percent. Japanese, a startling forty-one-and-a-half percent. Combine those two races together you could control the government. Instead, Kuhio joined forces with Euro-Americans and suppressed the Asians. Your Prince caused the trouble that the Japanese are facing today."

"I don't understand this accusation," Sol answered.

"The sugar plantations wanted Congress to repeal the Chinese Exclusion Act of 1882. They intended in this way to replace Japanese workers, who have been striking for fair wages and working conditions, with cheap Chinese labor."

"So?"

"Hawaii's representative in Congress was Kuhio. He claimed: 'The control of Hawaii has been the Japanese objective for many years. His proof was the dual citizenship of Japanese in Hawaii. He blamed Congress for allowing Japanese to be imported to these islands. In my opinion the implication of his protests was that Hawaiians did not want Japanese in Hawaii. You know the results of his claims, the Japanese Exclusion Act of 1924."

"Oh, wait a moment," Grant interjected. "People on the mainland and especially in California were afraid of Japanese immigration to the continent. There was a 'Yellow Peril' hysteria in America. State laws were passed to suppress the Japanese and prevent them from owning land. American labor came out against any further Chinese or Japanese immigration. A Congressman pointed out that the Japanese were incapable of assimilation. The *coup de grace* came when a Japanese statesman wrote a letter to the Secretary of State threatening war. Congress passed the Exclusion Act right after that."

"Despite what you say, Kuhio was not a friend of the Japanese in Hawaii, who were his constituents. Instead, he worked in Washington as a tool of the sugar plantations and did their bidding," Robinson asserted.

"How can you say that? We Hawaiians are grateful to him for passing the Hawaiian Homes Act allowing natives of fifty-percent *koko* to receive homestead land," Sol protested.

"How naïve you people are. The only reason the bill got through Congress is that the sugar plantations pushed it. Why? Because the Organic Act of 1900 creating the Territory of Hawaii required termination of leases made during the Republic of agricultural land and opening these properties to public use. By the provisions of the Hawaiian Homes Act, prime sugar cane land could be retained by the plantations virtually in perpetuity at ridiculously low rent. Hawaiians will never see homesteads. Congress never appropriated money for poor people to build any kind of native community."

"What are you seeking from the Hawaiian people?" Joshua asked.

"The members of the Royal Order are the last dynastic chiefs of the Hawaiian monarchy. In ancient times, the Hawaiians obeyed their chiefs. I'm asking the Royal Order to join with the Japanese, the other people of color, and seek change in Hawaii. Together, we can break the one-party control by the sugar industry of island government. Together, we can create better working conditions for the common laborer. Together, we can elect a representative to Congress who will champion funding for Hawaiian Homes and end the plantation theft of Hawaiian lands. Unified, we can break the chains that bind working people created by the ruling elite, and achieve equality and freedom."

Sol exhaled loudly. "It is a huge request that you are making. I can take what you say back to my board. I don't know what they will do. Maybe we could arrange to have you speak to the membership of the Order."

"With that suggestion, gentlemen, I think the purpose of this meeting is over," Joshua said. "If I can be of further assistance please let me know."

Grant approached Robinson. "You seem to know a lot about what is going on within the Japanese community. They are very clannish. I'm wondering if you can help me. I'm seeking information about the attack on the HSPA office. It's been suggested that the Japanese are responsible. Can you prove or disprove that claim?"

Robinson became defensive. "What are you talking about? Are you suggesting that I had something to do with what happened? I know nothing and do not intend to be involved. Goodbye!"

Grant shook his head as he watched the two men leave. He turned to Joshua. "I guess I stuck my foot into a mud hole and just made an enemy."

Joshua pursed his lips and thought for a moment. "There is an old proverb: 'He who protests too much has something to hide'. That man bears watching."

"Why were you so abrupt in closing the meeting?"

"I thought Robinson's words bordered on sedition. I wanted to get away from treasonous talk before some do-gooder reported us to the police."

"That was wise of you. But I have to admit that the man is right. If Hawaiians don't get involved in politics, they will remain marginalized. They will just be complainers and troublemakers. Do you think the Royal Order will step to the plate and become a force for political change?"

Joshua emitted a huge sigh. "So far they seem only interested in attending events in their dark suits and royal capes. If you play it safe and go with the establishment you can't get hurt."

A secretary approached Grant. "Detective Asing wants you at the HSPA office as soon as possible."

# CHAPTER 6

Robinson hurried to his office. He felt frustrated with his meeting with Sol. The man seemed lukewarm to his suggestions. How to help Hawaiians overcome oppression appeared to be a very difficult task. He entered his private room and found his Filipino comrade working on a poster.

"*Privyet.*"

"I wish you would not use Russian words. I'm American. I speak English and you also. We do not want people to know that there may be Russian agitators in Hawaii," Robinson complained.

"My pardon, Excellency, I wanted to give you a cheerful "hello" in a language that all believers in Communism speak."

"You meant well, but we have not yet converted people here to the cause. Trotsky's demand for world-wide revolution has frightened the capitalists and led to severe repression in America. We dare not openly speak of our great goal, a classless society, or appear to be Bolsheviks in any way."

"I understand your concern; Hawaii is not yet ready for a revolution."

"There, you have it. I'm sure you remember what happened in your islands when the Philippines revolted against American Imperialism."

"I was a child. Did not know what was going on. My older brother and I were told to run into the jungle. I watched the rest of my family chopped to pieces by those filthy khaki soldiers."

"It is a pity that supreme tragedy came to you so young in life. But you can appreciate the results of a failed revolution, nearly 250,000 of your countrymen were butchered by Americans before the revolt ended. That is why we must exercise patience in what we do here."

"It is difficult for me to wait. Hawaii is much like the Philippines. Land there is owned by a few. The owners milk the poor farmers for all they can get. The government is corrupt, controlled by a small group of rich people. Like my homeland, deadly force is used here to keep the working man enslaved."

"You are speaking of the recent massacre in Hanapepe?"

"Yes, many Filipinos killed, many wounded. That is not all, a hundred of my people will be sent to prison. None of the plantation murderers will be punished. My brother was shot in the back! The Planters Association must pay for this!"

Robinson fell silent for some moments as he watched his comrade shaking and tears streaming from his eyes. "I did not know your brother died in the massacre. Let me express my sympathy—"

"He was the last of my family! I have no one left! Revenge is what I want, an eye for an eye!"

"Wait just a moment! You were sent to me by the party in the Philippines. You are to aid me in convincing the workers in Hawaii to join our movement. We cannot have a private vendetta sidetracking our important work of freeing the proletariat from their enslavement by the rich plantation owners. Hmm, I met a Mr. Kingsley today. Were you the cause of his father's death?"

"No, no, I had nothing to do with that incident."

Robinson studied his comrade closely. A medium sized young man, slightly built, his face still wet. Could he believe him? With a sigh he said, "It's important that you understand your role here. It is to convince people that **Capitalism is evil, and Imperialism must be overthrown**."

"Yes, yes, I understand."

"Good. Now go out and deliver your messages."

"*Dasvidaniya.*"

Robinson threw up his hands. "Say goodbye in English!"

## CHAPTER 7

David Kingsley stood outside the HSPA office. Grant noticed that he didn't wave or acknowledge his presence in anyway as he parked his automobile. "How are you?" he asked.

"Don't want to talk to you."

"I cabled Dorothy yesterday that Dad is dead."

"Yes, she knows. I talked with her this morning by long distance telephone. She is shocked by what happened. They're planning to come to Honolulu. She thinks it will be ten to twelve days before they can get here."

"Steve and the boys coming?"

"I think Jason, but not Jasper. He can't get out of college without hurting his chances to graduate."

"With that long a wait it will have to be a closed casket funeral."

"I can't deal with it. You take care of everything." David walked into the HSPA office.

Grant shook his head. A major rift had developed between them. Nothing good could come of it. *I don't know what to do to close the gap dividing me and my brother. Maybe when she comes, my sister Dorothy can help. They grew up together. She probably understands David better than I do.*

Asing strolled along the sidewalk and walked leisurely up to Grant. "Beautiful day, it's unusually mild weather for November."

"Balmy air, soft tropical breezes, and a gentle rustling of the coco leaves, who could ask for anything more, this is paradise." Grant answered.

"It will soon be turned into turmoil as we investigate the crime. Come, let's go in."

Patterson came out to the reception room. "Welcome, I'm happy to see you Detective Asing. Doolittle is still in the hospital, but Marston is here and David Kingsley of course."

*What a cordial welcome*, Grant thought. *It is very unlike yesterday when he seemed insulted to have an Asian investigating the crime. He's up to something.*

"May we examine the scene of the explosion?"

"Yes, come this way."

When they entered the conference room Asing shook his head. "The place is cleaned up. Wasn't there debris everywhere? Shreds of explosive material lying about? Walls smeared with black soot?"

"You may be right," Patterson agreed. "I don't know. After the blast I felt dazed, disoriented, my mind couldn't focus on the surroundings. Marston fainted and Doolittle, I'm told, was knocked out."

"What about you, Grant, and David?"

"I think what you describe fits what I saw," Dave answered. "I couldn't give you any more details.

"Neither can I. All I could think about was getting my father to a hospital." Grant paused. "I smelled rotten bananas in the room. A stink like exploded shells on a Great War battlefield."

"There you have it!" Patterson bellowed. "It's one of those convicted Japanese union leaders that tossed dynamite into this room. Arrest them for murder. Interrogate them, you'll find the killer."

"You can't arrest people based on suspicion without proof. Aren't you picking on Japanese because they led strikes against the plantations?" Grant said.

"I must agree with him. None of you saw anyone hurl dynamite into this room. On what basis do I arrest any Japanese?" Asing said.

"If you don't do something to stop these people from bombing the plantations, the HSPA will," Patterson threatened.

"Let's not add vigilante justice to the mistakes plantation management has made in dealing with labor unrest. My brother and I have suffered the most from this incident. I swore to him and I swear to you I will track down these killers and see them brought to trial. Give me the chance to do so," Grant begged.

"I agree. My department will do everything necessary to solve this crime."

Patterson pursed his lips. He stared at Marston who nodded. "Alright, The HSPA will not act at this time. But our patience is short. I expect progress reports. This gathering is over!"

# CHAPTER 8

Asing and Grant walked out of the HSPA building. "We should begin our work right now," the detective whispered.

Grant watched his brother leave without a word being said by him. He grieved that there existed this gap between them, widening and unbridgeable. Asing tugged at his sleeve. "Shall we start our investigation?"

"Sorry. Yes, let's begin."

"HSPA office is on Richard Street near the ocean. I judge the distance between it and the building across the street is fifty to sixty yards. There are sidewalks on both sides of Richard. There are no obstructions between the windows and the street. None of those in the room saw anyone on the sidewalk, nor any autos traveling the street. Weather was like today, clear and sunny. Where did the dynamite come from?"

"That is the puzzle. There are no shrubs for someone to hide behind. Could the killer have been on the corner of that building across the street and hurled his sticks?"

"That would be seventy-five yards away and at an acute angle, a very difficult throw, if not impossible. He would also have to be in plain sight to hurl his missile. One of those in the room or someone on the street should have seen him. I will check the neighborhood for witnesses."

"How about the roof of the building that is opposite us?"

"An acute angle, long distance, a tough throw to make."

"Another problem, those panes of glass in the conference room appear sturdy. Thrown sticks of dynamite might not shatter those windows. More likely they would bounce off and explode in the street."

Asing shrugged. "Many issues to discuss. We should consider motives and suspects. Let's head to my office on Bethel. It's more private, I can have a smoke, and some coffee."

The two men sauntered the few blocks to the downtown police station. Once settled, Asing retrieved cigarettes, offered one to Grant, who declined, and began to blow smoke into the room. Between puffs he asked, "Who do you suspect did this attack?"

"Patterson claims it's the Japanese. They certainly have lots of reason to commit the bombing. The harsh and cruel treatment of them during the 1920 strike, thousands of people kicked out of their homes, strikers beaten by hired goons. There were hundreds of deaths from disease and exposure."

"All true, and the harassment continues to this day. The plantations have passed laws suppressing Japanese language schools and taxing Japanese students who attend. In their efforts to rescind the Chinese Exclusion Act they instead ended Japanese immigration. The Big Five frightened Congress about the 'Yellow Peril' and the Japanese taking over Hawaii and California. The result - Congress excluded all Asians from entry onto American soil."

Grant nodded. "The Japanese have plenty of motivation to harm the HSPA. My father was not a target of the killers, but the other men in the room were. Do we just look at the Japanese as the prime suspects? What about the Filipinos in the strike just ended? Their working conditions are so harsh that many men died shortly after their arrival in Hawaii. Their pay is the lowest given to any race. Because the plantations did not want dissent, uneducated Filipinos were chosen to come here. That allowed the plantations to treat them like slaves. And those poor strikers from the Makaweli Plantation on Kauai, massacred in Hanapepe town."

Asing shook his head. "We have two suspect races, but in police work we trust no one. Let's consider the Koreans?"

"I don't understand, why would they hurt the HSPA?"

"They hate the Japanese for their takeover of the Korean nation. They might have done the bombing to pin the blame on them."

"A little farfetched, but since Reverend Syngman Rhee is in town, their revolutionary leader, you could speak to him about this."

Grant looked at Asing, a wicked smile on his face. The detective stopped smoking; his eyes fixed on Grant. "What about your people, the Chinese? Don't they have a mighty axe to grind for harsh treatment in the early years of their work in Hawaii?"

Asing inhaled a lungful of smoke and blew out three perfect O rings. "It is true that the plantations were cruel to my people. There was an attitude that Chinese lives were worth nothing. That's why many left Hawaii when work contracts ended. Those who stayed and became merchants were discriminated against, denied the vote, and not allowed to become naturalized citizens. But you will find that my people have great patience. This has allowed Chinese to survive hardships inflicted on them over the centuries by cruel governments.

"Our great revolutionary leader, Doctor Sun Yat-Sen, who helped overthrow the Manchu Dynasty in China, saw the Chinese situation in Hawaii as a glass half full instead of half empty."

Asing paused for some moments and laughed. "Did you know he had a certificate of Hawaiian birth? This made him an American citizen. He could avoid the Chinese Exclusion Act and travel between China, Hawaii, and America, raising money for his revolution."

"I take it he was born in China and the certificate was fraudulent. What did you mean by 'a glass half full'?"

"Sun was a pragmatist. He saw that the Hawaiian Monarchy and people did not produce wealth. But the missionaries, their descendants, and foreigners who came to Hawaii understood economics. They began sugar plantations and, recently, pineapple farms. This has brought huge sums of money to these islands. There is a trickle-down effect which allows entrepreneurial races to prosper. Chinese living here have made lots of money."

"They have no reason to attack the HSPA."

"Precisely, but what about the Hawaiians, Mr. Kingsley? Don't they have the greatest of grievances to strike at the ruling business interests?

Your people are in poverty. They lost their monarchy and Queen through the revolutionary efforts of a few sugar millionaires."

"There is truth in what you say. Hawaiians are landless. A once sharing society where private land ownership did not exist, is no more. Now, large tracts of land are owned by a few who plant sugar cane and pineapple. Hawaiians say, '*aole ka aina no ka po'e Hawaii*'. "There is no land for the people of Hawaii." But our Queen Liliuokalani, when overthrown, said not to fight and to avoid bloodshed. Hawaiians did not battle the few revolutionaries then and they do not attack those in power now. But I will try to determine if there is a hidden movement to end Big Five rule."

"There we have it then, the possible racial suspects in the dynamiting attack. The Portuguese and other European races that live here have no cause to be trouble makers. In fact, our criminal statistics show the races we discussed are the ones in prison."

"But could it be they are arrested because of their color?"

Asing sighed, "Maybe so, but we must start somewhere. Let's divide the work. I will canvas the area of the crime to find any witnesses or evidence. I will speak with Rhee and influential Chinese I know. Have you taken the fragment from your father's side to be examined by the military?"

"I will, today. I gather my part of the effort will be to probe the Japanese, Filipino, and Hawaiian communities for possible suspects in the crime."

"Yes, we need to move forward with great speed before Patterson does something foolish which would totally polarize Hawaii."

# CHAPTER 9

Two Marines stood at an entryway into Pearl Harbor Naval Base. Grant marveled at how much the facility had grown since the last time he had visited. A dry dock had been completed; large fuel tanks jutted into the sky on his left. Ahead and to his right were rows of buildings. An aircraft droned above; its presence marked by the throb of its engines.

One of the guards leaned into the window of Grant's car. "I'm here to see Captain Trask, name is Grant Kingsley."

"You are on my visitor's list. Go a block straight. Turn right, second building"

Grant drove as directed, noting the large number of men in white marching or working in the area. The military had decided to make Pearl Harbor and Oahu a first-rate naval base. To defend it a half dozen forts had been built, including the honeycombing of Diamond Head with tunnels and artillery emplacements.

He slid his vehicle into a parking stall and walked into a two-story office building. A sailor behind a counter directed Grant into the office of Captain Trask. "It's good to see you, Mr. Kingsley. It has been awhile since you helped us with information of a Japanese military buildup in the Mandated Islands."

"I'm happy to be of assistance to our country anytime. Is the Navy still concerned about war with Japan?"

"Yes, the army and navy have recently adopted a joint plan, ORANGE, that will govern the conduct of war in the Pacific. We will have a military exercise early next year simulating an invasion of Hawaii.

One-hundred-and-thirty-seven ships and 45,000 men will take part in the operation. That's because Japan made a vague threat of war after the passage of the Exclusion Act."

"An ill-advised threat on their part, but since they beat the Chinese, Russians, and Koreans they believe their military is on a par with ours."

"Bingo, you have hit the nail on its head. Japanese hotheads are angered by the Washington Naval Treaty of 1921, the five-five-three agreement. Britain and America will be allowed to build five battle ships for each country and only three by Japan. Tension has increased significantly since passage of the treaty. But let's talk about why you are here, before I make a request."

"Fair enough, a couple of days ago an explosion wracked the offices of the HSPA. My father died from the blast and three men were injured. The head of the HSPA vows that it's Japanese dynamiters who are guilty. A strange piece of metal was removed from my father's body. It doesn't look like the residuals of dynamite. The police thought your ordinance department might be able to identify the explosive device it came from."

Trask fingered the metal that had been kept in a small box. "From feel and observation, I can't tell what this was once a part of. With your permission let me consult with army ordinance."

"Agreed, and what do you need from me?"

"I know you are on friendly terms with the Japanese Consulate in Hawaii. These islands are forty percent Japanese. There are persistent rumors that their loyalty is with the Mikado and the emperor wants to possess Hawaii. A Japanese fleet will be docking soon in Honolulu. Presumably these ships are on a training mission, but maybe the intent is to spy on Pearl Harbor and our military installations on Oahu. Naval Intelligence would also like to know if the Japanese are abiding by the 5-5-3 agreement."

Grant rubbed his hand over his forehead that had suddenly become damp. "That's a difficult mission. But if you will identify that metal and give me any information that piece might reveal I will do what I can."

"Okay, I'll rush the analysis."

# CHAPTER 10

A multitude of stars pinpointed the heavens. Nuuanu Valley lay in darkness except for the occasional lights from the mansions of the rich. From a window, Miguel heard laughter coming from Patterson's home. Tonight, the man would pay for his sins.

He had left Manoa Valley earlier in the evening and biked his way to his enemy's home. This time he would not fail in his mission of revenge. He did not regret the death of James Kingsley who had not been his target. But unforeseen events occur in war, and the man was a plantation owner. Ending his life just meant one more capitalist was dead. But Miguel felt disappointed that the three HSPA criminals had survived his grenade attack. Tonight, and in evenings to come he would carry out his revenge.

Darkness, light wind, warm but not muggy air, and the sounds of merriment streaming from the window of Patterson's dining room reminded Miguel of that evening months ago when he attacked the imperialist soldiers of America. After the chaos caused by the rifle grenade he had been rewarded by the head of the Communist movement in the Philippines. He wore the award on his shirt, the "Peoples Medal of Freedom."

Miguel believed that the evil man he planned to kill armed the forty plantation thugs who gunned down his brother and the other Filipinos in Hanapepe. There was a nagging doubt in his mind as to the truth of this claim, but what of it. Suspicion was good enough. Besides, the Hawaiian Planters Association was the guilty party in suppressing workers strikes.

He faced a tactical problem. An iron fence surrounded the evil man's home. The target window lay seventy-five yards beyond the metal barrier.

He would have to fire his Mosin-Nagant through a gap between posts into a first-story window. It was not a serious problem. He could do it. His training at the CHEKKA and later at the KGB had taught him how to overcome difficulties in order to carry out his terrorist missions.

But he would perform his attack in an urban area without a jungle to run into and hide from the hunters who might come after him. Miguel shrugged as he moved toward his firing position. It was just another problem that he must overcome. He thought of Robinson and his promise to him, but revenge was more important than the mission of convincing people to adopt Communism as their choice of government. He would try to do both, but killing those who had caused the death of his brother came first.

He heard the throaty engine of a car climbing up Nuuanu Street. Its headlights lit up the roadway. He panicked. Could it be a police car? He thought he saw a red light.

Miguel pressed against the fence, his dark clothes blending with the iron that he pushed against. He watched the twin orbs of light draw closer. Discovery seemed certain. Suddenly he felt weak as a feeling of helplessness swept over him. Should he run like a frightened deer away from the brightness that threatened him?

No! He remembered his KGB instructor shouting: "Fear is the killer. When it is dark, make yourself small to avoid being seen." Miguel shrunk closer to the fence. The headlights of the car lit up the road as it approached. He steeled himself to inevitable discovery.

The lights came toward his position. They spread out to the width of the macadamized pavement. The auto chugged on up Nuuanu, passing the terrorist without a pause.

Air escaped from his lungs. He had held his breath fearing that the sound of his breathing would cause the imperialist vultures to discover him before he completed his revenge. He was thankful that he could complete his attack.

Miguel looked through the iron bars as he came opposite the window where the laughter flowed into the night. It would be a difficult shot, thrusting his rifle through the gap between the fencing. But he felt he had no other option.

He studied the lit window. Maybe it had a screen maybe not. No matter, his bullet would break through and the heavy grenade should be enough to get through whatever was left. His rifle poked between the poles of the fence. The sounds of merriment inside the dining room of his enemy drifted across the distance toward him. He aimed through the iron bars. Miguel fired, loaded and fired again.

A violent explosion. Screams. Despite being flung back onto the roadway by the recoil of his gun he wanted to yell with pleasure for killing imperialists. He took from his knapsack a stone wrapped in paper and hurled it over the fence onto Patterson's lawn. Miguel shouldered his rifle and fled.

# CHAPTER 11

An incessant ringing forced Grant awake. He looked at the bedside clock. What idiot would call before six in the morning? The past two days had been stressful, and the pain of his father's death had robbed him of sleep.

Then he realized that life would never be the same after the deadly attack. This early call could only mean another disaster had struck. He rose wearing only undershorts. It covered the only light skin on his body, the rest was nut brown. At Punahou School he had been bullied for his darkness. But hazing ended when classmates learned his mother was *alii*, an elite. Missionaries who came to the islands to preach Christianity to the natives had married Hawaiian royalty to gain status and land. Half-brown descendants of these unions were not uncommon at the missionary school.

Selena slipped from the sheets. "Damn the fool who is calling us," she muttered as she hastened down the stairway to the telephone in the hallway.

For a moment Grant hesitated. He listened. Fortunately, the shrill ringing had not awakened Daniel. He ended his hesitation and moved down the stairs.

When he reached Selena, she said, "Detective Asing."

Despite his pounding heart Grant felt annoyed. He took the phone. "What's so important before six in the morning?"

"Patterson's home got bombed last night. He is on the warpath. Meet me there in an hour."

"Anyone hurt?"

"Maybe. Nobody dead." Asing hung up.

"What's going on?"

"Patterson got bombed, we got big—"

The phone rang again. Grant answered. "This is David. Patterson's angry. We must talk."

"About the explosion at his home?"

"Yes, and more."

"I'm heading to his place. Meet me at the office around ten?"

"Sure." The telephone went silent.

"Your brother?"

"Yes, he's scared. Patterson must have said nasty things to him."

"Troubles are adding up for us. Your father's murdered, last night an attack on an HSPA official, this morning a threat by Patterson."

"And I have no leads to find the killers plus the navy wants me to spy for them."

"How did that happen?"

"I asked for a favor and they asked for something back."

"I'll make coffee and eggs; you get ready to go."

Grant motored to Patterson's Nuuanu mansion. A six-foot wrought iron fence protected the property, its iron spears pointing to the sky barred entry. Within the grim border lay a manicured green lawn with beds of flowers surrounding a large, two-story white house. A strange show of wealth, he thought, a prison-like exterior and a crown of beauty within it. That's how the elite of Hawaii chose to live, keep away the riffraff and show off their wealth.

Grant maneuvered his car through the entry and onto a roadway leading to the front porch of the home. As he turned in, he saw the right wall of the mansion smeared with dirt and caved inward. The flower beds below were uprooted and scattered about as if some powerful animal had dug into the soil and flung the plantings into the wind.

Asing stood at the front door talking with a man in a dark suit, white shirt, and black bow tie. Grant slowed his eight-cylinder Packard to a stop. He exited the auto and climbed the front stairs to the two men.

"Mr. Patterson's manservant, Jonathon Welch, and this is Mr. Kingsley." Asing made introductions. "Welch has been telling me the events of last evening. His employer had guests for a late dinner. There was a smashing of a window, followed by a thud against the side of the building, and then a huge explosion outside. Patterson, who had his back to the wall got injured. His wife is in shock and maybe hurt. They are in the hospital. The guests are fine."

"Any warning of trouble before the explosion?"

"Not that I know of, Mr. Kingsley. The master did not mention anything to me."

"Was the front gate secured and all entryways into the property locked down?"

"Oh yes, Mr. Kingsley, everything closed. Only reason the gate is open this morning is Detective Asing requested it."

"I expected you to come and…" Asing emitted a great sigh. "Mr. Patterson will soon be here fuming like a lighted fuse in dynamite. Thank you, Mr. Welch, we will have a look at the side of the house.

"Quite strange, a massive thud against the wall by the dining room window. Then an explosion. And consider the distance the dynamite had to travel between the fence and the home. I'm not sure what to make of it," Asing said.

"The attacker meant whatever he threw to go into the window and explode in the room. His missile missed the opening and detonated into this flower bed." Grant pointed to the churned leaves and petals strewn over the lawn. "Earth and debris were flung against the wall and some objects penetrated into the room. Hello! Do you have a knife, Asing?"

Grant dug the tool into the partially caved-in, dirt-smeared, wall. He moved from place to place prying into the wood. "Let's dig into the earth and see what we can find. Careful, it may be sharp."

Working with their fingers the two men uncovered a small, jagged piece of metal. "Very similar to what came out of my father's side. Compare it to the shards of metal I dug out of the wall. It's the same. I suspect we are not dealing with dynamite."

The roar of an automobile streaking onto the driveway drew their attention. The car came to the stairway and skidded to a halt. Patterson jumped out of the vehicle, stared, then stalked to the two men. "Dynamiters," he yelled. "I want you to make arrests."

"Arrest who?" Asing answered.

"Isn't it obvious? Those convicted Japanese Union leaders who dynamited at Olaa Plantation. They are bent on mayhem."

"It may not be dynamite that caused the two explosions nor any Japanese," Grant interrupted.

"And you, Mikado lover," Patterson fumed. "Your continued support of yellow-bellies will cost you. The HSPA will shut your plantations down."

Grant bottled his rising anger. He knew that fighting fire with fire would only lead to disaster. "Mr. Patterson, we have just started to investigate—"

"I'm not going to listen to your claptrap!"

"Sir, please, control your temper and listen," Asing interrupted. "We have been studying both scenes of crime. Any person who hurled an explosive had to throw it more than a hundred and fifty feet each time."

"You're trying to say it can't be done! Back in 1899 Robert Wilcox invaded the grounds of Iolani Palace with a hundred men seeking to undo the Bayonet Constitution that the sugar planters had imposed on that corrupt king, David Kalakaua. I was a volunteer with the Honolulu Rifles who fought those revolutionaries. We skirmished with gunfire until Wilcox and his men retreated into a wooden building on the Palace grounds. The structure was impervious to bullets, but it had a metal roof. Someone got the idea to use a baseball pitcher to hurl dynamite from a building across the street onto the roof, a distance of three hundred feet. The dynamite blew open the tin covering and killed seven of the revolutionaries before they surrendered."

"But that had to be a wide and long roof. In both of our incidents small windows were the intended entry points of the explosive," Grant observed.

"Why should I listen to you? You're with the enemy."

"Please be patient Mr. Patterson, we are still investigating. We can't go around taking people into custody on suspicion." Asing pleaded.

"Why the hell not?" Patterson answered his face florid with anger. "If you won't arrest those criminals, the HSPA will ask the Governor to call out the National Guard and declare martial law to protect lives and property."

"You are proposing a military takeover of the Territory! That is a serious step, something only considered in war time. The HSPA will go down in history as an undemocratic fascist dictatorship!" Asing countered, his vehemence visibly shaking Patterson.

The men fell silent. Grant wondered if he should speak. Would Patterson's anger toward him cause a further explosion of threats? Somehow the conversation needed to be steered into quieter waters.

"Please, Mr. Patterson give Asing and me a chance to find the truth. There is a suspicion that dynamite is not the explosive used. Here is metal we scraped from this wall and an object found in the dirt similar to what struck my father. Because of his death, I have vowed to find the killers no matter the race. If they are Japanese, they must be tried and if guilty, hung. I swear to you I will not stop until I find who did these crimes."

Patterson hesitated, began to speak, and fell silent, his jaw falling to his chest.

Asing interrupted, "Give the Honolulu Police a chance to investigate these attacks. I remind you we are not ready to accuse anyone. If you proceed without us, and the HSPA is proved wrong in its accusations, you will never recover from the stamp of tyranny which will condemn you and your organization."

Patterson took a deep breath, exhaled and breathed in again. The crimson in his face subdued to a faint pink. "I have always considered myself as a fair man. I am not a tyrant. Investigate and find the truth. As for you, Kingsley, your father was a good man. He helped the sugar people in the overthrow of the black queen. He helped the HSPA become established. In his memory we will not act against your interests. But both of you remember my patience will wear thin if we do not get results."

## CHAPTER 12

Grant entered his office shaken by the early morning argument with Patterson. *What was it about these rulers of Hawaii? They bellowed, bossed, and screamed at everyone who was not of the original group of Christian saviors of the natives. I despise their arrogance, but realize I must play along with their overbearing nature. The HSPA spawned by the Big Five companies held all the economic and political power.*

It was not yet ten o'clock. His brother stood in the reception room. Grant's heart sank. He did not want more confrontations and threats. The words: 'You killed our father', sliced deep into his heart. David was eighteen years older, but he had no right to make an accusation like that. He smelled the alcohol. Patterson must have laid into him, frightened his brother beyond his ability to reason logically.

"God, I thought you would never come! We must promise change or the HSPA will ruin us!" David shouted.

"Hold it in for some moments. Don't yell where clients may hear us. Come back into my office."

David staggered from the reception room into the hallway, his shoulders brushing both walls. Joshua peered from a door. "Good morning."

No response. David shuffled toward Grant's office.

"Sorry, he's upset."

"Your father's death?"

"Yes, and other things. Talk later." Grant followed his brother.

When he entered his office, he noticed that David had fallen into his chair leaving him to take a seat usually used by clients. *He's pulling rank, the elder brother is in charge.*

Seniority is something he had to deal with in the army, no matter how incompetent the officer was. Many times, he had seen men ordered to charge and die without a good reason to do so while a commander hid safely in a trench. There were times when such bullies were shot in the head. Who could trace the origin of a bullet? Maybe a sniper shot him or maybe not.

David burped. Alcohol-filled air swirled through the room. He waved his hand. "Got no flag, disloyal guy, brother dear. Wall pictures of surf riders, canoe paddlers, and women in grass skirts. Nothing about the plantations, you are not friendly to the HSPA, the hand that feeds us. This I will change—"

"Just wait a darn minute. You've been listening to the claptrap that Patterson spews out."

"What if I have? He says we broke ranks with the HSPA in dealing with labor. That a solid front is needed to stop their demands for money."

"So, he played the disloyalty card against me and, if you remember, your father as well."

"Damn you," David rose unsteadily from his seat leaning his two-hundred-fifty-pound bulk across the intervening desk. "If you hadn't goaded Dad into being fair to the workers, he wouldn't be dead today."

"That's where you are wrong! You spent so much time on Maui cozying up to the Big Five power brokers that you forget or ignored the labor history that got you where we are today. Dad lived through the monarchy, Republic, and early territorial years. He supported the sugar planters during those times, but when the 1920 strike hit with Filipinos and Japanese workers seeking fair wages and more reasonable working hours he changed. The violence against the strikers and the cruelty visited on their families, changed him. At the time I was not here because of military service. I only got back after the strike had started. By then Dad had become a liberal."

"What you say is frigging bull shit." David leaned back into his seat. "What's this history you're talking about?"

"When the first plantations started back in the 1830's there were only Hawaiians to tend the fields. They couldn't be forced to work. The sugar moguls decided to import cheap Chinese contract laborers. They were treated like slaves. When they eventually got too restive, running away, not re-signing labor contracts, or demanding better working conditions, the planters brought in Japanese and other races. They called the technique 'divide and rule—'

"So what," David interrupted.

"Let me finish. When annexation occurred, the Organic Act creating the Territory forbade labor contracts. Slavery ended in Hawaii. The Japanese began to strike for higher wages, better working conditions. The plantations imported cheap Filipino labor as strike breakers. Again, the divide and rule technique was used to keep wages low and force men to work for ungodly long hours. It proved to be a sure way for the HSPA to rake in huge profits."

"Just remember, we benefited from that," David needled his brother.

"I did not know what was going on at the time, too young, and then away at school. It's the 1920 strike which revealed a serious flaw in the plantations' methods, twelve thousand workers went on strike. The only answer by the HSPA: strike breakers, beatings, and forcing families from their homes. They did pay off the Filipino leaders who pulled their followers out of the strike, but the Japanese stayed on. The walkout was finally settled with concessions being made by the sugar plantations. You must recall that I got involved with making labor peace and the HSPA thanked me for my efforts."

"That's when you maneuvered Dad into being nice to workers."

"He was already at that point when I got back to Hawaii. What you have to understand about our father: he could see persistent troubles ahead for the HSPA if they placed profits above people and used force to make the colored races work."

"Why not!" David interjected then burped. "Got to go, where is it?"

"End of the hallway, door on the right."

David rushed from the room leaving Grant alone to think over the morning. *Patterson had threatened my brother. This had forced him to drink and make accusations. Despite his support of divide and rule I believe David can be reached. I hope that I can turn him toward my side and end his accusation of killing our father. I need to convince him to retract the ugly claim.*

A little steadier, David returned to the room and his chair. His eyes, once dull and sleepy had regained a renewed alertness. "You say Dad could see 'persistent troubles ahead'. What do you mean?"

"The severe force used in the 1920 strike upset him. He believed that brutality against strikers would only lead to people being killed and not ending labor strife. That the HSPA would persist in its divide and rule technique to control labor."

"Please explain how the technique figured into our father's death."

Grant felt elated. His brother no longer acted surly and appeared ready to listen to reason. "I can't say how it led to Dad's death. I'm still investigating it, but divide and rule creates enemies. The HSPA after the 1920 strike decided to approach Congress to repeal the Chinese Exclusion Act and permit importation of those people to Hawaii. The effort created terrible trauma for the Japanese here as well as in California. There were accusations flung about that the Japanese intended to take over these islands and the West Coast. This 'Yellow Peril' hysteria affected the Chinese as well. Congress ended all discussion by passing the 1924 Japanese Exclusion Act and did not repeal the Chinese Exclusion Act.

"The HSPA suspected all along that they might not get what they wanted from Congress. They knew that Filipinos could be brought into Hawaii without restriction. These people are not united. They are tribal. Two groups of recruits from the Philippines were brought in, Ilocanos and Visayans. The HSPA figured they could be used as strike breakers, if the Japanese walked out. And if some Filipinos went on strike, one group could be pitted against the other. That is exactly what happened in 1924. Visayans were on strike on Kauai. They captured two Ilocano strikebreakers and held them at a rented schoolhouse in Hanapepe town. The sheriff tried to rescue the two captives. He was backed by forty armed men. A fight occurred and sixteen Visayans were killed and many wounded. A hundred were arrested, tried, and the majority were convicted and imprisoned."

David nodded. "I'm beginning to understand. It isn't just the Japanese who have a grudge against the HSPA, the Filipinos hate them also for the massacre at Hanapepe. There may be other races who have hard feelings against the association because of 'divide and rule'."

"Exactly. I think Dad happened to be at the wrong place at the wrong time. The bombing at HSPA headquarters was not intended to kill him, but the other three men. Last night's attack on Patterson proves it."

"But what are we going to do? He threatened me this morning with putting us out of business."

"I spoke with him today. He is going to let me find the killers and, in the meantime, hold off on any reprisals against us."

"That's good. I'm sorry I accused you of Father's death. The threats I had received from the HSPA unhinged me. My whole working life has been for our plantations. I couldn't stand the thought of losing what we have. I think we must rejoin the planter's association. In unity there is strength. I know your feelings, but trying to be fair to workers will not cut it with Patterson. When Dorothy arrives, we will discuss the future, unless, of course the HSPA threatens us before then. I pray that you find the murderers soon and they are not Japanese."

# CHAPTER 13

Grant felt a weight on his shoulders had been lifted. *It was difficult enough to lose my father, but horrible to be accused of killing him. David seemed to accept my explanation: the bomb was not meant for our dad. But if I cannot find the killers soon, then I agree with my brother: the HSPA would take reprisals against the family, and our properties would lose enormous value. I have my law practice that would sustain me. But David has only the plantations. If we are threatened by the hierarchy would I give up my liberal values? I don't know if I could.*

He parked the Packard and walked into Trask's office. The orderly ushered him into the captain's room. "You have some information for me?" Trask asked.

"Not yet, I visit at the Japanese consulate after I saw you. Is there anything new on the lump I brought in? I have more pieces from last night's explosion to be examined."

"Nothing to report, but assuming you have more metal to show me, it looks less and less like the explosions were caused by dynamite."

"That's what I've been thinking. But what could it be? The distance the missiles traveled in both instances were maybe a hundred and fifty feet."

"That's a long way for someone to throw dynamite."

"I'm told it's been done before in Hawaii, during the 1889 revolution."

"We will keep working on our end of the puzzle for you. Bring me some intel on the Japanese."

Grant left for the consulate.

After he parked, Grant studied the old building that over-looked Honolulu Harbor. *Little had changed since the last time I visited. Salt air ravaged the outside walls causing paint to peel. However, the grounds had been improved with flowers and a few cherry trees. I remember the Japanese gave hundreds of saplings to America as a peace offering in the early 1900's. They lined the Potomac River and, in the springtime, blossomed in beautiful umbrellas of pink and white flowers. But, like so much in life, relations between the two countries has deteriorated since that time.*

In the building he found everything neat and tidy. The inside was freshly painted with the floors shiny with light oil. The clean look was very Japanese, he thought. He asked for Consul Sakamoto and the clerk directed him to the second floor.

"Greetings, Mr. Kingsley. It is some time since we have last met. It is so kind of you to ask to visit. Cigarette? No. If you will permit me, I will smoke." The consul affixed the cylinder of wrapped tobacco to a holder. He lit the white paper, breathed in, and released smoke from his mouth and nostrils.

"I'm sure this is not a pleasure call. How may I be of assistance?"

"You are perceptive. We have had two explosions affecting members of the HSPA. It is believed by some that they have been caused by Japanese dynamiters."

Sakamoto lay his cigarette in a tray. Took off his glasses and polished them. "It seems these days that Japanese are blamed for everything that goes wrong."

"I assure you I do not believe your people are involved. I'm trying to prove that they are not."

"But suspicion falls on us because fifteen Japanese dynamiters from an Olaa Plantation incident have been convicted. I assure you that the Japanese community finds these men unacceptable."

"Is it possible that others who have a grudge against the HSPA did the bombing?"

Sakamoto carefully replaced his glasses and peered over them with an owlish look. "Japanese people are peaceful. Violence is not done by them, but to them. Yet I know there are outside agitators who wish to stir them up for their own evil motives. For example, this new editor of the *Hinode*

*Times* has written an article condemning: 'Imperialistic America due to its colonial attitude toward the workers'. The writer suggests that laborers unite and make regime change, whatever that may be."

"I think he means revolution. Weren't the Japanese driven to the brink of war by the Exclusion Act?"

"Nonsense, we would not be that foolish."

"What about the Washington Naval Treaty, the 5-5-3 arrangement?"

"You ask many provocative questions. I excuse your probing curiosity since you have been a good friend in the past. A Japanese fleet will be coming very soon. I invite you to be part of the delegation that receives them. You may gain some interesting information about Japanese views regarding the treaty. In return for this I have a small favor to ask of you."

Grant hesitated, what could Sakamoto want? He knew that in return for the invitation he must give something. "If I may be of assistance please do not hesitate to ask."

"*So desu ka*, we have a problem with your chief immigration officer. He claims that because of Bubonic Plague our staff women who arrive from Japan must strip naked, and their breasts and genitals examined. White women passengers are not subjected to this indignity."

Grant sighed. "That is something I can help you with."

"Good, our fleet arrives in several days. Watch for an announcement. Please meet me at the harbor on their arrival."

Grant left the consulate puzzling over the meaning of the *Hinode Time*s article. *Did the author want to overthrow the existing Territorial government? That is impossible with the thousands of military on the island. But revolution had occurred in Europe during the Great War, with the Bolshevik takeover of Russia.*

Grant worried as he drove toward his office. A light rain had purified the air. A perfect rainbow arched over the Koolau Mountains. Everything around him lay beautiful, languid, and serene. *Revolt and war meant bloodshed. This must not happen*, Grant thought.

# CHAPTER 14

When he arrived at his office, Asing had left a phone message asking that he stop by on his way home. Grant worked through the lunch hour and into the afternoon wondering what the detective had to say. He hoped the news would be positive for he had not been able to uncover anything useful.

When the sunlight began to fade Grant abandoned work and headed for the Bethel Street police station. Asing's office had its usual dank smell of burnt cigarettes. "Do you ever do anything other than smoke those horrible smelling weeds?" Grant needled his friend.

"They keep my mind sharp and awake. I do better with something in my mouth and warmth in my lungs," Asing answered. Then needled back, "And what have you accomplished without the guidance of smoke?"

Grant sighed, "I've been putting out family fires and sleuthing Japan for the U.S. Navy."

"Must keep in mind our goal and not wander off into other avenues."

"I had to deal with an angry brother. On the positive side, the navy will help us with the shards of metal. In return Trask asked me to spy for him. I spoke to the Japanese Consul in Hawaii and he told me the union men convicted of dynamiting at Olaa Plantation are no longer welcomed by the Japanese community. They will be forced to leave Hawaii once released from prison. You do not have any Japanese suspects to arrest."

"Mr. Patterson will not like that. You recall he promised not to take any action. I got a call from the Governor's office inquiring about our investigation. He urged that we use all resources to find the guilty parties who did the bombing."

"Were there any threats of martial law?"

"No, but he did stress the need to move quickly to solve the crimes."

"Any luck in your investigations?"

"I sent officers to Richards Street to canvas the area. No witnesses to anything unusual, meaning no one saw a person hurling sticks of dynamite. I checked the roof of the building across the street from HSPA office. Found nothing, talked to the building manager, he couldn't help us. He's got my card if something shows up. I sent officers to canvas Patterson's neighborhood. No one saw anything unusual that night. But—"

"What is it? A clue?" Grant interrupted, anxiety in his voice.

Asing paused for some moments. "I really don't know what to make of this message Welch gave to me. It had been wrapped over a stone and apparently thrown onto the lawn at Patterson's home."

"Let's have a look."

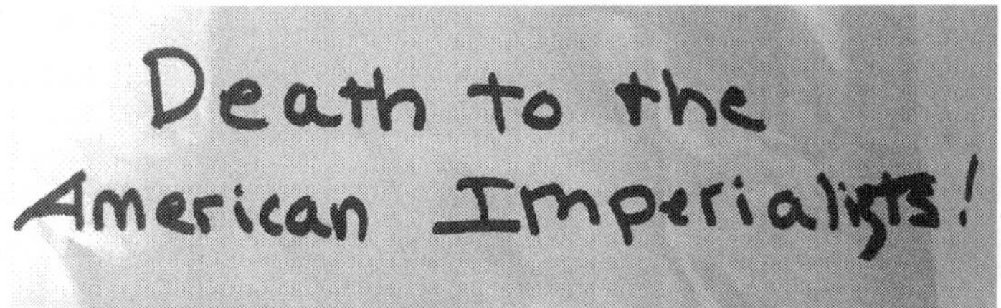


"That's a cryptic message. It's clearly a warning of future violence. Strange, at the Consulate, Sakamoto showed me an article in the *Hinode Times*, it spoke of ending imperialism in Hawaii and making change. I wonder if there's a connection between the death message and the article."

"That is hard to say. There are several Japanese newspapers in circulation, some favorable to the plantations some not. The words 'imperialism' and 'change' have appeared in more than one story. It's not unusual for labor leaders to use the two words to stir their followers to action. For the moment we keep an eye on the *Hinode Times* and what they publish."

"What's our next move?"

"We spoke of eliminating racial suspects. I called Syngman Rhee. He is an impressive man and has been fighting to free Korea from Japan ever since that country took over the peninsula in 1912. He has just been elected as permanent President of the Comrade Society; an association dedicated to Korean independence. I suspect that if ever Korea is free, he will be its leader. I asked the question: 'Would Koreans dynamite the HSPA so the Japanese would be blamed for it?' His response: 'Never, Koreans might be strikebreakers against the Japanese, but not foolish enough to attack the HSPA.' That eliminates Koreans as suspects."

"And you have ruled out the Chinese, that means we have only 80,000 people to deal with, Hawaiians, Filipinos, and Japanese."

"I'd say a little less, discount the women and children and we are dealing with 40,000 men."

"But why discount the women? Can't they commit crime?"

"Yes, but they don't like explosives, too messy. A poison cocktail, that is what they use."

"Alright then, let's see if we eliminate another race, the Hawaiians. My partner Joshua has got friends in that community, I'll find out if he can help us."

"Good, I'll check on the convicted Japanese dynamiters from Olaa Plantation and locate any union leadership that still exists. Pablo Manlapit is the number one guy for the Filipinos. He may have fled to California to escape a criminal indictment because of the recent strike."

"The HSPA works fast to suppress the union leaders. My experience is that they are not concerned about guilt for a crime. They use the court system to squash dissent."

"That is true. There are very few Caucasians in jail, but hundreds of Filipinos, Hawaiians, Chinese, and a few Japanese. That racial group is getting smart. They are finding ways to stay out of trouble. They are also using the Constitution and appealing to the federal courts to correct wrongs against them. The territorial laws suppressing Japanese Language schools for example; they challenged them and lost in the local court. Now they are pursuing the federal side and are presently headed for the United States Supreme Court. I can cite other examples, but currently that's the most interesting case to follow. Their approach, using the Federal Court, makes me think their dynamiting days are over."

"Then we concentrate on the two other races?"

"We can't. We must suspect the Japanese as well until we can determine who the guilty parties are. Let's pray there are no more attacks. If another occurs, repressions will be severe, and you and I may not be able to stop it."

## CHAPTER 15

It was a ring that refused to stop no matter how satisfying his dream. Grant pushed himself from the sheets damning Graham Bell's great invention. Why couldn't awful crimes happen during the day after a decent night's sleep? It seemed to Grant that all things bad or evil happened at night. He reached for the telephone that Serena held out to him. "What is it?" he answered; his voice surly.

"Marston's been bombed. Patterson screamed at me, 'Japanese criminals will pay'. He wants the governor to declare a state of emergency, and round up Japanese. This is serious."

Grant came fully awake, fearful for the terrible racial chaos that would happen. *I have seen the damage done to families when Germans were rounded up in America during the Great War. What did the HSPA propose to do, gather aliens and citizens and put them in concentration camps like the British did to the Dutch during the Boer War? It would produce an unbridgeable gap between the white elite and their Oriental workers. Would Japan go to war to protect their people in Hawaii?*

"Bad news?" Selena asked.

Grant paused. His wife looked smashing. *How could she be so gorgeous without makeup after a long night's sleep*? He focused in on her question, his voice a little throaty, "Asing said: 'Masterson got bombed. Patterson wants to roundup Japanese and put them away.'"

Selena stood taller, emphasizing her feelings. "How foolish. We would be like a dictatorship. The leader orders and soldiers fling people into cells whether guilty or innocent."

Grant nodded. "That's exactly what happened to the Russian Tsar. He tried to silence protest by military force. He had striking workers shot and the net result, his soldiers turned against him, he lost his throne, and he and his family were murdered."

Grant drove up the rising roadway of Nuuanu Avenue. The homes he passed were beautiful - *the expansive green lawns, gardens of flowers, and forbidding fences surrounding them. The Big Five elite had established their residences in the cool valley that once Hawaiian royalty had made exclusive to themselves.*

He entered through an open gate in the lava rock wall surrounding Masterson's home and parked near a group of uniformed men. Asing left them and came to Grant, "Patterson is on the war path," he whispered.

From the middle of the pack of police officers, Patterson separated himself and strode to Asing and Grant, "You aren't going to persuade me again to be lenient to the Japanese. They caused this bombing. Masterson's wife is in the hospital and those yellow bellies must pay. I've called the governor. I'm going to ask him to declare a state of emergency and put away these Asiatic anarchists who are attacking us." The HSPA leader thrust out his jaw and poked a finger into Grant's chest.

*He is beyond reason*, Grant thought. *Mrs. Masterson's injuries had unhinged him. I have to be careful what I say.* "Farrington is your friend and would want to do whatever you ask, but would he want to destroy the economy of the islands?"

Patterson reared back, "What's your meaning?"

"If you are merciless to one race won't the others fear that you will harm them and react?"

"Ridiculous, everyone knows who butters their bread—"

"And controls their lives?" Grant interrupted. "But if you use force against one race without evidence don't you think that the workers of Hawaii will know that they are not living in a democracy but in a slave state?"

"You're trying to infect me with your liberal ideas again. It will not work."

Grant noticed that the policemen were drawing near to their conversation. "I am not trying to win you over to my way of thinking, but simply pointing out that our appointed governor has come up with a new tactic to control the population. Americanize the children by forcing them to learn democracy and convert the adults to Christianity so they can be taught from the pulpit to be good and industrious workers for the plantations. By your blood and iron method you would destroy the current scheme of controlling the workers."

Patterson swore, "Damnation, what do you mean by 'blood and iron'?"

"It's an expression that Chancellor Bismarck used. He meant that Germany should solve troublesome political issues by force. In my opinion it helped lead to the Great War which led to the destruction of empires."

"What a farfetched example," Patterson said, his voice and posture less confrontative.

"Not really, Democracy and Christianity seek peaceful solutions to issues that divide people. To rule arbitrarily by force and not reason is to court regime change. I saw that when I fought in the Great War. The carnage and huge destruction caused empires to fall and surviving governments to realize that force is never the answer to social issues. You call me 'liberal'. Maybe to you, I appear to be, but I think of myself as practical by avoiding drastic solutions to problems. I know the hurt you feel from this attack and the harm to Marston's wife, but don't make it worse by punishing the Japanese."

A policeman interrupted the silence that followed. "One of us found this on the lawn." He handed a paper-wrapped stone to Asing. The detective unwrapped it and read its message. He lifted his head and stared at Patterson. "It would appear from this that you and the governor will need to arrest the Filipinos as well as the Japanese." He handed the document to Patterson. In huge black letters were the words:

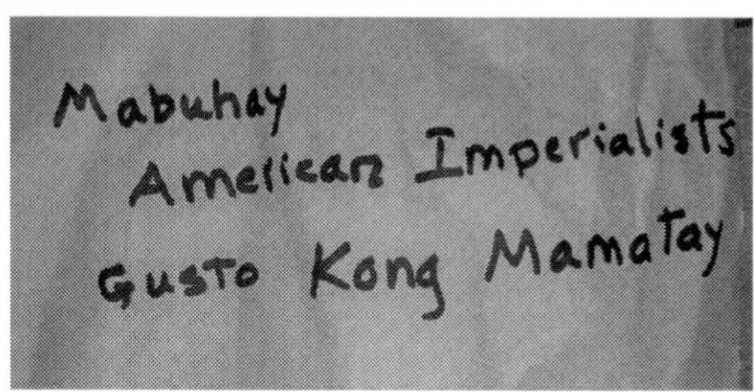


"What's it mean?" Patterson asked.

"The foreign words are Filipino," Asing answered. "I believe the message is: 'Greetings American Imperialist Prepare to Die'."

# CHAPTER 16

Patterson sat in an overstuffed red chair. Grant noticed that he relished the comfort and power that the big seat gave him. Doolittle, his arm in a cast, and Marston with a stitched wound on his head sat next to him. On the opposite side of the table were the Police Commissioner, a representative from the Governor's office, Grant, and Asing.

"I want to thank you gentlemen for coming to this meeting. We have had a grave problem over the last few days. Mr. Kingsley's father died in this room from an explosion which injured Doolittle. Marston's home was bombed and mine also. We appear to have an epidemic of dynamiting in Honolulu, all directed toward the HSPA. Our belief is the Japanese are the guilty ones since they used that explosive in their attack at Olaa Plantation. That is why I have asked the Commissioner and a representative from the governor's office to come here and discuss the problem. Earlier in the day I thought that a roundup of Japanese and incarceration would solve the attacks."

"That is an overly drastic solution," the governor's representative interrupted. "Can't the police cope with the troublemakers?"

"We have just begun our investigations," Asing volunteered. "But the attacks have come with unbelievable speed and by a means we have found difficult to determine. Motive is always important in capturing criminals. While the Japanese may have cause to harm the HSPA, the messages received from the attackers have not been about past wrongs, but instead are death threats against imperialists."

"This is an interesting wrinkle to these attacks," the Police Commissioner said. "It is not the usual invective by labor for higher wages, better working conditions, or the like. It's a blatant threat against Americans who colonized this territory."

"Then it's the Hawaiians who are responsible. They are always complaining about lost land and the overthrow of the monarchy," Doolittle said.

"Wait just a darn minute," Grant protested. "There is no evidence the Hawaiians are involved. If you examine the written threats that have been received it may be the Filipinos who are the guilty parties in these attacks. We need time to properly investigate and find the truth."

Patterson's voice cut through the discussion. "I called this meeting because of my anger over the attacks. But much as I dislike giving up on my suspicions against the Japanese, Mr. Kingsley has convinced me that a thorough investigation is needed before we make accusations and imprison people. Blood and iron are not the solution to political issues."

"If the gentlemen of the HSPA are in agreement we will allow the police to continue their investigation," the governor's representative said, looking at the men across the table. Doolittle, Marston, and Patterson nodded.

"By the way, what did you mean by 'blood and iron'?"

Patterson glanced at Grant before answering, "It's a statement that Chancellor Bismarck used to describe the need to use force to establish an empire. But look what happened to Kaiser Wilhelm. I've become convinced that there is a more intelligent way to deal with political troubles than forcing people into submission."

# CHAPTER 17

Grant strode into his office elated by the success of the day. In the early morning, he was in despair. He needed Selena's love to raise his spirts. He thought the confrontation with Patterson had gone well. His appeal to the man's intelligence and innate fairness had worked. Now he and Asing had time to find the guilty parties. The Police Commissioner had been extremely helpful promising Asing complete support.

"Brother, where have you been?" David complained. "I've been calling all over for you. We need to do something fast. I want to sell everything and leave."

"Whoa there, we don't want a forced sale. We could lose the true value of our properties. Has Patterson frightened you again?"

David hesitated, shuffling his feet. "Let's go into your office and talk."

Grant followed his brother into his private room. David again took the chair behind the large oaken desk. His assumption of the power position irritated Grant. *This elder brother game needed to stop, but at the moment I am at a loss as to how to end it. David needed all the psychological support he could get, I will humor my brother, at least for a time.* "Patterson got you frightened?"

David evaded a direct answer. "This is a time of great prosperity for America. President Coolidge has declared it the very best of times."

"I know, the stock market is up, but you haven't answered my question. Are you spooked by HSPA threats?"

"Yes and no. Concerns over the HSPA's attitude toward us is a factor, but I also have no appetite to operate a sugar plantation."

"Is your wife's decision to leave you the reason you want to sell our plantations? I know Dad was an important factor in keeping things running smoothly. But up until Marge left, I thought you were managing the business very well."

David shook his head and began sobbing. Grant went around the desk to comfort him. "Her leaving has been painful. I don't know why she left. Maybe, m-a-y-b-e…" David stuttered.

Grant almost finished the sentence, but thought better of it. *Marge had run off with someone else. Add to it our father's death and my brother is emotionally beaten down. Patterson's battering only added to David's psychological devastation. What can I possibly do to help him? I will talk with Selena.*

For the moment he said, "You don't have to be worried about Patterson. He won't pull the plug on us. I'm taking care of all arrangements for Dad. You have nothing to be concerned about. Let's wait until Dorothy gets here before making any decisions."

David wiped his eyes. "Everything hinges on finding the bombers doesn't it? If you can't find them, we are in trouble. What have you discovered?"

*It was a question I do not want to honestly answer recognizing the fragile state of my brother. I know it was more than the threat of the HSPA that drove David to ask. I also want to get the killers of our father.* "We are making great progress," Grant lied.

"Oh, that's good to hear. Keep me informed of developments in the investigation."

"Dinner at our house tomorrow night?"

"I'll let you know. I haven't had much appetite lately." David heaved himself from his chair and shuffled out of the office.

Grant folded his hands over his chest and stared at the ceiling. *I feel lost. There were no clues to the identity of the criminals. Asing and I have only narrowed the field of suspects to three races. I hate lying to my brother, yet I feel I needed to give him some comfort. The reality of where the investigation led struck: it led nowhere. I will talk with Selena. Maybe she could help me find the criminals, but as important, I need to have her help with my brother.*

# CHAPTER 18

Grant gave his wife a passionate kiss. She looked beautiful in her dinner apron covering her favorite Shantung silk dress. He knew that she loved it. Although the silk is a little rough it is still smooth to the touch. A perfect business outfit, wrinkle free and holding its shape throughout the day.

"Dan okay?"

"He's fine, bathed and ready for bed. I know you wanted to talk. Go upstairs, make sure he's brushed his teeth, put him to bed, and read a story until he's asleep."

When he came into the bedroom, Daniel leaped into his father's arms. "Miss you."

"Missed you too. Ready for bed? Teeth brushed?"

Dan nodded, then said, "Throw me."

Grant tossed his son onto the mattress making the little boy laugh as he bounced on his bed. He grabbed a pillow and flung it at his father.

"Want to start a war?" Grant threw it back. They exchanged soft blows for a couple of moments before Grant said, "Time to rest and listen to a story."

Daniel said a prayer. When finished Grant tucked him under the sheets and began to read. "The little engine said: 'I think I can, I think I can.' But it was a high hill. It chugged slower. 'I think I can, I think I can. I know I can, I know I can.'" Grant saw his son's eyes close. He tucked the sheet around his chest, kissed his forehead, and turned off the light.

Once he was in the living room Selena said, "Sounded like you two boys had a great time."

"You gave me a wonderful son. He's so easy to love. Makes me forget all the troubles I face."

"On the phone it sounded as if you were worried about your brother."

"Yes, and finding the killers of my father, and the bombers of the homes of Marston and Patterson."

"Why are you talking about killers and bombers, maybe it's only one person that is involved in these attacks."

"We got onto that track because Patterson believes the Japanese are conspiring to destroy the HSPA by dynamiting. Now there is a new rub, maybe it's the Filipinos."

"Why them?"

"A message in Filipino found at Masterson's home threatened to kill American Imperialists. Asing says we must consider the Japanese, Filipinos, and the Hawaiians."

"Why?"

"The Hawaiians lost their monarchy and land to what they call 'Western Imperialists'."

Selena frowned. "I think you can forget about the Hawaiians. Their losses occurred more than thirty years ago. The last time they tried a revolt was in 1895, it failed. They have been quiet ever since."

"I agree, but Asing says you suspect everybody until proved wrong."

Selena thought for some moments. "At the University strange messages have appeared. They damn imperialists and call for revolution. Maybe I can find one for you. It might be a clue."

"Whoa, that adds another area of investigation. We can't solve the crimes if we pursue too many avenues. We need to eliminate possibilities one at a time."

"If you want to start by ruling out races contact my father, since his business is in the middle of China and Japan Town. He might be able to help you. What about your brother?"

"He has me worried. I think he's losing it. Dad's death and the badgering he got from the HSPA made him lash out at me. But I think it is more than those two things that unhinges him. The divorce from Marge is a big factor."

"Never really knew her. She didn't like Orientals."

"I didn't know her either. Marge is a military officer's daughter who was stationed at Pearl Harbor at a time when vast construction occurred. Millions of dollars poured into the islands. The Big Five companies made huge profits. They gave lavish parties for the officers. At one of these gatherings, Dave met Marge and fell in love. She was half his age. They had no children."

"My remembrance of her is that she loved to party, always too busy for a family get together. She didn't even come to our wedding. I suspected she didn't like Chinese."

"But you're half-Portuguese."

"That's a lower-class white. Didn't they get divorced about a year ago?"

"Yes, she sprung it on Dave, said he was always too tired to take her out. She got her settlement and left with someone else. My brother has been devastated ever since."

"He was already psychologically cracking when your dad died and the HSPA laid down their threats?"

"Yes, and he is living alone with no one to comfort him."

"He needs a long vacation where he can heal."

"That's why I believe he wants to sell and get away from Hawaii."

"You have a carload of problems to solve. Maybe, until after the funeral, he can stay with us and get to know his nephew better. After that he should take some cruises. They say there is always a rich widow or two looking for a man."

"Get married again? Isn't that like jumping out of one frying pan into another?"

"Your brother needs love. He doesn't have to marry to find it, but he needs someone to tell him how handsome he is and smart. Praise, that's what your brother needs. Tell him to come over. We will feed him well and I'll get a friend or two to date him."

"Perfect, I've been worried. Maybe you can find him a pretty Portuguese blonde."

"Or a servant Chinese woman."

Grant put his hand on Selena's shoulder, smiled, and said, "There aren't any."

# CHAPTER 19

Grim faced, Dan Choy stared at his son-in-law through narrowed eyes. He shifted his great weight in the large black chair pushed close to his desk. He mopped his forehead with a cloth then smoothed his thin hair with his hand. "What you are telling me is not only is your father dead, but several plantation men were injured by unknown attackers."

"Who are believed to be Japanese dynamiters," Grant finished the statement.

"How do you know this?" Dan asked, a finger of his hand resting against his right cheek, his heavy jowls cradled in the remaining fingers.

"Patterson of the HSPA believes this, but the police and I don't know who. It could be Filipinos, or Hawaiians. The other races have been ruled out. Selena suggested I come to you since you know much of what happens in Japan Town.

"My daughter, you have beaten her into being a subservient Chinese wife?"

Startled, Grant stood from his chair. He pounded his fist onto the burnished oak wood frame of the desk. "I don't know what your customs are. I don't beat women, especially Selena. I also believe you would cut off my arm if I did such a thing."

Choy's face wreathed into a smile. "Just testing you, I'm happy that you are not like other men who treat females like a piece of furniture to be used and kicked around." Choy sighed. "I know that it is not easy being a woman. Usually they have no chance in life other than as a man's servant.

But Selena is different, brilliant. I raised her to be unafraid of the world, to be strong, and challenging."

Grant nodded. "She is a special woman, a PhD in Botany at the University and highly respected in the field of soil and fertilizer for growing pineapple and sugar cane in the tropics."

"She never told me. It makes me proud of my daughter. But you did not come to talk of Selena. The Chinese are not involved. Possibly the Hawaiians, they've been badly treated. Despite what I said, they are not dynamiters and would not attack the ruling class in a sneaky way. More face-to-face antagonists. Japanese, maybe, and the Filipinos have the most recent grudge against the HSPA."

"Anything you can tell me about those two races?"

"Not at the moment. I might suggest you speak to your old nemesis, Rudy Tang."

"Never, the guy hates me. Almost died dealing with him."

"He might be able to help you."

"I know you do business together. For now, forget it."

"Selena called me. Your brother needs a comfort woman, you want young or sophisticated?"

Grant looked away studying the pictures on the wall. *What was best for a fragile middle-aged man? Despite their differences he had to do the right thing for his older brother. Did he need someone worldly-wise and a challenge, or a woman with knowledge of the art of making men happy, or a young flower eager to please but an amateur?* "Choose someone who knows the art of Kama Sutra."

Grant left.

# CHAPTER 20

Puzzled, Grant sat at his desk considering what he knew, which he decided was next to nothing. *In the Great War the enemy lay in the trenches ahead. They were protected by barbed wire, land mines, and shell craters. At least you were aware of what to overcome to get them. They shot you and you shot back. But in these HSPA attacks you did not know the face of the enemy. In the war a Kraut looked just like you. But what did the HSPA killers look like? Were they* short, *brown-skinned, skinny Filipinos, or short, yellow-skinned, skinny Japanese? I don't know.*

Joshua popped his head into the office. "Come in?"

"Sure."

"You look like hell," Joshua quipped.

"Thanks a lot. To tell the truth, I feel pretty good. Last couple mornings wake up calls before six o'clock. Today, nice and serene, it's almost uncanny. I'm wondering when the next shoe will fall."

"Any leads?"

"Nothing, except we have narrowed the races down to three, the Japanese, Filipinos, and Hawaiians."

"Eliminate the Hawaiians."

"That's what Selena says, why do you think so?"

"Bombing is not what they do. They have no knowledge of things like dynamite. Hand-to-hand combat, that's how Hawaiians fought in the old days."

"I hear you, but Asing doesn't want to rule anyone out just yet."

"Besides wanting to say hello, the reason I stopped by is to tell you that Robinson, the editor of the *Hinode Times*, is scheduled to give a talk to the Royal Order of Alii and any other interested parties. I think you ought to come."

"Explain?"

"His subject is: 'Imperialism, Colonizers, and Regime Change'. It might be interesting. You'll also meet some movers and shakers in the Hawaiian community."

"Okay, when?"

"Three days, mark your calendar. Any luck in your search?"

"Not yet."

"Nothing to worry about, killers can't keep quiet. They're always bragging about what they have done."

"I have been told that. But what if it's a single man, a lone wolf?"

"Then it is much harder. Something will show up, it always does."

"I hope you are right. Remind me later about the talk, I've got a lot on my mind."

Joshua walked out. Grant pulled a file from his desk and studied it, a new probate. He scribbled a note to his secretary to do 'Letters Testamentary' for the executor of the deceased. He shuddered. He needed to start the legal process for his father, get his hands on the will, and find out what it says. He prayed it contained nothing controversial. *Three heirs and their children, divide the wealth among them and be done with it.* He heard the phone ringing outside.

A secretary knocked and entered. "Telephone for you Mr. Grant, Detective Asing."

He walked to the reception room and took the phone. "A development. Janitor in the building across the street found something. Meet me on Richards and have a look."

## CHAPTER 21

Grant hurried to Richards Street. Wind whipped into him. He leaned into the gusty breeze like a sailor peering into the water on a rolling boat. At any moment he thought he would lose his balance and fall on his face. Maybe driving would have been better. Turning onto Richards, the wind weakened, and he moved more freely.

Asing waved a hand at a door across the street from the HSPA offices. When Grant reached him, the detective ushered him inside where a tall man stood.

"This is Mr. Cox," Asing said. "He's the manager. Tell Mr. Kingsley what you told me."

Cox offered his hand, and they shook. "I believe you know that we rent offices. Our janitor sweeping in a second-floor room found this."

Cox unwrapped a shell casing from some tissue.

"What do you make of it?" Asing asked. "It's not a caliber I am accustomed to."

Grant examined the brass cartridge. "Not familiar with the caliber either. It's been fired. You can see by the ident on the percussion cap."

"Maybe it has something to do with the attack that killed your father?"

"Mr. Cox, the second-floor room, where does it face?"

"Directly at the HSPA conference room, I looked after this was found. I suspected it might be important."

"Thank you. Asing, let's go across the street."

The office receptionist was far from helpful. "Why do you want to examine the room?" she asked. "Everything has been cleaned and repaired. Only the painting needs to be done."

"Good, that's what I hoped for," Grant said. "Let's see the room."

"But—"

"This is police business." Asing drew out his badge.

The woman threw up her hands, picked up the keys from her desk, and unlocked the conference room door.

"What are we looking for?" Asing asked.

"A hole in the wall, and a metal bullet wedged inside it. We'll just check the wall that faces Richard Street."

The two men inspected the side wall by dividing it into sections. Nothing.

"If there was a hole in the wall, maybe the cleaners covered it up?" Asing asked.

"Possible, but we haven't been able to examine any higher than the height of our eyes. We need a ladder."

"I'll find one," Asing answered.

When he returned with a ladder, Asing said, "The receptionist was not very helpful. Finally found a janitor's closet and this was in it," as he unfolded a wooden ladder. Grant climbed up and continued his inspection using the imaginary grid. After an hour Grant shook his head. "Looks like a dead end."

Patterson entered the room. "What are you two men doing here, searching for HSPA files?"

"We are not spying on you. A brass cartridge was found across the street. We were looking for the bullet that fits it."

"Bullet! A bullet didn't cause that explosion! Dynamite did!"

"Maybe not, we have to check every clue to piece this puzzle together."

"A colossal waste of time. Arrest Japanese, interrogate them using your usual methods. You will find the killers."

Grant winced. *He remembered the beatings he received three years ago from the police trying to secure a confession from him. A rubber hose strike on the kidneys or stomach left no marks. Then there was the water torture. And if that didn't work there came the Big Tank. Once inside, a frightened man would confess to anything.* Grant sat in the brown sofa staring at the second story window across the street. He tried to eyeball the trajectory of a bullet.

"If a shot did come through the window, wouldn't the pane blunt the bullet and the slug become misshapen and fall anywhere?" Asing asked.

"If it's lead, that's what Civil War slugs were made of. Before the Great War, manufacturers developed alloys of harder metal. These new bullets could penetrate thick wood and not lose their shape. I hoped we would find something like that in here."

"That's tommyrot. This conference room has been restored. Go out and arrest Buddha heads instead of wasting your time here," Patterson scoffed.

"You have changed your mind since we last talked about how best to proceed?"

"Yes, I had a long talk with Marston. He is incensed by the attack on his home. He says this is the beginning of a revolution by the Japanese to take over these islands and present it as a gift to the Emperor. He has convinced me that the white races must stop the 'Yellow Peril'."

"And you do this by arresting Japanese without cause?"

"They have attacked the HSPA, killed your father. They have declared war on us."

"Just a moment," Asing interrupted. "I'm not going to arrest every Japanese in the Territory based on a suspicion of being involved in what's happened."

"I don't see why not," Patterson demanded. "We know they love to use dynamite to harm the HSPA. Fifteen have been convicted of a previous bombing. I say round them up and you will find our killers."

"Asing, we haven't inspected this couch! We moved it from the wall, but we didn't check it." Grant stripped off a small dark brown patch and stuck a finger into the hole that appeared. "It's the right trajectory. Mr. Patterson, we need to tear this couch apart."

"You want to destroy Association property! I forbid it."

"I would remind you," Asing said, "we are conducting an official police investigation of a murder. This is a crime scene. You have already obliterated much of the evidence. You may not interfere with our efforts to solve the homicide."

"But what will tearing apart a couch prove?"

"An expended cartridge was found in an office across the street. If the bullet from it is in this couch then we will know where the attack came from that killed Mr. Kingsley. We could then find out who used that office at the time of the killing."

"But death came from an explosion, not a bullet."

"An interesting point, Mr. Patterson. What the connection is, I do not know, but it is a clue to finding the killers."

"While you two have been chatting," Grant interrupted, "I've been checking the back of the couch. At the bottom of the frame something is sticking out. Based on what has been said, I assume I have your permission to cut it out?"

Patterson nodded.

Grant dug his knife blade into the fabric and wood that surrounded the object. It was a bullet. He wormed the metal out and handed it to Asing.

The detective took the expended cartridge from his pocket and pushed the blunt end of the round object into the empty cylinder. "It fits!"

## CHAPTER 22

Grant fumbled with the door knob of the entryway into his home before finally succeeding in turning the handle. He entered the cool hallway just as Selena came from the kitchen. "Where have you been?" she demanded.

He sighed, his shoulders slumping as he shrugged off his coat. "Been investigating, I'm sorry. I thought we had a good lead, but so far, a dead end."

"Come to dinner, food's a little cold. I'll warm it up. You can tell me all about your day."

"Daniel?"

"Fed and in bed. He couldn't wait for you. It's after eight o'clock."

Grant fell into a dining chair, "You needn't warm anything up. My fault, should have called, but couldn't find a phone, too involved in a wild goose chase anyway."

"Wash, then come back. I'll have everything ready."

Grant didn't argue, spent ten minutes cleaning up, changed his clothes, and returned. Steam from lemon chicken and egg foo young rose from the table, and he piled into the food realizing how hungry he was.

"I think you haven't eaten all day."

"Not since your delicious breakfast."

Selina frowned. "Tell me, what kept you so late?"

Grant took a long swallow of plum wine. "The food's great, thanks for preparing it." He glanced at his wife and realized he needed to explain the day. "Asing retrieved a fired cartridge from an office across the street from the HSPA. We searched the room where my father was killed and while I went to gun shops to try to identify the bullet. Caliper measurements showed it was not an American made shell. None of the shops I went to could identify where it was manufactured. I took what I had to the navy to seek an answer. They'll investigate and let me know.

"I met Asing. He had talked with the rental agent of the office on Richard Street. They had a name and address of a lessee. Other than at the time of renting, they hadn't seen the person at all. No coming or going."

"That is strange. How long before the attack was made did the person rent?"

"Within the month. What is also interesting, no furniture was moved in and no one at the building could tell Asing if anybody used the room."

"Did anyone at the rental office describe the lessee?"

"Only the secretary who took his money and had him sign a lease. She said, 'He was of medium height and build, light brown skin, wore dark glasses, and a hat that covered his hair. He paid in cash'."

"Too bad, no bank account to check on. What did you do then?"

"That's why I'm late. Asing and I went to the address given in Kailua. No such place. We asked around the area, no one had heard of Mr. Johnson, the renter."

"Your investigation has come to a dead end."

"Yes, but we have established several things. A bullet was fired before the explosion. Whoever did the attack was one man, not a group, and may have been any of the dark-skinned races of these islands or a well-tanned white person, Italian or Portuguese."

"That leaves out the Hawaiians, they're either big and fat or just fat," Selena laughed.

"There are slender types like me," Grant winked.

"You want praise, but you're not going to get it." Selena smiled.

Grant reached over to take her, but Selena stood and pushed him away. "I told you there were strange flyers left for students at the University. I picked up one."

EXPLOITATIAN

Of the WORKING MAN

MUST END!

RISE UP! REVOLT!

DEATH TO AMERICAN

IMPERIALISTS!!!

"That's just like the other messages left at HSPA homes. Anyone seen passing these out?"

"No, most were left in student mailboxes during the night. Do you think there's a connection to the attacks?"

"Maybe, it's worth investigating."

"Then I'll ask around the campus and do some checking."

"Oh no you don't, it's too dangerous. The man's a killer."

"What is wrong with you? Do you think I'm a helpless female, whimpering in fear at the first sign of danger? Have you forgotten how we worked together to solve the Ku murders?"

"What I recall is you almost got killed trying."

"But we fought the murderer together and won."

Grant sighed. "We did, but I was terrified for your safety throughout the final battle. I don't want to experience that again."

"Do not worry, I will be careful. Did my father help you?"

"He suggested seeing Rudy Tang, but I don't want to go to him. I think your dad is playing it safe. He's the main source of Chinese labor for the HSPA. At the moment he doesn't want to make waves."

"But Congress has shut off all Japanese and Chinese immigration with their latest Exclusion Act."

"I don't know what he's got going, but he is up to something which may not be legal. The less we know the better."

Selena sighed, pursed her lips, began to speak, stopped, then sighed again. "I agree, it is better that we do not know what is going on. I love my father and that love will remain no matter what, but I prefer to be blind about his business dealings. One last thing, I have decided with your brother to have dinner tomorrow night at the Moana Hotel, seven o'clock sharp. Be sure you are home in time to take me there."

"Is it just the three of us?"

A Mona Lisa smile arched Selena's lips. "My father has arranged a special treat for him. We will pick her up along the way."

# CHAPTER 23

Asing sat in his office chair plucking at a ukulele, his fingers moving rapidly along the strings at the neck. Grant liked the pretty melody, but could not identify the song. The detective seemed enchanted by the tune, his hands moving flawlessly along his instrument. A rousing crescendo ended his playing. "What, no *aina ho*?" he asked, smiling broadly.

Grant applauded his friend. Two other police officers looked in and also clapped. "We would like to hear another tune," one of them said, "but work to do."

Asing placed the instrument on a shelf, his face crinkling into a smile. "Love the *uku*. Portuguese brought it to Hawaii forty some years ago. Hawaiians took to it. Small, easy to hold and play. They called it *ukulele*, jumping flea, because your fingers had to move rapidly over the strings to make beautiful music."

"Where did a policeman ever learn to play it or have the time to learn?" Grant asked.

"I was a cowboy, *paniolo*, at the Parker Ranch on the Big Island. I learned all the ranching skills, especially using the whip. After work, I didn't want to play cards, so I practiced on the ukulele. One thing all Hawaiians have in common, they know how to sing. Of course, if you have no money, playing music and singing is the cheapest entertainment."

"*Paniolo*, where did the name come from?"

Asing rose in his chair as if to give a lecture. "Captain Vancouver dropped off cattle in Hawaii on one of his trips. Kamehameha let them loose and put a *kapu* on them. Like the Sacred Cows of India, they could not be harmed. The animals prospered. The wild cattle bred by the thousands causing havoc.

King Kamehameha III sent some of his chiefs to California to discover how to corral and tame them. Three Spanish *vaqueros*, cowboys, were brought back. They taught the Hawaiians the trade of cow punching. The vaqueros spoke *Espanola*. Paniolo is a Hawaiian corruption of that word."

"Is that how the Parker ranch got started, corralling wild cattle, and fencing them in?"

"Not quite. John Parker jumped ship on the big island. A great shot with the musket, he began shooting cattle for food when the *kapu* laws ended in 1820. Soon he began salting the beef and started a thriving business on the Big Island. He founded his ranch on Mauna Kea, leased and purchased land until his family owned the largest cattle farm in America."

Grant sighed. "I love learning this history. There is much about Hawaii I do not know and never will. But dwelling on the past will not solve the murder of my father and the attacks on Patterson and Marston. Got any ideas where we turn to next?"

"It takes time and much investigation to unravel puzzles. We earlier decided to concentrate on three races and thought that some group among one of them were the killers. At least that is what Patterson insisted upon, 'Japanese dynamiters are the culprits,' he said. Today we know that one man leased the office where the first attack began and despite my asking several people in the building no one can say that a group of men occupied or used that room. It makes our task doubly hard. If you have conspirators, usually one of them talks. It is how the Olaa Plantation dynamiting was solved; one of the twenty-one men involved talked."

"I hear you. Out of the thousands in the islands, we must find one man, and you believe he is from one of the three races, Japanese, Filipino, or Hawaiians. My wife insists it can't be Hawaiians, the suspect is too small."

"We cannot exclude them. The man could be Hawaiian, not all of them are huge."

"But by the same token, can we exclude other races who are tan like the Portuguese and Italians?"

"Not the Portuguese. I told you they are huge supporters of the plantations. They provided much of the militia in the early days of the Republic and the Territory. Italians, there are very few of them in Hawaii."

"True, but they supported the monarchy in the past. At least six of them were involved in the Robert Wilcox revolt against the sugar people. From their history they have been supporters of revolutionary causes. Consider the two Italian anarchists, Sacco and Vanzetti. They wanted to bring down the American government. Can we rule these people out, however few there may be?"

Asing palmed his hair, lit a cigarette, sat silent for a moment before he spoke. "I think we must concentrate our efforts on known racial groups who have grudges against the HSPA. The Japanese, because of the harsh treatment during the 1920 strike, the persecution they have received since. The Filipinos are angry for the sixteen men killed in the Hanapepe massacre, and the Hawaiians are unhappy due to the overthrow of the monarchy and the loss of their land."

"Are we making a mistake by looking at races with a grudge? How about the "Reds"? Here's a message found at the University of Hawaii, 'Death to American Imperialists, Revolt'. We know there were dynamite bombings on the East Coast of America. That's what Bolsheviks do to start a revolution."

Asing's brow furrowed, he loosened the collar of his shirt, wiping away sweat from his neck and brow. "It's hot in here and I cannot say your words aren't adding to the heat. Yes, I know there was a 'Red' scare started by Attorney General Palmer in 1920. This was generated by the revolutionary threats of the Soviets. Palmer predicted widespread bombings and attacks. It created huge hysteria and a flood of sedition laws, thirty-five states including Hawaii passed them. Thousands of aliens were deported. But Palmer's prediction of a May 1920 blood bath fizzled.

"It ended the 'Red' scare everywhere. I think the Russians are too involved in coping with their internal problems to cause bombings in Hawaii. Our laws are tough enough that any sedition would lead to a lengthy prison sentence, even death. Let's not get sidetracked by 'Red' scares."

"Patterson is breathing down my neck and wants arrests. I hate to say it, but we may have to take Japanese into custody to please him, maybe Filipinos as well. I'll do more checking at Richards Street and try to track down Pablo Manlapit, the Filipino union leader. You work on the Japanese."

# CHAPTER 24

Puzzled about what to do next, Grant entered his office, sorted through the mail, then pulled out a probate file. Before he could review it, Joshua knocked and entered. "I'm glad you're back. Been covering for you the best I can. Maybe you can give this woman a call, sounds like a good case. What's happening on the murder investigation?"

"We have a suspect. Tan-colored man, medium build, but nothing more. Asing wants to work the race angle first. I'm to sleuth the Japanese, but I have no one to talk to. The labor leaders I once knew, I lost touch with. I suggested to Asing that maybe we should consider the Communists, but he discounts it as irrelevant. It seems the 'Red' menace was a big thing in 1920, but on the mainland only, not in Hawaii. There has not been a whisper of Soviet agitation here says Asing."

Joshua palmed his silver hair, flattening out wayward strands that made his appearance unruly. He put a finger to his chin as he eased into a chair. "I have a client by the name of Saiki. He has a business and lives in Japan Town. From my experience with him, he knows a lot of what goes on in the local community. To my knowledge he never got involved in controversy. He'd be a good source to start with. As for the Communists, I think you will want to listen to Robinson's talk to the Royal Society two evenings from now. I've read some of his articles in the *Hinode Times*. The man's trying to stir things up, talks about world-wide revolution occurring."

"I want to hear him. Lenin died recently and there are two men vying for leadership in Moscow. One is a guy by the name of Stalin and the other is Leon Trotsky, head of the Red Army. He's the architect of the Bolshevik revolution. What's important is he advocates for world-wide revolution to happen now."

"You know a lot about the Russians. How did you learn what's going on in that country?"

"I fought in the Great War. You knew that. What you didn't know is that we invaded Russia, Siberia to be exact. President Wilson wanted to stop the Bolsheviks from taking over. He joined with the British and Japanese in fighting the Communists. When the Great War ended my commanding officer asked me to volunteer to combat the Reds. I thought it over and learned what was going on in Russia. At the time, I was a little mixed up over my mother's death. I decided not to volunteer and returned home. Ever since, I have had a special interest in what is occurring in Europe and especially Russia."

"That's a country so far away that I can see why Asing might ignore any threats that may come from it."

"Yes, he believes that, but Communism has a great appeal, especially among enslaved workers like we have here in Hawaii. The Big Five elite are the wealthy few and the plantation laborers are the 'downtrodden poor'."

"Don't leave out the Hawaiians. We didn't want to lose our kingdom and land to the sugar-rich folk nor to America. Our protests were in vain. We couldn't stop the takeovers and are viewed as American Indians. At least that is what our Queen said."

"Thanks for the Saiki information." Grant left.

# CHAPTER 25

Colorful banners with Chinese writing waved above the street. Grant couldn't read them though he knew they were advertisements. What puzzled him is how Asians could memorize the thousands of symbols of their written language. *But was a twenty-six letter alphabet any easier to use? Combinations of these letters made up hundreds of thousands of words. The American dictionary seemed much more difficult to memorize than the symbols flapping above him.*

He threaded his way through the crowds on Maunakea Street and worked his way to a roadway he thought was River Street. Next to it Nuuanu Stream flowed to the sea, a quixotic waterway which could rise suddenly by ten feet and dwindle as quickly. In times past the stream would overflow and flood the area around it. On the border of downtown Honolulu, it once served as the city's waste matter drain with many drains projecting over the water. But the sewer system ended their use.

Grant searched for Saiki's home between the Queen and Beretania Street bridges. After many inquiries, often using a one syllable word and sign language, he was directed to a modest two-story green structure with white trim around the windows and door. A Japanese calligraphy sign in front had the name Saiki as part of the script.

Adjacent to the green building lay another two-story house which stretched to an intersecting street. In a queue before a side door were half a dozen Asians. Grant watched the men slowly walk in as others joined the line.

Beneath the Saiki sign was a lacquered black door with a brass knob. Grant twisted the handle left and right, noticing it moved freely, but he could not open the entryway. He knocked. No response. He knocked again, saying, "*Ohio gozaimasu*, Mr. Saiki, my name is Grant Kingsley. My law partner is Joshua Kanakoa, may I speak with you?"

"You police?" a gruff voice answered.

"No, Kanakoa thought you might help me with a problem. May I come in?"

A latch screeched and the door opened part way. A pale face peered out. "What you want?"

"Talk story. Get your help, my partner say you know much of what goes on in J town."

"Why Kanakoa no come? He good man. Help me plenty, no charge. You say him your partner?"

"Yes, this is my business card with his name on it. We work together," Grant answered, noticing a slight thaw in the initial hostility of the man's voice. Hearing noise to his left he glanced at the queue. It had grown longer, and an argument erupted. After a brief scuffle a man moved to the back of the line.

"What's going on next door?"

"If you don't know, I no tell. Come inside."

Grant entered a dark space with shelves along the walls. A door ahead opened into another room. To his right a stairway led to a second floor. A low counter stood to his left where sheaves of paper were piled, illuminated by sunlight piercing through a window on the outer wall of the building.

Saiki moved over to the counter. Grant followed, noting the man's slight build and average height. Skimpy light from the window fell onto his short black hair, oval face, slanted eyes, and delicate nose. Through thin lips that barely opened to thrust out words, Saki asked, "What you want?"

It was a question Grant had debated for some time as to how to answer. *The truth would cause Saiki to refuse to help. A lie could result in eventually losing my credibility. Something in between the two extremes seemed best.* "My family has suffered a great loss. It is claimed that Japanese may have caused the *pilikia.* You know much about Japan Town. I thought you might help us."

Saiki scowled. Coldness spread over his face. "Trouble you say? What makes you think I can help you? Even if I could, why should I help you?"

*I must keep him talking, don't let the conversation end*, Grant thought. "*Hai*, I understand, for your help I must give something in return. I don't think it is money that would persuade you, but some service I can perform for you?"

"*So desu ka*?"

"That is so. You have wanted to bring to Hawaii a 'picture bride.' The recent Exclusion Act prevents it. I can arrange to get her in."

Saiki reared back, his brown eyes staring at him. "Kingsley-san you can do this? How?"

"That is my secret. Will you help me?"

"*Hai*, for a wife I will if I can. What is it you want?"

Grant took a deep breath, choosing his words carefully. "An explosion in the HSPA office killed my father. Since that time two other bombs have been used at the homes of HSPA executives. These people believe it is Japanese dynamiters who are behind the attacks. I do not, but I can't prove what I believe. Can you help me?"

Saiki did not react. He stood impassive behind the counter for many moments before his lips slipped away from a frown and formed an answer. "Japanese were not involved. But I can see you might not believe me."

"Mr. Saiki, Patterson of the HSPA does not. The only way to convince him is to capture the bomber who is a man, tan in color and of medium height and build. I'm told you have many contacts in the Japanese community. Find out what you can. Help me and I will help you."

"What you ask could be dangerous. If the man is Japanese and I revealed his name, I would die. That I would not do. If he is of another race you must pursue the information I give you alone. I will not be part of his capture."

"You drive a hard bargain. It is difficult to foretell what I may be getting from you."

"You have made a tempting offer. I am getting old. I need someone to take care of me and keep me warm on chilly nights. Yes, and there is the matter of children. I have none. A boy and a sweet girl child would give me great comfort."

Grant smiled. "I understand your needs. Get me good information leading to the bomber and I will reward you with what you want. You have my card, contact me when you know something."

"We would make an exchange then?"

"It depends on what you reveal. Let me add we must move quickly. Patterson wants to arrest Japanese and beat them to find the guilty ones. I have been able to delay such criminal acts. But one more attack and I may not stop him."

"Hai, I see why Japanese should help you. I will do what I can."

Grant left. As he walked along the pathway, a voice yelled, "What you doing here, spying?"

When he turned there were three young Japanese wearing soft shoes, khaki pants, and white T-shirts that clung tightly to their muscular chests. "Just visiting, not causing trouble"

One thug pointed an accusatory finger at him, "You police, we no like your kind." He stepped forward and swung his fist at Grant's face.

Instead of rearing back, Grant stepped under the punch and smashed an elbow into the attacker's throat while placing a hand behind his back. He pulled the man into him. The quick push-pull brought a scream from the thug and he collapsed to the ground. The other two Japanese backed off and watched their companion writhe on the pathway.

Grant assumed the '*moku moku*' position, knees slightly bent, fists closed and arms hanging by his side. He glared at the men. "No need for further trouble. Take your friend and walk away and I will too."

For a moment there came no response. Only the groans of the injured man in the dirt broke the silence. One of the thugs signaled that his companion should go to the right while he went left.

Grant did not hesitate, he moved forward, pivoted on one foot and smashed his metal-laden shoe into an attacker's side while he thrust an open palm into the man's nose. A weak punch hit his jaw, but did not daze him. Blood flowed from the thug's broken nose over his face and white T-shirt and he staggered backward.

Grant felt a foot hit his ribs. He winced, turned and saw a knife. He stepped to the side of the attacker's arm and swung an open palm between the man's legs as the knife sliced into his coat. He felt a sudden pain, heard his opponent howl and drop his hands toward his crotch. A head butt finished the fight.

Grant removed his coat and checked the slice on his left arm. It bled onto his torn shirt, but fortunately the cut appeared shallow. He eyed the wounded thugs. They made no moves toward him. "I'm sorry you attacked me. I would prefer to be friends with Japanese and help you. Goodbye." He backed away, watching his opponents for any movement toward him. Men in the queue stared, but did nothing, instead they jabbered with each other.

Grant turned onto an intersecting roadway and headed for Queen's Hospital.

# CHAPTER 26

With a half-dozen stitches in his left arm, Grant stepped into his office building and strode to his reception room. Joshua stood as he entered. "I got a call from Saiki, very agitated. Yakuza visited him—"

"Yakuza?" Grant interrupted. "Who the hell are they and what did they want with Saiki?"

"I gather you don't know anything about them. Today they are Japanese gangsters, but in ancient times they were like Robin Hood and his Merry Men. Around 1600 there was a lot of turmoil in Japan. The peasants were starving. Master-less samurai, Ronin, roamed the country. No warlord wanted them. Some of these banded together and helped the poor at the expense of the rich. They were called yakuza, meaning 'losers' or 'outsiders'." Joshua smiled. "But what I said may just be a myth told by criminals to mask their crimes.

"What could be closer to the truth is that The Tokugawa Shogunate that began in 1600 banned gambling in Japan. Wandering peddlers took advantage of this law and ran illegal games of chance. Soon these men organized themselves into gangs with a simple hierarchy: a father who is the boss and the brothers. Because they were criminals, when jailed, tattoos were placed on them. All yakuza today have tattoos."

"I did see ink markings on the three men who attacked me. Why would yakuza challenge me to a fight?"

"In the area you were in, see anything unusual"

"There were men constantly joining a line to get into a house."

"You have your answer, the yakuza started as gamblers and, from what I know, when they came to Hawaii ran houses of prostitution. You wore a coat and tie to visit Saiki, right?"

Grant nodded, "And they called me 'policeman'. They suspected me of spying on their illicit operation."

"Yes, you were not the usual clientele that whores entertain."

"I still don't understand why they confronted me. Don't the police permit brothels to exist in Honolulu?"

"Yes, in restricted areas. I can't say for sure why you were attacked. There is a legitimate concern that yakuza are using juveniles as slave women. Plus, there are moralists in Hawaii who want the laws enforced. And there is a growing belief that without regulation, ugly diseases will pollute the population. When Cooke first arrived, our nation had robust and healthy people. Hawaiians had been isolated from disease for centuries. The captain forbade his sailors from having intercourse with the native women. He left the islands and a year later returned. Men and even women were sickly, and the death rate among the natives had increased noticeably. This is a story repeated many times throughout Polynesia when white sailors first arrive to pristine islands. All the rules that men like Cooke would make to stop sex between whites and browns were useless. The passions of human beings will override any law against love making."

Grant laughed. "And I understand the Hawaiian women were open in their wantonness for sex with the sailors. They challenged their manhood and aggressively engaged in love making with them any time and any place."

With a loud sigh, Joshua shook his head. "That's why the missionaries, when they got here, thought Hawaiian women were naked, wanton trollops. It is hard for people to understand why a stone-age society might be enthralled by what a Western world can give. Exchanging sex for an iron nail is a great bargain when you have no metal."

"An interesting discussion, but I still have an uncanny feeling that there is a different explanation for the confrontation than what you suggested."

"There is more below the surface than meets the eye. It is an old Chinese proverb. But isn't this diverting you from your investigation?"

"Yes, but criminals know how to find other criminals." Grant smiled. "That's a proverb I just made up. I believe it is true. If I could get the yakuza to help me, I think we could find the murderer of my father."

"Unfortunately, you have made a poor start at making friends. Maybe Asing can assist you?"

"A great idea, I'll call and see if he's available."

Grant phoned, then left his office heading for Bethel Street. As he passed an alley way, he heard a man beg, "Sir, my grandfather has taken ill. He may be dying. Can you help us?"

Grant saw what appeared to be a bearded old man lying among the trash. He bent down. Something hard struck his head. He faltered and was hit again. He fell to his knees and received a kick to the side of his cheek. As he dropped into the garbage in the alley, he heard a voice say, "Stay out of Japan Town or the next time you die."

# CHAPTER 27

A bright light forced Grant awake. A voice said, "Eyes are responding, pupils are open. Close your fists. Raise your arms. Good. Can you hear everything I have said?"

Grant nodded.

"Except for a swollen knob on the side of his head your husband is fine, Mrs. Kingsley."

"Does he stay overnight?" Selena asked.

"No, take him home." The doctor left.

"How did you wind up at Queen's twice today?" Asing asked.

Grant slowly rose from his hospital bed. His bare feet touched the floor's tile, its coolness made him shiver. "Neither time by choice. I went to Japan Town to enlist a Japanese to help us. Three yakuza were unhappy with me being there. We fought. I got cut. Came to Queen's and got stitched. I went to the office, called you, and headed to Bethel when I got sucker-punched."

"You got beaten by yakuza? They are a tough bunch, a brotherhood of men who are the real criminals among the Japanese. Before the Great War they exerted extraordinary power here. They controlled the vice. When police tried to make arrests, they would be surrounded by Japanese who would force the officers to release the gamblers and return their money. Law men didn't carry guns at the time just like the British bobbies. I still don't, just use my whip.

"Yakuza made no secret about their prostitution activities, but did agree to keep it in one area, Iwilei, near the train depot. Government allowed the oldest vocation to exist. Why? Honolulu is a port town and you have to keep sailors happy, plus the plantation moguls wanted to be sure their wives and daughters weren't raped or seduced by common laborers or a traveling seaman. During and after the war their influence waned. But Oahu is becoming a major naval base. Lots of military construction, mainland workers, soldiers, and sailors have come to Hawaii. They need comfort women. What you just experienced means those thugs are back in force."

"Yeah, it seems there is a major whorehouse next to where Saiki lives. Asians were lined up to get in. I didn't see any military guys."

"That's because of sanitation." Asing laughed.

Selena gasped.

"What do you mean by that?" Grant asked.

"There is another entryway into the 'boogie house' where the whites go in. That's because they believe that if a brown man enjoys the same women, then they will suffer from loathsome diseases."

"Disgusting," Selena said. "But it is true, many a time have I been approached for sex by a white, and when I say emphatically no, they insult me by saying "You have a dirty Oriental pussy." and then add other insulting remarks about my cleanliness."

"Selena, you never told me that."

"It's because I don't want you to get into fights, especially with some men who are friends—"

"Name them—"

"Stop this squabble," Asing interrupted. "We have more important things to work on. Besides you well know this is a man's world. Take the Japanese in Hawaii for example, they sell their wives into prostitution. The going rate is $100, but it can be more if she is especially skilled."

"Enough! This is not the place or the time for this," Selena said. "Grant is hurt and needs to be home where he can rest."

"Yes, whatever we need to talk about can keep until morning."

"But my only contact in J Town may be in grave danger. I need to protect him."

"You can do very little for him in your beaten condition. I would go to see him, but I am well known in J Town and may cause him trouble."

"Then I shall visit the man," Selena insisted.

"No, too dangerous," Asing said. "River Street is not a place for a lone woman at night. Besides, Saiki doesn't know you. I think we have to ask Joshua to check on him, it's his client."

"He's an old man. They could kill him," Selena objected.

"But his age may keep him safe," Asing answered. "I will speak to him. We will come up with a plan. Take Grant home, we meet in the morning at my office.

# CHAPTER 28

Grant's sleep came quickly after Selena slipped a warm blanket over him. Her tenderness comforted him like his childhood when mother gave him warm milk and tucked him in bed. *She would sing pleasant, peaceful Hawaiian songs which told of the winds in the forest, the flowers growing by a waterfall, or the graceful movements of a seagull. From her singing and kind nature, he had developed a love for the land and the Hawaiian belief that the aina is family because it feeds and provides for all who live on it. Because of what it gives, there is a duty to care for it like a family member.*

Selena came into the bedroom, "Up, up sleepy head, time to meet Asing. Daniel's off to school. Your breakfast is on the table. I'm leaving for the university, and you're expected at Bethel Street at 9:30."

"Have you heard from my brother?"

"He's fine. Says he is very happy with the woman we introduced him to. He is seeing her again. No need to live with us. He enjoys his independence, but dinners together from time to time will be welcome. He's upbeat. The date we arranged has done wonders for him."

"That's good news." Grant kissed Selena, watched her leave, then completed his morning routine. He arrived at the police station on time and walked in to find Joshua sitting in Asing's office.

"I'm happy to see you. I worried about asking for your help with Saiki, but I wasn't in shape to do anything last night."

"Understood. Asing and I worked out a plan. I called Saiki, arranged to meet him in Chinatown. Asing and another undercover officer were hidden near where we ate. Everything went smoothly. No problem."

"That's the way I like it," Asing said as he entered his office. "But things are not smooth with Mr. Patterson. He called my lieutenant who summoned me to his office. The HSPA guy ranted about shoddy police work and demanded I be taken off the case and some 'smart, white officers appointed'. I got to give Hitchcock credit, he defended me as a good detective. However, he appeased Patterson by saying he would assign white officers to investigate the bombings of his home and Marston's. He left it up to you to decide if I stay on your father's murder case."

"You know I trust you to get the job done right. I'd like to hear what Joshua has to say about last night."

"A simple story, the yakuza boss man talked to him about your meeting. Saiki told the truth about what you asked him to do. At first the boss was skeptical, but took interest when the 'picture bride' offer came up. In the past, some Japanese are getting those women to come into Hawaii and selling them into prostitution, that's why the boss man got interested."

"He's trying to figure a way to get around the Exclusion Act and get 'picture brides' in again. What a disgusting practice, this selling of women into sex slavery. Can't the police stop it?"

Asing shook his head, "A deal has been made with the yakuza: 'Do your dirty work in one area of Honolulu, and we will leave you alone'. It's not my call to break the deal. There are thousands of unmarried men descending on Honolulu, we have to let those guys burn off their heat. Giving them prostitutes is the best way to do that."

"How many whores are we talking about?"

"There's at least three hundred if not more."

"Servicing thousands of military personnel?"

"Grant, the big bosses have a system. Acquire or build a two-story house and divide it into compartments, eight feet by ten. Soldier goes into one room, gets undressed and walks into another where a woman waits. He's got three minutes to get it done. When he is finished, he enters a third room, dresses, and leaves. That way one gal can provide comfort to maybe a hundred men in one day and night."

"That's unbelievable, why would a woman accept that kind of animal behavior?"

"Some of them are slaves and have no choice. But just remember this, if a woman works in the sugar fields, she gets $7.50 a month. That is one-half the pay of a man. But she can get $1.00 or more a trick. That's good money for easy work. You have heard the *hole hole bushi* song? I see you shaking your head. *Hole, hole* is Hawaiian for stripping leaves from the sugar cane stalk. *Bush*i is Japanese for a song. Japanese wives penalized by the plantation system sing:

*"If I work in hole hole, all I earn is twenty-five cents.*
*If I sleep with a Chinaman, I get one dollar.*
*Tomorrow is Sunday, come visit me.*
*My husband will be watering the fields.*
*I will be alone.*"

A knowing smile curved Joshua's lip. "It's very hard being a woman in this world. You work like a slave and receive half of what a man gets. If your husband falls into debt, he can sell you to pay his bills. If you make money as a whore, your pimp takes what you earn. For a poor woman, there is very little chance to escape an awful life. I guess that's why the Cinderella story has a lot of charm."

"You gave a thoughtful analysis of the hopeless lot of women-kind, but we have a murder to solve and how do we do it? When I heard of the yakuza, I thought those criminals could help us find a criminal. But can we trust them? What can we give to get their help?"

"How about picture brides?" Asing said, a wry look on his face.

"So that yakuza can sell them into slavery. It's a repulsive thought."

"Coin of the realm, money has always been a universal inducement to buy information," Joshua suggested.

"Yes, but what would we be buying? We have narrowed the possibilities to three races, one of them, the Japanese. Would yakuza turn on their own people?"

"To do so would be a one-way ticket to heaven or hell," Asing said. "There has to be a way to get truthful information from them. I agree, when it comes to criminal activity those tattooed birds would know who the good guys and the bad ones are."

"Speaking of races, you were to check on the Filipinos, any luck?"

"Pablo Manlapit and the other union leaders have been imprisoned or run out of the islands since the massacre at Hanapepe. It was a disorganized strike in April this year. On Kauai, out of the 5,500 Filipino workers on the island only 575 went out. The rest kept working. On September 9th when the fight occurred there were only 120 Visayans in Hanapepe still on strike. This is when the HSPA hit them with forty armed men. Who was at fault for starting the fight, none are sure, but after it finished there were twenty dead, four of them sheriff's deputies, and many wounded Filipino. Trials led to four-year sentences handed out to seventy-six strikers.

"The plantations took advantage of the 'Red Scare' following the Great War and passed an Anti-Syndicalism law, an Anarchist Publication law, and recently an Anti-Picketing law. The penalty for breach is ten years in prison. With the imprisonments, the massacre, the harsh laws, and the loss of union leaders, the Filipinos do not want to cause any trouble. I could not find any information of an active conspiracy among any of them to seek revenge on the HSPA."

Grant shook his head. "That only leaves the Japanese and Hawaiians as racial suspects. I don't think the Japanese are guilty of the attacks."

"Nor are the Hawaiians guilty!" Joshua said emphatically.

"We can't rule out the Japanese. They are clannish, stick close to each other and do not mix with other races. They have much to be angry about: the terrible 1920 strike when many died; the Ozawa case where the Supreme Court said Japanese could not be naturalized since they were not whites, but 'Mongolians'. Then laws were passed to close the language schools. Couple these injuries with the attitude of the Big Five that there is a 'Yellow Peril' that seeks to take over Hawaii and the result is the Japanese Exclusion Act," Asing said.

"But the only lead we have to Japanese involvement in the recent attacks are the Japanese dynamiters of 1920 who are in prison," Grant objected.

"Hitchcock will be taking into custody anyone connected with the Fair Wages Union and family members of strike leaders. Patterson's demands are to beat the truth out of them. I truly hope it does not go that far, but it is out of my hands."

"We have a local tragedy in the making and no clues as to how to stop it." Grant sighed.

"What about the metal and bullet you gave to navy ordinance?"

"I haven't heard from Trask; I'll check on it. Let's talk about Saiki. Joshua, did he tell you he would help? Did he have any information at all when you saw him?"

"He just said he wanted a picture bride—"

"To sell," Asing interrupted, sarcasm in his voice.

"No, I think he genuinely wants a woman to comfort him in his old age. At this point he has no information to give us. He will try, if the yakuza will let him. But I know he will not point the finger at any Japanese."

"It looks like we are up against the proverbial rock and a hard place. We have nothing fresh to go on. I hate to think we are at a dead end," Grant said, wistfully.

"I don't know how this affects our investigation of your father's murder, but since Hitchcock took me off the dynamiting cases, I've been assigned to investigate counterfeiting. What's interesting is that bogus bills showed up just before the attacks on the HSPA. We have never had this crime before."

"Asing, you are wrong. The first counterfeiters in Hawaii were the Lahainaluna School boys back in 1832," Joshua said.

"How so?"

"When the missionaries got here one of the first thing they wanted to do was create a Hawaiian alphabet so they could print the Bible in our language. Lahainaluna is a school they founded on Maui to begin educating the people and printing the Bible. Young ones learned the art very well. Hawaiian currency or coins did not exist, only Yankee dollars and Spanish Real. The school boys began to print foreign money. They got away with it for a time, but what they created would not pass close inspection and they were caught and shut down.

"An interesting part of history, Ben Franklin is the first American to learn how to defeat counterfeiters. His method was to simply misspell a word on the currency. Counterfeiters would correct the spelling and get caught. Kalakaua introduced coins and paper money to Hawaii with his image on it. Some Chinese tried to imitate it, but couldn't get away with it. The Hawaiian legislature passed drastic laws against counterfeiters, life imprisonment at the discretion of the judge. I think those laws are still in force in the Territory. All Kalakaua money has been phased out with annexation. His coins are very valuable. They make nice jewelry."

"This is all very interesting, but how does it help us in our quest?" Grant asked.

Asing pursed his lips. His brow wrinkled like waves on a pond. "It is hard to say how information can be useful. Obviously, the yakuza are protecting something, otherwise why fight and later beat you. They are protecting something."

"With the queue I saw next door to Saiki's shop maybe they were defending their whorehouse?"

"Not necessary, there is an agreement with the law: keep your harlots in J Town and we will leave you alone. I think with the increased military in Honolulu, the Big Five will want that deal to remain in force. There is something else being protected by the gang and Saiki is a factor in whatever scheme they are engaged in."

Grant stood. "This speculation is most interesting, but I'm going to Kaneohe to meet a friend to talk about Hawaiians and dynamiting. Something's going on in that rural area that's worth investigating."

"I've told you before," Joshua interjected, "Hawaiians wouldn't commit these attacks."

"Probably not, but I think visiting in Kaneohe might be worth a trip."

"Good luck, please remember we have a Royal Order meeting soon. Robinson from the *Hinode Times* is the guest speaker."

"He is?" Asing interjected. "I've been reading that man's newspaper, his articles border on violating the anarchy laws. He had best be careful of what he says, or the sugar people will chop him off at the knees and those that attend could be charged with sedition." The detective smiled.

"Then I will definitely be at the meeting despite the danger."

"Count me in." Asing winked.

Grant left.

## CHAPTER 29

Grant turned his auto onto the dirt pathway that led to the banana patch and then the Makanani house. There were two new grass shacks to the left side of the unpaved roadway. As he motored along, he saw a long earthen berm that stretched several hundred feet toward the steep blue-green walls of the Koolau Mountains. A new taro patch was under construction.

He winced as he thought of the poor Hawaiians who were being pushed out of Honolulu by the rapid development of the capitol city caused by sugar, pineapple, and an expanding military. Grant remembered the HSPA touting to Congress: "Hawaii is the American outpost in the Pacific that guards against unfriendly hands."

This accelerated growth had made the Hawaiian an itinerant farmer forced to move from place to place. No longer did he grow taro in the traditional areas of Nuuanu and Waikiki. Now he had to move out to the countryside. Grant wondered how long it would be before this agricultural haven in Kailua and Kaneohe would be swallowed up by development. He hoped never, but he knew that change would come, and the fields of green leafy plants would disappear like the one hundred ponds that had once provided the Hawaiians with a bountiful supply of fish.

He parked his Packard by a banana patch and pushed his way through the tubers. His friend Kawika had wanted it this way. "Eh, 'brah," he said. "No want nobody finding where I make *okolehau.* If you want come my house you go through the bananas first." Grant knew the fastest way to his friend's home lay through the fruit field. It also could be the most dangerous, since the alcohol still lay in the middle of the growing plants.

"No want anybody finds my stuff. If they come through, I bust them up," Kawika said.

Grant easily picked his way through the plants, following a route Kawika had shown him. He emerged onto an open field of grass. In it lay a neat brown bungalow. At its entry Kawika sat on a wide straw chair chewing on a stick and dipping his fingers into a bowl. "Eh, 'brah, come eat, *pulehu* meat some good. The poi, *ono*, real sour."

"Go ahead and enjoy yourself without me. That fermented taro is a terror, makes you sound like a back-firing automobile." Grant stepped up onto the veranda of the home and took the chair that Kawika pointed to.

"I'm sorry about your father. When's the funeral?"

Grant sat silent for several moments, the horrible events playing over his mind. He took deep breaths.

"Sorry, 'brah, I can see hard on you. Never mind. We talk other stuff."

Grant wiped his eyes. "We are waiting for my sister to get here from Los Angeles. Maybe nine, ten days from now."

"Let us know, I'll bring the family over. Say, if you want, we can make a luau for the reception."

"Thanks for the offer. I know we will do something. You mentioned to me on the phone that you wanted to talk about weird things that are going on."

Kawika wiped his sticky hands on a cloth, stood, and walked into his house. He returned with a paper in his hand. "Some guy, maybe Filipino, is passing this out."

The message read:

Hawaiians!!

Your land has been stolen by the Imperialists!

They are militarizing it with forts, guns and soldiers.

Unite against the Oppressors of the People!

Make them leave Hawaii! Free yourselves from them!

Come to a meeting in Honolulu

THURSDAY NIGHT 7:00 PM

ROYAL HAWAIIAN HALL

"Us kine guys don't know what's what. Maybe you can tell us?" Kawika asked.

Grant paused for some moments choosing his words carefully. "Six years ago, during the Great War the people of the nation of Russia revolted because they were poor, starving, and dying. Men put the ruler, the Tsar, in prison. They were anti-military and anti-imperialists, which means they were against rule by a few rich people like the Big Five. These men wanted to have a world-wide revolution of the common folk, like the *maka'ainana* of Hawaii. They were called 'Reds' for the flag they used."

"Meeting about Hawaiians be like da 'Reds' fight da kine Big Five?"

"I think so. Hawaiians have much to be angry about. You're dying by the thousands since the foreigners came, you have lost most of your land, you are poor, your kingdom is gone, taken by a few haole revolutionaries and given to the United States."

Kawika scratched his head, "You know, 'brah, we doing okay. Got plenty taro, fish, raise pigs. Yeah, there's Hawaiians who got less, but we share, that's the style. We take care, *malama* each other."

"That's how it's been for our people, share and care for each other. But this is not the style of the new world we live in. It's run by capitalism which is all about making money. The reason we have strikes is the sugar plantations don't care about the workers, pay them very little, make them labor long hours six days a week. Why? You make lots of money when you profit from the sweat of the working man."

"You say da rich guys work us for all they can get, and give back *opala*."

Grant smiled. "Yes, rubbish, and the worker is treated like *opala pala unu*."

"Like junk people, that's why I no work in the sugar fields, no respect."

Grant looked out at the ponds of taro next to the Makanani house. Green leaves above the water waved in the late morning breeze. A rooster crowed and hens made their busy noises as they scratched into the earth. *What a peaceful scene*, he thought. *Was this what it was like in ancient times?* "Would you like to go back to the old, old, days?"

"No way, unless I a chief. Dem guys told you what to do. You obey or die. They got the most food, the best of everything. The maka'ainana work their butts off for da *alii*."

"What you're saying is there will always be the few who have the power and the many who work for them."

"You got it. You kick out the old bosses and new ones come in. Da people still suffer da same."

"Okay, let me ask this, three bomb explosions, one of them killed my father. We don't know who did it. Would Hawaiians do that?"

Kawika shifted in his seat. "We know nothing about that kina stuff. If we goin' fight you, it's face to face, man to man."

Grant nodded, "I agree, besides Hawaiians don't like to hurt the land, it's family. But what about this Filipino guy that passed out messages, can you describe him?

"Yeah, maybe this tall," Kawika gestured with his hand.

"Looks like about five-foot-six inches."

"Yeah, and maybe one-hundred-forty. Tan, with no hair on the face."

"Recognize him if see him again?"

"Sure thing."

"Great, maybe we'll see you Thursday night at the talk?"

"Long way to go."

"Think about it." The men embraced, Grant went to his car and drove to Honolulu.

# CHAPTER 30

David rushed to him as Grant stepped into his office. "Where have you been? I've looked all over for you. Patterson's going crazy, threatening all kinds of retaliation against the Japanese and us."

Grant flinched. "What did we do? What's he angry about?"

"A train blew up in the depot. Killed the foreman and burned the engineer. He thinks the Japanese planted dynamite in the engine. He blames you and Asing for not acting faster to arrest people. He blames the both of us for being cozy with the Japanese. Kind of crazy, but we are the bad guys! I can't stand these attacks, time to sell and leave."

"Where did it happen?"

"Iwilei."

"Let's go."

The brothers entered the train yard which had a roundabout, an engine house, workshops, and a red-roofed station painted light brown. Three police cars were parked nearby. Grant wondered if Asing would be one of the investigating officers. He was the chief detective in the murder division.

After inquiry, they were directed to the back of the station. There, Grant noticed several officers examining a small locomotive. He and Dave strode along the tracks until they got to the train. An officer challenged them, "What you want?"

"I'm working with Detective Asing on an explosion case like to this one. Is he here? If not, I'm sure he is on his way."

"Don't know about that."

Grant didn't wait for any more questions from the policeman but bluffed his way into the investigation. "Doesn't look like dynamite from the lack of damage to the cab. What happened?"

"Engineer said they were getting steam up. The gauges showed the water hadn't reached boiling point. The fireman shoveled a load of coal into the fire chamber and an explosion occurred right after. Damaged the boiler and inside the fire pit, and did minor outside damage as you can see. The fireman caught burning material on his face and body. He didn't die right away. He got cooked by his clothes catching fire and the engineer got burned also. Funny thing is the engineer didn't see anything unusual about the coal, no red sticks of dynamite."

"I had thought these engines burned wood?"

"Yes, they once did," a voice interrupted.

"Sorry, my name is Grant Kingsley and you are?"

"Station master Alex Hamilton, as I said, the first engines burned wood when they got to Hawaii in 1880. We didn't have natural coal and lumber was available. The trouble is that the whalers had chopped down too many trees to cook blubber and people kept burning up wood without reforestation. We have run out of lumber. It's the same problem that ended the Hawaiian sandalwood industry, Hawaiians cut down trees without replanting. Plus, there's another downside with wood, insufficient BTUs."

"BTU, what's that?"

"Steam engines were first developed by the British in the 1800's. They created the term BTU, British Thermal Unit, that refers to the amount of heat required to raise the temperature of a pound of water by one-degree Fahrenheit. A pound of wood can produce 8,600 BTUs. A pound of coal can give you almost twice as much. We are turning to fuel oil to heat water. It's cheaper and provides more BTUs than coal."

"This engine that exploded burned coal. Have you had any blow ups from coal in the past?"

"Never, coal is a very stable substance. In its natural form it does not blow up. To have any effect as a catalyst for an explosion it would need to be ground down to a fine powder. But we don't use grains of coal to make steam, we use lumps of coal."

"Somehow coal was involved in the blast that killed the fireman."

"What are you two men doing here?" a loud, angry voice interrupted.

Grant turned to see Patterson striding toward them, his face red either from exertion, anger or both. "You have made accusations against my brother and me. We came to determine the truth."

"You, Mr. Kingsley, very well know who caused this explosion, Japanese dynamiters!"

"There is no evidence of dynamite in the blast that occurred. Shoveled coal into a fire pit caused the blow up."

"That is utterly ridiculous. If it was not dynamite maybe a defective steam kettle exploded."

"Not likely," Hamilton interrupted. "The water had not been heated enough to boil before the blast occurred. It had something to do with the coal that got thrown in. What it was I can't fathom."

Grant pursed his lips, rubbed his face with his fingers thinking back to his days in the trenches. Patterson swore and berated Hamilton for not being more careful with equipment. Grant raised his hand and said, "I may have an answer, it might have been sabotage."

"Sabotage, what in heaven's name is that?" Patterson blustered.

"The word is well known in undercover warfare, it comes from sabot, wooden shoes that Dutch workers wore. They were afraid of machinery that was being introduced in manufacturing, believing that they would lose their jobs. Sabots would be thrown into the gears of the equipment to destroy them. Business owners did not know who did it, hence the name saboteurs to describe these unknown men who could grind an enterprise to a halt. The term became very popular in wartime to describe hidden activity that caused great damage to the means of making war."

"You're talking fantasy stuff. We are in Hawaii, not a war zone," Patterson sneered.

"That's where you are wrong, with four explosions and two dead there is someone who has declared war on the HSPA. Have you ever heard of a "coal torpedo"? If my suspicion is correct, more coal burning engines are in grave danger."

"Whoa there." Hamilton smacked his palm against the side of the damaged train. "What are you talking about, 'coal torpedo, more danger'?"

"Don't listen to this kind of claptrap. Torpedoes! We are not at sea but in a train yard." Patterson laughed as if a joke had been uttered.

"But maybe we should hear what Mr. Kingsley has to say about danger," Hamilton admonished.

Grant was not intimidated by Patterson's head shaking. "When I soldiered in the war, we had hours of boredom between attacks and patrols. We talked of many things including saboteurs. There were men in my battalion from the South. They spoke of a special unit during the Civil War run by a man named Courtenay who invented a coal bomb. In the hollow of a mound of iron, gunpowder would be inserted. The lump would be sealed and covered with coal dust. Then the device would be tossed into a Union ship's bin. When sailors shoveled lumps of coal into a fire pit it exploded, sinking or at least damaging the ship. For a time, the Union military were baffled about the cause of the blasts until they discovered the truth. They dubbed the device a 'coal torpedo'."

"And this is a contraption used in wartime. How many ships were lost by this device?" Hamilton asked.

"At least sixty Union boats. The Confederacy didn't use the bomb until the last few months of the war. Had they started the sabotage sooner, maybe they could have won."

"It's obvious," Hamilton interjected, "we have to examine all the coal to be used in the engines."

"That would grind sugar operations to a halt. I say it's a defective boiler or dynamite," Paterson protested.

"But the temperature gauge hadn't reached a boiling point and dynamite without a detonator will not explode when burned. A stick of it would have been obvious with a detonator and fuse," Grant said

Hamilton shook his head. "We can't take the chance that it isn't a coal bomb. We have been replacing coal burners with fuel oil equipment. It's possible we could get by with the retooled trains. I'll get men to start examining the coal right now." Hamilton hurried away.

Patterson stood silent, his eyes shifting from place to place, finally resting on Grant. "You have stirred up unnecessary turmoil in our business. You know who is responsible, the Japanese."

"It may be there was only one bomb placed in a coal bin. But does it take finding other explosive devices in this train yard to convince you that the Japanese are not involved in these attacks, but another foreign agency is?"

"Who? Is there some dark, unknown power conspiring to undermine the sugar industry? Since annexation all we have imported are Japanese, Koreans, and Filipinos. The Koreans hate the Japanese. We use them as strike breakers. The only ones that are clearly visible as enemies of the HSPA are the Japanese who are proven dynamiters, and those dammed Filipinos. Those people were taught a deadly lesson when they decided to defy the law. Force will be met with force even if it means shooting people."

Grant shuddered; the man appeared on the brink of insanity. "If I am right about the coal torpedoes will you leave the Japanese alone and stop badgering my brother with your threats?"

Patterson smirked. Here was the weak spot in the Kingsley empire, David. He would work on his fears until he could buy their two plantations cheap. "It remains to be seen what I will do. If there is someone other than our imported races behind the attacks, I might reconsider my opinion." Then he stared directly at David, his voice deathly cold. "But you had best toe the party line and know whom you must listen to or else there could be dire consequences."

Grant shook his head. *It was the same all over the world, the ruling power, no matter what it called itself, bullied the weak. Anger rose within him. Should I meet threats with threats? He decided to be conciliatory, no need to play all his cards in this train yard.* "As Asing and I continue to investigate and uncover the truth I believe you will be forced to agree that the Kingsley family will be proven right. Let me add that we will not sit idly by while you attempt to steal what we have like the plantations stole from the Hawaiians."

Patterson stepped back, swearing. "Damn you, are you accusing the HSPA of being thieves?"

Grant's eyes turned steely as he looked directly at Patterson. "No, only suggesting that we will not be run out of town with our tail between our legs. We will not allow anyone to take what we have without a fight."

David looked at his brother and then at the HSPA man. "I agree."

# CHAPTER 31

Hidden in a nearby tool shed, the saboteur wanted to scream. This wild man from the HSPA advocated death for the working man. He remembered American imperialists killing thousands of Filipinos in their conquest of the Philippines. Recently, British imperialists in India had shot at thousands of peaceful protesters until the soldiers' ammunition had been exhausted. On Kauai, the military had trained machine guns on strikers in Kapaa town. Many Filipinos would have been killed if they hadn't fled the deadly weapons. At the schoolhouse in Hanapepe scores of men had been killed and wounded by the rifle fire of HSPA gunmen. One of the dead was his brother.

Through the screened window of the shed, he heard everything the men had said. They had shouted at each other, Patterson being the noisiest. He cursed his bad luck that the first bomb he had planted went off before the locomotive had been harnessed to wagons and put to work. A spectacular derailment had been spoiled by the premature explosion.

The three other bombs he had tossed into bins might have wreaked havoc on the railroads, maybe even caused a permanent shutdown or, better yet, a vicious campaign against the Japanese. But that nosy Grant Kingsley had guessed correctly about the sabotage device and suggested that it might not be the Nipponese who were the guilty parties for the bombings.

Despite this failure, the saboteur congratulated himself. His teachers would be proud of him. He had correctly measured the amounts of potassium nitrate, seventy-five percent, crushed charcoal, fifteen percent, and sulfur, ten percent and blended the brew together with mortar, pestle, and a touch of water. The explosion of the gunpowder-filled iron container had been spectacular. But that miserable rat Kingsley had spoiled the rest of his plan. For his interference he would be placed on his list of imperialists to terminate.

Kingsley would die. But the HSPA men would come first, unless, of course, an opportunity arose to finish the interfering lawyer.

The saboteur stepped out of the shed and easily blended into the crowd of workers that had come to the Iwilei rail yards. He threaded his way through the throng considering what device he would use to blow Patterson to Catholic hell.

# CHAPTER 32

As Grant strode back to his office, he thought of his brother. *David had stood silent during the meeting at the train yard and the vicious harangue by Patterson against the family enterprises. But in the end, he supported what I had to say.* He asked his brother about this.

David answered, "A saboteur can undermine a nation's ability to fight. A bully can do the same thing to a family enterprise like ours. I realized today that I have been pushed around by Patterson. He knows I am the weak one and he has preyed upon me. No more will I let him beat upon me using the usual plantation tactics of divide and rule. What's that saying? 'United we stand, divided we fall.' Today, I set aside my fears and decided to stand up to that bully."

Grant felt thankful that his brother had come around to his way of thinking. *This "Mikado Lover" bull that Patterson had been dishing out was just a ploy. He had other motives for calling the Kingsleys traitors to the cause of the HSPA. What was it about the Japanese that made him pick on them? I'll ask Joshua. The older man knew so much.*

Grant entered the reception room and headed for his partner's office. Though he had been in it many times, he realized when he entered, how sparse it was. On the far wall stood a picture of the deposed Queen autographed by her in the right corner. On each side were certificates. The one on the left recited he had successfully completed his law training by a judge of the Hawaiian Kingdom. The one on the right side recited he had successfully passed the requirements of the Territorial Bar and was admitted to the practice of law before the courts of Hawaii.

On the left wall stood a bookcase filled with law books. That completed the simple decorations of the office. Joshua looked up, smiled, and said, "Good day to you, my boy. To what do I owe the pleasure of your company this noon?"

Grant slipped into a chair, studied the wrinkled face of the older man and said, "I've just had a very interesting morning. Tried to solve a crime at the railroad yard and suffered through brutal accusations by Mr. Patterson. He hates the Japanese. I don't know why. I thought you might give me some insights."

Joshua rubbed his nose, fingered his ear, thought for some moments before answering, "I can't rightly say what has angered the man about them. They were first imported to Hawaii by a labor contractor. Many were the derelicts left over from the fall of the Tokugawa Shogunate, unemployed samurai, plus young men trying to escape from conscription into the army of the Meiji government. They didn't know a thing about farming and became very unhappy plantation workers. This first try at Japanese labor failed. Then King Kalakaua traveled to that country and made a deal with the Emperor. By the way, that is how the Japanese embassy was established in Hawaii, to protect the citizens of Japan imported to work in the islands. These new workers were mostly farmers escaping from the severe depression and poverty in their homeland. They proved to be capable. The plantation folk decided to import them by the thousands to counteract the Chinese who had become very restive due to low wages and horrible working conditions."

"The usual tactic of divide and rule, play one race off against another. But the Japanese were no better off than the Chinese. That must have led to trouble," Grant asked.

"It did, especially when the islands became a territory. We were subject to American law which abhors slavery. Before annexation the plantations could force the contract laborer to work according to the written agreement. The Hawaiian courts enforced the agreements that the men had been duped into signing. They were contract slaves. But once we were part of the United States, such contracts had no effect. Starting in 1900 a series of strikes and work stoppages began. This is when Mr. Patterson first got involved with the HSPA. The credo adopted by the planters' organization is to exert power 'out of the barrel of a gun' and 'use the militia' to teach strikers a lesson. Throughout this first decade of the twentieth century the National Guard was called out to deal with troublesome Japanese laborers. Shootings injured many workers."

"You are telling me that Patterson received his labor education at a time when the plantations were merciless and exerted their power with an iron hand."

"Yes, and to an extent such treatment achieved results, but divide and rule continued to be the method to control the demands of the Japanese. Koreans were brought in as strike breakers, seven thousand of them. They came to escape Japanese imperialism and were not friendly to members of that country.

"It was the 1909 strike that caused the plantations to turn to the Philippines to find a rich source of strike breakers. Filipinos were not affected by exclusion laws or deals made between countries, like the Gentlemen's Agreement. This strike-breaker mentality of the HSPA and the use of force against the Japanese must have affected Patterson, especially when the plantations won the 1909 strike."

"I see your point, if you use force and harsh treatment against militant workers you can achieve labor success. But this did not work as well in the strike of 1920."

"To some extent what you say is true. Harsh treatment like evictions and police brutality led to deaths. The flu also killed many. Despite all this, the Japanese hung in there for six months and the HSPA made concessions."

"I recall that very well. To some extent I was involved in negotiations to end the strike."

"Did you notice what the HSPA did after it? They put twenty-one Oahu labor leaders on trial for a minor dynamiting on Hawaii Island. It broke the union. Look what has happened to the labor leaders of the Filipinos after their latest strike, they have been persecuted, jailed, or run out of town. Your friend Patterson is still dealing with workers with an iron hand."

"I think you are saying that he has cowed the Filipinos by a massacre in Hanapepe and he is trying to suppress the Japanese by blaming them for the latest round of attacks on the HSPA."

Joshua smiled. "I don't believe Patterson knows what to do. He is striking out at the Japanese because he can't think of any other race that would put his life at risk along with his HSPA compatriots. He's too accustomed to dealing with massive racial strikes. He can't get it into his head that it might not be the answer to his problem."

"I agree with you. We have been looking at these events as a racial conspiracy to do in the sugar people. But maybe it is not that at all, it could be a personal vendetta by a few people or even one person."

"Yes, we have to move away from what we think are the obvious reasons for the attacks and consider other alternatives."

Grant sighed. "What those alternatives might be, I can't figure out. Could the coal torpedo bombing of a plantation train give us a clue? Is there a conspiracy to have warfare by sabotage to bring down the plantations? It doesn't make sense to damage something that gives people jobs."

"Think on it for a moment, if you wanted to destroy capitalism and redistribute wealth what would you do? You attack the profit-making enterprises. You rile up the workers, the poor people, preach toppling the existing power structure and making change."

"You're sounding like a Bolshevik."

Joshua went to his bookshelf and withdrew a volume. "This is *Ten Days That Shook the World* by John Reed, an American reporter. He tells the story of that revolution. Don't you think that is possible in Hawaii?"

"Anything is possible, but at this point I don't see a 'Red' movement in the islands. I don't reject what you say, but I think Asing is of the old school: "First investigate the usual suspects."

"And that would be the Japanese, Filipinos, and Hawaiians. Exclude my people, they would never be involved in bombings or constructing weapons like coal torpedoes."

A receptionist entered the office "Detective Asing would like to see you at Bethel Police Station."

"Okay, tell him I'll be right there."

Grant left.

# CHAPTER 33

The saboteur had carefully planned everything to this point, but making the coal torpedoes had nearly exhausted his supply of weapons. He had bullets for his rifle and deadly poisons, but he needed more explosions to bring down the capitalist dogs who preyed on the working class.

He held his breath, did not move. A Filipino worker stood near the plantation shed that housed the dynamite. It would be easy to kill the man, a collateral casualty in the war against the imperialists. Would that be a victory for the cause? No, only the HSPA leaders should die, not the immigrants who made them wealthy.

For a moment, as he slowly exhaled, he wondered if he should give up, not kill the guard, and leave. His thoughts returned to what Trotsky had lectured to the students at the CHEKA School of terror. He told of how the revolution had been won by men who dared to do what was needed. "If there are comrades who haven't the courage to dare what we dare, let them leave with the rest of the cowards and conciliators." The saboteur realized then that despite danger, the brave will do what must be done to win freedom for the proletariat. It was a credo that he believed in ever since he heard Trotsky speak.

Patience, he would wait. Watch for an opportunity, no sense to leave a trail of death. His theft needed to go unnoticed. The saboteur recalled what had made the Bolshevik revolution successful: a willingness to kill enemies and make them drown in blood. Lenin had preached: *We must stop at nothing to save the rule of the workers and peasants to save Communism.*

He would follow this dictate until the overthrow of capitalism became complete.

A voice from a long distance away called, "Hey *manong*, come help."

The saboteur glanced from his hiding place and saw a cart many feet from the shed with a wheel mired in a hole. The watchman moved from his post at the storage building. Bending low the thief hurried to the door and picked its lock. He entered and realized in the dim light of the interior it would be difficult to find what he wanted. He had no choice but to light a match to explore the inside. But as the burning sulfur wrinkled his nose, he suddenly worried that the flame would explode the shed.

He felt the heat of the flickering light on his fingers and dropped the match to the dirt floor, extinguishing the last spark with a twist of his shoe. He breathed shallowly listening for the return of the watchman. He heard nothing. Before the flame had died, he had seen on the far wall a box marked with four Xs. He quickly moved to it, loosening a knife at his side.

He placed it against the wooden top prepared to jimmy it open. He worried: would the sounds of his prying alert the guard?

As luck would have it, the top cover moved easily as his knife pushed into the wood. But now a new dilemma. In the dim light, did he dare strike a match to see what lay inside?

He debated with himself for a moment, then reached in, felt round objects and pulled a cylinder out. He could tell what he held felt like a stick of explosives. But is it dynamite? "Damn it all," he swore. Light from a nearby window suddenly glowed and he rushed to it before the sunshine disappeared. "It's dynamite red," he whispered.

"But what about the detonators and a fuse?" he asked himself. Panicked that he had little time to spare he returned to the box, dropped the red cylinder in, took a deep breath and lit a match. Beads of sweat rolled down his cheeks as he peered at the shelves near the dynamite.

Just as his light faded into a thin stream of rising smoke, he saw it: a box of fuses. He reached into the dynamite container, retrieved four sticks, took fuses, and placed them all into a bag. He moved toward the door.

Would the watchman be there? He unsheathed his knife. He didn't want to kill the working man, but for the cause he would.

At the door he listened and heard nothing. Were the hinges rusty? Would they emit a loud shriek as he opened the portal? When he entered, he hadn't heard any sound, but any noises would have been masked by the voices outside yelling instructions on how to free the cart.

With great care the saboteur eased the door open, his knife ready to plunge into anyone outside. He peeked through the slender opening, saw no one, pushed the door wider, and slipped out of the building. Bent low, he could see men hovering over the cart. He put the lock back on the latch and carefully moved toward the shrubs nearby.

A voice yelled, "Hey!" His heart raced. He almost ran for the bushes. But he held back resisting his panic. The voice yelled again, "Hey, lift that wheel onto solid ground."

Sweat dampened his shirt, as Miguel worked his way into the spiky foliage. He felt elated. He had found the means of destruction. Patterson and the HSPA would soon pay dearly for their sins.

## CHAPTER 34

Grant walked into the downtown police station, and said to the desk sergeant, "Asing?"

The officer nodded to the left and Grant stepped into the hallway then entered the first door he came to. The Chinese detective sat at his desk, a cigarette between his lips and a cloud of smoke spiraling toward the ceiling. In an ashtray sat several squashed white butts. The room felt dank from burnt tobacco. Despite this, Grant enjoyed the smell of the hot ash of a cigarette. "What's up Chinaman?" Grant smiled.

"Watch your racial slurs you dumb kanaka." The two men laughed and clasped hands.

"How goes the great Inquisition of the Japanese?" Grant asked.

Asing winced. "As you recall, I have been removed from the case and am not involved."

"Come on, there are always leaks in your department. You can tell me what's going on."

Asing stood and shut his door. "What I will tell you is not to be repeated, understood?"

Grant nodded.

"You remember that there were twenty-one indictments in the Olaa Plantation dynamiting. All the defendants were Japanese labor leaders in the Fair Wages labor movement. Most of these men lived and worked on Oahu.

"Olaa Plantation is near Hilo, Hawaii, hundreds of miles away from this island. The dynamiting occurred at a Japanese worker's home on June 4, 1920, near Olaa Plantation. There were no injuries, only property damage. At the time it was considered a minor incident and the police investigation ended within a week with no charges being made.

"A year and two months later, the HSPA caused indictments to be issued. The primary charge was a claimed conspiracy of Japanese labor leaders to form 'an assassination corps' to carry out a campaign of terrorism. The Honolulu Advertiser wrote that those indicted: 'Intended to burn, assault, dynamite, and do other acts of violence during the 1920 strike'.

"But none of those dreadful events ever occurred. Only the Olaa incident provided the overt act necessary to show a planned criminal conspiracy of terrorism. The evidence to convict was flimsy, but fifteen labor leaders were found guilty and sentenced to four years in prison. The convictions were intended to teach a lesson to those who opposed the HSPA, just like the recent prosecutions against the Filipino labor leaders.

"What Hitchcock is learning so far is that those convicted are still in jail and family members questioned know nothing of a conspiracy to dynamite or continue terrorism. In fact, the Japanese community wants nothing to do with acts of violence or with those that were found guilty. They are like pariahs in a pond, to be avoided."

"I would guess that Patterson may not be satisfied with denials, but seek to press on with this witch hunt."

"That is correct. Until it is proven the Japanese are not involved in the recent attacks, the HSPA will continue to suppress what they are calling 'the Yellow Peril' a claimed attempt of the Japanese to take over Hawaii, and that is what I want to discuss with you. From what I have learned about Hitchcock's investigation and your description of saboteurs and coal torpedoes, I'm beginning to believe the Japanese are not conducting the latest attacks. But I have no concrete proof of this.

"I've been told to concentrate on counterfeiters and other crimes, I'm thinking that the counterfeiting angle may be a way to disprove Japanese involvement in the attacks on the HSPA."

"Now that is a stretch of your imagination. Explain yourself."

"We know the yakuza controls the major crimes on Oahu: gambling and prostitution. Rumor has it that the counterfeiters are Japanese. The logic is that the ringleaders are yakuza."

"Okay that makes sense, but how is that information useful in proving the Japanese are not involved in the current bombings?"

"Bear with me, the heart of Japan Town is from River Street west toward Maunakea. You found a major brothel on River Street and next to it is Mr. Saiki's shop. He is a printer, your partner Joshua told us this. Why were you attacked by yakuza after leaving Saiki's place? It would not be because of the whorehouse which is protected by Honolulu police."

"You're suggesting that maybe Saiki is involved with the counterfeiters? I did notice something peculiar when I visited him. There was a stack of what looked like greenbacks when I came in. He immediately covered it over with a table cloth. But explain where we are going with this."

"It's a wild idea I have. If the yakuza is involved with counterfeiting, we could use that information to make a deal. For an agreement to end the operation and a promise not to prosecute we could enlist them to find out who the bombers are."

"That is a wild idea. You would agree not to press charges of counterfeiting for information about the attackers. It sounds like tricky law enforcement."

"Grant, in police business deals are made all the time with criminals in order to get the real big fish. What is more important: stopping the attacks on the HSPA or convicting counterfeiters?"

"You know my answer to that. Somehow, we have to stop the persecution of innocent Japanese. What's your plan?"

"Sadly, that is why I need you. I can't tell my department of what I intend to do, too many leaks and people who will obstruct our efforts. Before we can make a deal, we must have proof, we need information we can bargain with and that is where you come in."

"Explain."

"This is an investigation that involves just you and me. Despite our suspicion, we can't just barge into Saiki's shop and search it. What if we are wrong about him? I think the whore house will provide us information about the counterfeiting operation. There is a back alley that services both Saiki's business and the boogie place. We need to scope out that pathway. City plans show you can access the alley from both places."

"You keep using the term 'we'. Where do I come in on this investigation?"

"I am too well known among the yakuza, but you are not. I want you to go into that whorehouse, check it out. Get into that back alley and find out what you can."

"You have to be crazy. Do you realize the danger? What do you think my wife would say if she found out? What about the length of time I would be in there? You said three minutes a trick. Not much time for an investigation."

Asing pondered for a moment. "There is danger I know, but isn't this a risk we must take for the many who are presently being persecuted? I understand about your wife, but you do not have to break your marriage vows. You do not have to have sex with a prostitute. As to a quickie, you can buy more time. Purchase twenty minutes with a woman for twenty dollars and you will be given a special room for love making on the second floor. Change for money is key to what we need to find out what is going on."

Grant put his fingers to his hair rubbing them against his scalp. "This plan is getting more mysterious by the moment. What does the receipt of change have to do with our investigation?"

"Counterfeit money has been showing up in ten-dollar bills. If you were to pay with a fifty-dollar President Grant your change might be counterfeit. I think that is likely. What better place than a whore house, where cash is king, to distribute phony money."

"Okay, assuming I went along with this plan, if I entered on the street where Saiki's door is, the yakuza that cracked my head might recognize me. They seem to be watching his shop very carefully."

"There is another entrance on King Street, for whites only. That's the entry for the military and business folk."

"I may be a little too tan to be considered white."

"It will be dark when you go in. That may be enough to hide your color. The lighting is very dim in the building. What you would expect in a place for pleasure. We have to chance it."

"You said dark, when are we going to pull this off?"

"Tonight, they service men until two o'clock and even later for a price."

"That is sudden! Will I have backup if something goes wrong?"

"I'll be outside. I will have help. They will not be told why they are there, only that it is a stakeout. Here is a police whistle, use it if you're in desperate trouble. Also, a small .32 caliber pistol if death is imminent. I pray you will not need it."

Grant breathed in and out several times. "I can't tell Selena what I will be doing tonight. She would try to stop me. If something does happen please explain to her that I did this task to help people."

## CHAPTER 35

Grant stood in a short line, wondering why he was here. *Deep inside he knew that he acted to uncover the murderer of his father. There was nothing altruistic about his motives for engaging in this wild scheme of Asing. Find the killer and kill him. He went along with the detective's plan because he had no clue as to who fired a bomb that had ended James Kingsley's life.*

The line moved slowly forward. He rebuttoned the long sleeve of his black shirt. Darkness, dark clothes, and a grey hat pulled down to his ears would disguise the features of its owner and the color of his skin.

Grant stepped through the door into a small reception room. A long hallway stretched to his right ending in a wall with an exit sign over it. Many doors were evenly spaced along the hall with some men walking in a door, and others coming out and heading to the exit. To his left was a stairway leading to a second story.

Two men sat at a desk. They were obviously yakuza with arms heavily tattooed and blue-inked symbols covering their necks. He searched their faces and felt relieved that he did not recognize either of them. When his turn came, he said, "I want the twenty-dollar job."

"Ah so," a painted goon answered. You want twenty minutes. You can last that long?"

"Cut the crap, here is fifty-dollars, change please."

The sarcastic yakuza looked at the bill and smiled. He paid out thirty dollars in tens. "Upstairs, end of the hall by exit, room 45."

Grant took his money and went to the stairs. He passed a third man seated behind the reception desk who stared intently as Grant passed by. He felt the man's eyes on him as he mounted to the second floor.

He entered a decorated room with exotic pictures of nude women hung on the walls. Males ahead of him were entering in or out of the hallway doors as in the floor below. But there were fewer in number in the upstairs area.

Grant thought to examine the money, but realized he had no expertise in counterfeit paper. At least one part of his mission had been completed. Worried by the scrutiny of the man downstairs, he headed for the exit sign. A stairway led down with men exiting the building. This must go into the alley that Asing had shown him on the city's map. He stepped down, a voice from the decorated room yelled, "Hey you. Room forty-five behind you, on your left."

Grant didn't stop. He rushed down the stairs as he heard heavy footsteps coming down the hallway. He got to the alley door and stepped out. His heart sank, to his right two men were exiting from Saiki's office onto the same narrow street between the buildings. Behind him he heard footsteps on the second-floor stairs.

# CHAPTER 36

The saboteur hurried in the dark, thankful that street lights did not brighten Nuuanu. Only the windows of the mansions lining the roadway cast feeble light onto the pavement. He wore dark clothes to blend into the night. His approach to the target must be undetected. When the occasional vehicle came along, he shrunk into the shadows.

He felt conflicted. His handler had argued against blaming the Japanese for more explosions. "Why?' he had asked.

"Because they are the exploited ones, our cause is to incite revolution. We must unite the workers of the world against the bourgeoisie and the wealthy. These people from Nippon are ripe for social change. Why burden them with more harassment from those in power?" his handler answered.

"But Lenin said: 'We must stop at nothing to save the rule of the workers.' If the Japanese bleed from the harassment of the sugar people, they will be more responsive to our call to revolt," the saboteur answered.

"But if they are cowed into submission by the imperialists they may not respond to our arguments for change."

"That is where I believe you are wrong. Trotsky said: 'The struggle to create a classless society is filled with violence, hate, and destruction. It is a crusade that leads to progress for humanity.' For the good of the cause, if there is blood that must be given from the masses, I say, so be it."

The handler had reared back as if slapped in the face, "You think I am afraid? I provided all the funds for the cause in Hawaii. I am the one who has taken you in and given you sustenance. You are an ungrateful wretch and should leave my presence."

The saboteur knew he had gone too far in his zeal to wreak havoc on the HSPA. He hadn't dared to reveal to the man the reason he had come to Hawaii. Revenge is what he sought. He must have it at all costs.

He meekly addressed his handler, "I apologize, I said things because of my love of Communism. I will continue to serve the cause as you may direct. Let me do this last bombing. Mr. Kingsley is getting too close to us. He has much knowledge from the Great War. I want to keep him away from us. Blame the Japanese for the dynamite explosions."

Reluctantly, the handler had agreed to the attack. But the saboteur had no intention of abandoning more violence. Tonight, he would deal with Doolittle. Tomorrow it might be Patterson or maybe Kingsley.

He approached the pine hedge that bordered the home. It proved easy to work his way through the bushes. He bent low as he scurried across the green lawn. His feet sank into the sod and he realized he left a trail to his entry point. No matter, he would be far away when the dynamite exploded.

With a jolt he heard a dog barking. This he had not counted on. Should he retreat and try again another time? But his presence had been memorialized by his footsteps imprinted into the grass. Would the lawn spring back by morning and hide his entry? He could feel the arteries on the sides of his neck throbbing. He knew his heart pounded wildly with the threat of discovery.

Damn that dog, he thought.

A veranda light came on and a pale face peered through a partially open door. The saboteur sank to the level of the green grass.

The face searched the outside. "See anything?" a female voice asked.

"No, nothing," the face answered. "Maybe some animal spooked Lady into barking."

"Don't let her out."

"All right, take her into the kitchen, feed her, and let's go to sleep."

"Perfect, when all the lights are out, I will plant my dynamite. The explosion will strike fear in their hearts," the saboteur muttered.

He waited, his thoughts dwelling on the anger he felt for the killing of Filipinos. Americans did not care for his people. They had slaughtered them without mercy. They were like the British, exploit the natives, kill them if they protested. Tonight, as he had done before, he would strike back.

Slowly he moved to the home, looked up at a second story window that he guessed to be the master bedroom. He placed his dynamite below it and lit its fuse. It sputtered into life moving slowly toward the three red cylinders wrapped together.

No longer concerned about barking dogs, he hurried back to his entry point and stepped onto Nuuanu Street. He ran to his bicycle and sped away. Breathing hard from his furious pedaling he listened for the explosion that would kill the imperialists.

# CHAPTER 37

Grant felt a chill descend his spine. He had only a moment to decide: run, blow his whistle, or fight his pursuer? But there were two yakuza in the alley, surely, they would help their brother behind him. The pathway lay dim in the scant light. Men walked the alley toward the main street. He felt the presence of someone in back. He prayed that it was a person who had just finished his 'quickie.'

Grant backed up and knocked the man toward the stairway. "Sorry," he said and leapt out into the pathway. He moved into the darkness beneath a building wall and huddled into it. He squashed his hat and found some cover in the heaps of garbage piled against the building's side.

Someone swore at the exit door. Another voice yelled, "Damn you, out of my way." Grant saw a tattooed man come out and look up and down the alley. He called to the two yakuza loafing at the far end, "Hey, you guys see anybody leaving?"

"Sure," one of the men laughed. "Ahead of you, them that already done it."

"I mean just a few seconds ago. A guy wearing a hat.

"Kina hard to tell. Kina dark. Maybe, don't know."

The yakuza at the exit door shook his head. Men were moving out of the alley onto the main street. Men behind him complained, "Out of the way. We want to leave."

With a long last look, the thug turned back into the building. Grant slowly released his breath. He felt instantly nauseated by the smell of the offal he lay in. A bath, he needed a bath to cleanse himself of the stink. But he had not completed his mission.

The parade of satisfied men out of the whore house ended. Grant bent low, hugged the wall, and moved carefully toward the yakuza still standing at the far wall. He wondered whether they were on guard or just having a long smoke break? Once he heard their voices he stopped.

The two men spoke in Japanese. Grant could barely understand what they were saying. He knew their conversation concerned money and what they would buy with it. They laughed a lot. They talked of gambling, mah-jong, hanafuda, often giggling when they spoke. He worried; how long could he hide by the side of the building before discovery?

The men chain smoked. Finally, one of them said something like, "We go…Saiki…finish…make money." They entered the shop.

Worried, a shaft of fear coursing down his spine to his toes, Grant padded to a window that gave him a view into the shop. Saiki stood near a press. On the table that supported it were stacks of currency. Saiki placed the bills into a suitcase while the two yakuza watched. "They are going to take the fake money somewhere," Grant said in a low tone. He had seen enough. It's time to leave and find Asing.

He hugged the alley wall padding toward the main street. A couple of men walked ahead of him, one of them whistling a merry tune. Good, he thought, the satisfied sounds would mask the noise of his movements.

He reached the exit and paused. He worried. He studied the doorway. He recalled a proverb: "He who hesitates is lost. Self-doubt brings disaster." Resolute, he strode past the dimly lit exit and headed for the main street. He must find Asing and if they were lucky, they could intercept the couriers.

Grant turned the corner onto the road. Traffic was sparse. From far away he thought he heard an explosion. Where could Asing be? Had he left? Stay cool, he thought.

The detective stepped from a closed entryway of a building. "Aloha, my, my, you have a very distinctive odor. Swimming in a sewer?"

"Don't joke. Where are the men who are with you?"

"I am alone."

"What! You are the only one to save me if I got in trouble!"

"I wasn't worried. You're a war time soldier. You know how to handle dangerous enemies."

Grant scowled. "The next time you want someone to go into serious danger without backup you can do it yourself."

"Why are you complaining! You made it safe and sound. I knew you could do it. Besides you had me, whom else did you need?" Asing smiled as if he had told a humorous joke.

Grant stopped his complaints. The detective appeared immune to criticism. "If you and I are all there is to deal with the yakuza, I suspect two of them will be walking down this alley in a few minutes with a suitcase filled with bogus bills."

Asing rubbed his hands together. "Pay dirt! Quick, back to the exit way, we will nab them as they come out."

"Shall I draw my gun?"

"No, my police presence should be enough. Besides, guns could hurt the wrong people."

The two men came to the alley. Grant drew a hood over his face. Neither peered down the pathway. They listened for footsteps. A man came out and Grant shook his head. Minutes passed by, before they heard conversation in Japanese. Grant nodded.

Asing stepped out from his hiding place. "Police, you're under arrest."

"Bakatare," the two yakuza answered in unison as they drew knives from the belts at their waists.

"It's a serious offence to threaten a law officer and resist arrest."

"You one dumb Chinaman. You die quick." A yakuza lunged forward as his partner moved to the left.

"Kiai!" Grant yelled a single martial arts word to startle his opponent as he swung his fingers onto the knife arm of the lunging yakuza. He followed the strike with an arm bar. He grasped the man's wrist, leaped, scissored his legs around his opponent's waist, brought him to the ground, and pulled the knife arm over his chest. Grant applied heavy pressure to it. "Give up the knife or break arm from its socket."

The pinned man squirmed, flayed his legs in an attempt to escape the hold. Grant applied more pressure on the trapped arm, the yakuza's muscles and ligaments were stretched to the tearing point. "Drop the knife or have your arm crippled forever."

The weapon clattered to the pavement. Grant released his hold and rolled upright. The yakuza came up as well. He tried a sweep with his leg. Grant danced back, pirouetted and slammed his foot into his opponent's abdomen. The man faltered and bent down in agony.

Grant ended the fight with a two-handed smash onto the back of the yakuza's neck. He glanced over to Asing. The second yakuza no longer had his knife in his hand. The detective stood a few feet from him, his whip at his side. The tattooed man turned to run. A quick movement of the wrist, and Asing's lash snaked out and wrapped itself around the man's leg. A sharp pull and he fell to the ground yelling, "Ayah, no more."

Asing went over and cuffed the man, dragged him to where Grant's opponent sat, and cuffed them together. "Help me take these guys to the station, then you best go home and wash, you smell like a dung heap."

# CHAPTER 38

He lost his concentration for some moments. His *olohe*, David Kamaka, grasped the shoulders of his exercise robe, rolled back, placed a foot into his stomach, and flipped him over his head. As Grant had been taught, he ducked his head under, rolled onto his back, onto his feet, and rose up turning to face his teacher.

"You were sleeping," Kamaka said.

"Hard night," Grant answered. He didn't add that he spent more than an hour at midnight explaining to Selena why he had returned home late, wore black, and smelled awful. He inadvertently said, "The smell is because of the garbage at the whore house."

This admission started a new round of interrogation that only ended when Daniel walked into the bedroom complaining, "Noisy, can't sleep." Breakfast in the morning had been frosty between them until Grant swore he had not had sex with any whore.

"Teacher, I'm thankful you showed me the flying arm bar and we practiced the move until I got it right. I used the leverage hold to perfection last night. I subdued my opponent in less than a minute."

"Good," the forty-five-year-old lua master said. "Why did you need to use it?"

Grant studied his olohe, a six-foot tall Hawaiian, solidly built with sculpted muscles on his arms, chest, abdomen, and thighs. His teacher had dark hair, brown eyes, like his skin, flattened nose, and full lips. He didn't have scars although Grant knew that Kamaka had engaged in many battles either for sport or survival. "I had to fight a yakuza bent on sticking a knife into my partner."

"Yakuza, mean guys, they know a lot of the tricks I have shown you. How did you get involved with those gangsters?"

"A long story, you know my father was murdered, and detective Asing and I have been searching for the killer. The HSPA believe the murderers are Japanese dynamiters. I don't think so. Asing and I thought the yakuza might help us find the guilty party."

"That is a stretch."

"Asing believes to find a criminal you need a criminal to catch him. Would Hawaiians use dynamite or any other explosive to kill an enemy?"

"No, that is not our style. We believe in man-to-man combat, not sneaking around kind of stuff."

"That's what every Hawaiian I talked to says. How about the Japanese?"

Kamaka scratched his head. "You told me about them dynamiting a place near Hilo. I don't know. I think if one of those guys wanted to kill somebody, they would do it in a more direct and certain way, not exploding dynamite. One thing I know about those guys, they are very clannish. They really stick together. I think it's because they have been smashed down by the plantation *lunas*. I got a good friend named Koichi; he knows plenty about what's going on. Maybe I can get him to help you."

"Let's save that until Asing and I have a chance of a deal with the yakuza. Last thing, I want to know about is the Filipinos, would they be dynamiters?"

"Those guys came as bachelors, no women. The Japanese brought wives and children. 'Picture brides' were encouraged to come, and many did. Plantations thought family people wouldn't be troublemakers like the Chinese. But the sugar folks soon learned that the Japanese wouldn't be satisfied with poverty pay. They started to strike. They were smart because they learned that American law is against slavery. They realized that labor contracts could not be used to force them to work.

"Filipinos were strike breakers against the Japanese. Besides not allowing women to come the sugar people did another devious thing, they recruited men who were uneducated and couldn't read or write. They thought they were a bunch of dummies who would do as told. Most Filipinos recruited were poor uneducated farmers. The only weapons they knew of were the hoe, rake, and bolo knife.

"Just because your skin has color doesn't mean you aren't smart. You take this guy Manlapit, comes in as a worker. He educates himself and learns to be a lawyer, starts unionizing and agitates for fair wages for workers. The trouble for him is, the plantations kept doing 'divide and rule' by hiring Tagalogs, Ilocanos, and Visayans. These men were from different islands or tribes in the Philippines. They couldn't unite together to get what they wanted."

Grant interrupted, "When Manlapit called the strike in April this year, only Visayans left work?"

"Yes, and the Ilocanos became strike breakers. On Kauai out of five thousand Filipinos only five hundred went on strike, all Visayans. That is how the trouble started. These guys were in a schoolhouse in Hanapepe and captured two Ilocano strikebreakers. When the sheriff tried to free them, that's when the shooting began."

"Olohe, you're making me think that Filipinos are so divided that they couldn't have planned attacks on the HSPA"

"Right on 'brah, you ask me would these people be dynamiters. I say they would not."

"And the HSPA is prosecuting Manlapit and other Filipino labor leaders and making sure they go to prison for what happened on Kauai. Manlapit wasn't even on the island at the time."

"Makes no difference, he stepped out of line and those in power are going to make sure he is behind bars for a long time."

Grant closed his fist and pounded it against a wall. "We are back to the Japanese as suspects and using the yakuza to help us find the guilty."

"If you are going to deal with those guys, I better teach you some dirty lua techniques, eye gouging, ball busting, throat biting, kidney punch."

"Throat biting, what for?"

"Two major arteries go up the neck to the brain. Chew one up and you die."

"That doesn't seem like a fair way to fight."

Kamaka gave Grant a quizzical look, "'Brah, if the other guy is killing you and all you got left is your teeth, are you going to use it or—"

Grant interrupted, "Bite him and live. I see your meaning: forget the Marquis of Queensbury rules and play dirty."

"Why not, it's you or him. You're not in a sports contest, but a life and death situation. That's why you used the arm bar. The good thing about the trick is that you don't kill the knife man you just ruin his arm."

Grant laughed. "Okay you have shown me the clean-cut martial arts techniques, now I'm ready to learn the dirty stuff. Let me ask you olohe, if we need help in dealing with the yakuza would you back us up?"

"I think there is a better way, see my friend Kouchi, but sure, if you need me let me know."

For the next hour the men worked on dirty tricks techniques.

# CHAPTER 39

Grant felt exhilarated by the morning workout. Despite his elation he thought of what his olohe said. "Use what you have learned only in the direst moments of a combat where there is a thin balance between life and death. Serious, if not fatal, harm may come to your opponent if you strike as I have just taught you."

Up until today, he had been satisfied with the martial arts moves he had perfected. Use of them could injure an opponent, but rarely could they lead to death. But this morning his olohe had said there were twenty-five ways to kill with the bare hands. What he taught were only a few of the methods to kill or seriously maim someone without using a weapon.

Suddenly, he realized: *If I can kill using these tricks so can my opponent.* Grant felt vulnerable. *I have learned only four deathly attacks. What were the other twenty-one? Damn his teacher. He's playing with my mind, just like a kahuna does when he uses fear of death to psychologically destroy a victim.*

*What's the purpose? Bring me back for more training? I would return even if I knew nothing of the twenty-five ways to kill with bare hands.* A frisson made him shiver. *Was my olohe preparing me for serious trouble lying ahead?*

Grant stepped onto King Street and noted the policeman in his kiosk with the umbrella fixed above his head directing traffic. Downtown Honolulu had become a busy place, not the backwater town that Mark Twain wrote about. There were street cars to dodge and throngs of two-and four-door autos to thread through as you crossed the street. The officer in the kiosk tried in vain to direct the traffic, constantly blowing his whistle and using his white gloved hand to manage the ceaseless flow of machines.

Grant walked under colorful awnings shading the sidewalk and entered his reception room. His employee announced, "Detective Asing asked that you call ASAP." He noted that his nine o'clock appointment sat in the room. The policeman could wait.

The interview did not take long. Grant had pre-prepared forms for probate cases and rapidly got the essentials about the decedent's estate. Grant thanked the new client, gave the completed forms to his secretary and dialed Asing.

When he finally reached him the detective's first words were, "Where have you been? The shit has really hit the fan over here. Patterson is demanding martial law and a roundup of Japanese."

"Has he gone crazy?"

"Yes. Doolittle's home got dynamited last night."

"Injuries?"

"No, husband and wife were sleeping on the second floor. They got knocked out of bed that's about it. Lots of damage on the ground floor, plenty of smoke. Eerie thing, it's very much like the Olaa dynamiting."

"That's why Patterson has blamed the Japanese? What's your department going to do about it?"

"Strangely, Hitchcock is trying to keep him under control. He's learned that the original defendants are in jail, that the family members he has questioned deny any knowledge of a conspiracy, and, most important, he is convinced that only one person planted the dynamite."

"That's a revelation. How did he come up with that bit of detective work, he's always been a toady to the power structure?"

"When he investigated the scene, he found only one set of tracks leading to the house where the dynamite was placed and another set going back to the fence line. Apparently, there had been a lot of rain and over watering that made the grass soft, there were telltale footprints. But I think most important, the Big Five knows that more than half of the workforce is Japanese, that's maybe a 100,000 people, where are you going to jail them? What's going to happen to the economy?"

"Yeah, but that might not stop Patterson. He will push until he gets what he wants."

"That's why we have to work harder to solve these crimes before things get to the breaking point. That is the real reason I called you. After you left the station last night, I thought that I should gather in all the evidence before it disappeared. Two officers and I broke into Saiki's shop. There were counterfeit plates and more fake bills. Saki's in jail. Then I decided to hit the whore house before it closed down. We nabbed three yakuza at the front desk and more counterfeit bills. I put two in custody and sent one of them to the boss man with a message.

"You worked fast, what's the message?"

"We talk or everything gets closed down including the whore house."

"Can you do that?"

"I don't know. The top dog has got a lot of protection. But we got leverage, the counterfeiting. That everyone wants to stop, especially the federals."

"By bringing in other officers aren't you in a very weak bargaining situation? You are like a tight rope walker trying to go from one building to another on a slender piece of string. It would be easy to fall off and end your career."

"Or be found dead in an alley. I know I told you I wanted just you and me to capture the counterfeiters. But things changed last night when you got fake bills in the boogie house, saw Saiki at work, and we captured the two yakuza with a case full of fake cash. We have overwhelming evidence of a serious crime, a criminal enterprise that at one time in these islands would have caused the guilty to be sentenced to life in prison."

"Yeah, that's why I felt you became a tight rope walker when you busted this case wide open last night. Frankly I wasn't comfortable with the idea of covering up the crime in exchange for yakuza cooperation."

"I know how you feel. I had the same concerns myself. But please forgive me when I say this to you, there is no one in this department who could have done what you did last night. I apologize for using you in the way I did. Yes, I'm in a tight spot with the evidence that we have, but there is still a good chance that we can make a deal that accomplishes what we both want and also end the counterfeiting."

Grant smiled; his narrow grin widened as he spoke. "I knew I was being used as an undercover agent for the police. But there was merit to your plan. We were at a dead end and had to pursue any straw we could find. There isn't a Japanese conspiracy to bring down the HSPA. But how do we prove it? Why not use a criminal to catch a criminal?"

"I'm thankful you are not angry with me, but I have put you in grave danger, a key witness to counterfeiting activities."

"When I entered the whore house, I thought one of the yakuza might have recognized me. That is the only one who could be a problem."

"If I can't make some kind of deal you will have to testify at trial. That would make you a marked man."

"We are both on a tight rope and I am more likely to be killed because I am not a police officer."

Asing sighed. "You have great wisdom. Police have some immunity from serious harm or death. Criminals know they will be hanged if they kill an officer. It doesn't work the same way for an ordinary citizen."

Grant rubbed his head. "Maybe this is why my olohe is teaching me to kill with my bare hands. He sensed I had put myself in grave danger by helping the police."

"I pray I can keep you safe and make a deal without using you. I have told no one in my department who is the undercover man who broke the case, but unfortunately there are always leaks, missteps, or good guesses."

"Keep me informed if the father contacts you and what Hitchcock and Patterson do. Tonight, there is a meeting at the Royal Society. See you at the event."

# CHAPTER 40

Grant pondered what should be done. Even with what Asing had seized, he felt uncertain what the crime family would do. In the past, they had not engaged in counterfeiting. They were gamblers and girl providers, that had been their historic role in Japan, and, to his scant knowledge, in Hawaii. Would they be willing to make a deal?

He entered his office uncertain as to what they needed to get the investigation moving to a conclusion. Patterson's threats could upset the fine balance that had kept the largest group of imported workers subservient. Then his secretary shocked him. "Japanese consul Sakamoto called. You are invited to be on the reviewing stand when his country's training fleet docks in Honolulu. You also are invited to a reception."

Could this visit be a prelude to war? Rumors had been flying that the Japanese planned to seize Hawaii. That is what union leaders had allegedly suggested when they went on strike. The HSPA controlled press had been fanning the flames of sedition ever since. It led to the conspiracy trials of union leaders. More suppression followed with an all-out attack on the Japanese Language Schools. Today, Patterson demanded a roundup of Japanese and martial law. If that happened, would this tip the balance between peace and war?

Joshua interrupted his thoughts. "Aloha, partner, I've been trying to get your attention for the last minute. You are way, far away. Worried about something?"

"Yes, a lot happened last night and has spilled over into today." Grant then explained the cracking of the counterfeiting operation, the dynamiting of Doolittle's home, and Patterson's threats against the Japanese. "I'm worried about what could happen and we aren't even close to solving the case.

"Asing is intent on pursuing the race angle to solve the crimes, but maybe what has occurred has nothing to do with races being suppressed. Maybe it's someone's desire for revenge against the HSPA?"

"That's an angle I've started to think about, the coal torpedo, the single footsteps in the green lawn at the Doolittle house. But who is it? What's his motive?"

"On the other hand, Asing could be right. An organized crime group has the membership and the means to spread terrorism. The yakuza are criminals who can acquire weapons like dynamite and guns. Intimidation is a big part of how they operate. This terror is like a guerrilla war against the oppression of the Big Five. The only way you will know for sure if they are not involved in these bombings is to capture a top man and interrogate him."

Grant put his palms to his face, rubbed his eyes, and stared at Joshua. "We are back to suspecting the Japanese as being the prime actors in these explosions."

"It may not be all of them, but just one militant group."

Grant scowled, "We captured the counterfeiters to make a deal with the yakuza to find the killer, whether Japanese or some other race, and now you are suggesting that the yakuza may be the guilty parties in these explosions. Why?"

"Because you must think of every possibility that could be the cause of what is happening. There could also be a cause for killing that you have not considered."

"Partner, you have made this whole series of events more confusing than ever."

"I didn't mean to. I'm actually eliminating possibilities for you. If you think carefully you are down to the yakuza as the guilty ones or some person or persons seeking revenge for some wrong done by the HSPA."

"Interesting analysis, but we have to eliminate the Japanese as the guilty parties, if for no other reason than to prove Patterson is wrong.

Asing wants to use the yakuza to do that, and you're saying they may be the guilty ones. I don't know. We will just have to take it one step at a time and see what develops."

Grant heard the office phone ring. He looked at his receptionist as she answered the call. "It's detective Asing, he wants to see you right away."

# CHAPTER 41

Grant and Charles Kamaka sat in the shadows of the Honolulu train station of the Oahu Railroad and Land Company. Across from them lay the triangular-shaped Aala Park. Along its east side flowed Nuuanu Stream.

"In the old days this was mostly swamp land with some taro fields." Kamaka said. "But things changed with the big fire of 1900."

"Was that the one set by the health department to kill rats infected by the bubonic plague?" Grant asked.

"Yeah, that is what the Health Department claimed when they decided to burn some old buildings. Supposed to be a controlled fire but once it started, it burned down Chinatown, more than four square blocks of buildings. Seven thousand people homeless; half were Chinese and the other half Japanese."

"Where did they go?"

"The Republic in 1898 had decided to do landfill on the west side of Nuuanu Stream, to build Aala Park and improve the Palama district. After the fire this is where all the burnt-out people came to live. They built shacks, hovels, any kind of shelter. This area became the slums of Honolulu while the city Health Department built a sewer system before reconstruction in the burnt-out area would be allowed.

"Where the Palama Settlement is, just to the north of us, became the toughest, meanest area in Honolulu. I think that is where the big yakuza boss is located, and that is why he chose the Park to meet with Asing. Your friend is taking a big chance of getting killed."

"That's why he asked us to be backup for him, if things went wrong. Thanks again for helping him."

"Asing is a good guy he's done me some favors. That's why, when you called, I was willing to help. Besides, I didn't want to lose my best paying student to some gangsters." Kamaka laughed.

"I still think my friend Koichi would be a better source than these tattooed guys."

"Japanese identify with Japanese; they are close-knit people. Don't trust others, very clannish. Why would this guy help us?"

"He owes me big time. I used to work in the sugar fields. Hated it, but needed the money. Koichi was part of the working crew that I was on. A haole supervisor on a big horse started whipping him. He called him a bunch of names. It wasn't right, Koichi had done nothing to deserve a beating. I pulled the haole off his horse.

"Big guy, still remember his face, pig eyes, pug nose with a beard around his cheeks and chin. I smelled alcohol. The supervisor was fat. I knew he had a habit of picking on smaller guys. When he started to raise his leather snake, I moved into him. I think I surprised him. Other guys try to run away from a whip man. With my fingers closed, like I have shown you, I slammed them deep into his gut. He came down. I came up and my head clipped him on the jaw. *Pau* fight. I got fired, Koichi...hey look, some guys coming to Asing. I move slow to the right. You wait and then move slow left."

"Remember, we only move in to help if he blows the whistle."

"Okay, but be smart, undo your sling, get some stones ready."

Grant nodded and released his rock thrower from his waist. He watched his olohe moving away from the station and shuffling slowly toward the park. He fished out some small missiles from his pocket and held them in his left hand. He pulled down his straw hat over his ears trusting that the wide brim and increasing shadows of dusk would hide his features.

He moved from the station, his eyes on Asing. Several men had approached him. He couldn't tell if they had tattoos. One man stood out, big as a sumo wrestler. *Got to be the boss man*, Grant thought.

He ambled slowly across the tracks toward the tufts of grass that grew sparsely along the park's edge. Grant moved his eyes away from the meeting point. He searched for hidden soldiers of boss man. *They must be there, but where?*

There were a few people in the park, several playing catch near the point where Beretania Street met North King. He paused in his shuffle, went down slowly as if to tie his shoes. He glanced at the big man. He appeared to be talking to Asing in an animated fashion. Then he laughed and slapped his thigh.

Two men with the boss man moved toward Asing. Out of the corner of his eye he saw three men stop baseball play and run toward the confrontation. Asing loosened his whip and lashed out.

Grant rose from his stoop, dropped a stone in his sling, whirled, and let fly. The missile struck one of the men who ran toward Asing. He doubled up. A second rock dropped into the sling pad and rocketed out. A yakuza turned, and the rock caught him in his face. He screamed, "Bakartare," and stumbled onto the grass.

A loud, "Hai" came from Grant's right. He didn't have time to see who yelled as a third yakuza charged him. The man who he had struck on the side wobbled toward him. He felt an adrenaline rush as he ran toward the attacking man, saw the knife, leaped ahead like a baseball player sliding into second base, and smashed into the legs of the charging yakuza who sprawled head first to the ground.

Grant bounced up and felt a jolt of pain on his side. He saw a tattooed man with blood-smeared lips open his mouth full of sharpened canines. Like a piranha, his bared teeth moved to bite Grant's throat.

With death a second away, Grant countered with a move he had practiced with his olohe. He thrust the top of his head into the gaping mouth. Despite the pain of sharpened teeth cutting into the side of his scalp, he felt the crush of broken teeth and heard a howl. In one swift movement he brought an elbow up into the face of the biter. The man fell to the ground.

Grant sensed movement to his left, turned, and saw the yakuza he had slid into staggering toward him. With closed fingers over his hands, he swung his arms upward into the jaw of his attacker whose head flung back, Grant punched him in the throat. He went down.

One thought raced through his mind; *my friends need help*. He hurried to where the fat man had laughed at Asing. His olohe had released nunchaku sticks from his waist and had already put one yakuza down. Three others were dancing around him. The boss man stood to the side.

With a sharp intake of breath, Grant saw a frightening sight: Asing sat on his knees attempting to rise as a yakuza stood above him with his back bent gripping a bolo knife, preparing to deliver a guillotine strike to the detective's exposed neck. Without a pause Grant dropped a lead ball into the sling's pouch, whirled and flung it with all the strength he could muster.

The deadly sugar cane blade moved past the yakuza's head as it began its descent to the policeman's neck. The round piece of lead, the size of a Civil War musket ball, plunged into the hacker's exposed stomach. The man screamed, released his weapon, clutched his belly, and wilted to the ground.

The cry caused the three tattooed warriors to pause in their movements around Kamaka. They stared in Grant's direction. Another lead ball zinged into the side of the boss man. His extreme girth seemed to absorb the hit although he bent low as if in pain. "*Nanikakaru*," he gasped.

"*So desu, hashiru*, cried a yakuza still standing. The other two grasped the boss man and helped him off the field. Asing stood, his face showing great pain. "Let them go, they will not help us. Gather the fallen and take them to the station."

# CHAPTER 42

Anger made the saboteur's hands shake. His handler demanded that he cease making bombs to attack the HSPA. "Mr. Robinson, the members of this organization are the Imperialists that enslave the working man!"

"I do not deny the truth of what you say. But it is your vendetta that causes the Japanese to be punished. We need them to overthrow the Capitalists of these islands. They are forty percent of the population."

"All the better then if the bombings cause those in power to suppress these people. It will make them ripe for revolt."

"You do not understand the dialectic for a successful revolution. Yes, you need an oppressed class, but first you must give them reasons to revolt, a process of discussion convincing them that Communism is better than bourgeois Democracy with its pompous words and high-sounding phrases like 'freedom and equality'. The reality is, there is no freedom, and women and the exploited workers are treated as inferiors. This is what Lenin has said, but as an alternative—"

"I attended the meeting of the Third International," the saboteur interrupted, his voice rising as he spoke. "The purpose of the Communist party is world-wide revolution!"

Irritated, Robinson replied, "Yes, that is true, but I had begun to say before you interrupted me, that Lenin claimed that societal change comes from a catastrophe or revolution. As an alternative, if the means for the making of a revolution is not available, the best course is to seek tolerance of our beliefs, followed by securing acceptance, and finally force adoption of them. In Hawaii we do not have the means of a revolution as yet. We need to use the alternative approach of seeking tolerance of our beliefs. The American right of 'free speech' works in our favor."

"But what you advocate is slow. Why not overthrow the oppressors now, by using fear as our weapon? I can steal more dynamite, make explosives."

"I know you want revenge for the HSPA killing your brother. But you were not sent here by the party to carry out a personal vendetta. You are here to assist me in advancing the cause of Communism.

"You weren't in America when the Comintern called for world-wide revolution. Our believers carried out dynamiting as a means of spreading terror. All that accomplished was suppression. Attorney General Palmer prosecuted union activists as Communists. He caused thousands of immigrants to be deported. He manufactured a 'Red Scare' which made Russian people undesirable aliens. Criminal syndicalism laws, anti-anarchist publication laws, anti-picketing laws were passed in many states including this territory. What I am saying is, if you continue your attacks it will only increase the persecution of the Japanese and the unions. It could end our efforts to persuade people to our cause."

Reluctant to give up his desire for revenge, the saboteur argued, "Didn't Trotsky say something about comrades who are unwilling to take risks should leave the party? Aren't you saying that you are fearful of being caught and therefore unwilling to dare what I am willing to do?"

Angered, Robinson pounded his fist upon the table where they sat. "I know that Trotsky said those words at the start of the revolution. But he was in Russia backed by thousands of soldiers and workers when he said that. Here we have no one to support us. We must win friends. We will not do that if all we do is dynamiting. Stop, I tell you, and help me convince the oppressed masses that Communism is their best hope for freedom."

Despite his hatred, Miguel decided to mask his feelings and be conciliatory for the moment. "I understand. My schooling at the CHEKA caused me to believe in dialectical materialism: 'Social change can only come if there is perpetual conflict between classes until a classless society is achieved.' I was taught that the struggle is filled with violence and hate. It only ends when all who resist Communism are annihilated. Instead, you are proposing that in these islands we become persuaders to our cause. Despite my feelings I will set aside my beliefs and follow your lead until your effort fails."

Robinson sighed. "I gather we have a truce between us. We will prepare for our meeting tonight with the Royal Society and other Hawaiians. I want to convince them to unify with the exploited races and join in a united front against the sugar planters. Help me pass out these flyers and assist during the evening."

Miguel nodded then asked, "Why are we dealing with royalty? Aren't monarchists the oppressors of the poor?"

"There is much you do not understand about Hawaii. Once there were only two classes living in these islands, the chiefs, known as alii, and the commoners called the maka'ainana. There was no private land ownership, everything was shared, very similar to Socialism which is a step away from Communism.

"The alii dictated what the mass of Hawaiians could or could not do. When the western world occupied these islands, the communal system was replaced by the concept of private property ownership. This allowed large sugar plantations to develop. The capitalists took the place of the alii and Hawaii has been ruled by a few rich people ever since. Despite this change, many Hawaiians still obey the descendants of the alii, the Royal Society."

Miguel blew out a sharp whistle, "You want me to help you with people who parade around like kings and queens? What has this Royal bunch done to help the working man?"

Robinson shook his head, "Sad to say, they have done nothing. What is worse, Hawaiians have been used by the plantations as strike breakers to suppress the unions. I would not be surprised if they weren't some of the forty men involved in the Hanapepe massacre."

"*Ay, caramba*!" Miguel shouted. "You want me to help you with people who have killed my brother!"

"I'm sorry I upset you. Never should have said that. I don't know the truth of what happened on Kauai in September. Set aside your anger for the good of the cause. We need Hawaiians to be involved in overthrowing the oppressors of the people. Will you help me as you have promised?"

His eyes cast down, Miguel nodded.

"Alright then, let's go to the meeting."

# CHAPTER 43

Grant stared at the high ceiling of the church. He nudged his companion, Charles Kamaka. "You're telling me that all these walls and roof are constructed of dredged up coral."

"Correct, fourteen thousand blocks of reef were chiseled out of the harbor in 1840 by Hawaiian divers. A back-breaking enterprise, but converts were willing to dare the dangers of the ocean to create this monument to Christianity. It is a special place where all people can worship God."

"Is it the oldest church in Hawaii?"

"I think the one in Lahaina might be older."

"Was it hard for Hawaiians to accept Christianity? I mean, they were heathens, right?"

"Yeah, we were pagans once, believed in the kahuna, black magic, and kapu. Funny thing though, ten months before the missionaries arrived the king and queen ordered all idols and temples destroyed. After maybe a thousand years of believing in false gods, we got one God as a replacement. Took a little time to change over, but when Queen Kaahumanu accepted Christianity and other chiefs converted it became easy for the missionaries to enlist believers. The downside of all this is these same preachers of God's word became advisors to the kings and soon became the property owners of Hawaii. That's how the Big Five got started."

"You don't sound so happy about that."

Kamaka's face contorted into an angry frown. "They screwed us out of our land. That's how you convinced me to come here. This guy Robinson's talk is supposed to be: *Poho ka aina no ka po'e o Hawaii.* Which means, 'Lost land of the people of Hawaii'."

Grant nodded, "I know, older Hawaiians are angry about what happened in the monarchy years of these islands. Many young people don't know the true story. I don't either, since my family is white and had plantations. My mother was half-Hawaiian, but she never talked about it, I guess out of deference to my dad and grandfather. I don't know much about the history of those times and that's why I want to hear what Robinson has to say. He's supposed to cover it. Look, there's my friend Kawika Makanani. I'll signal him to come over to us."

It took a couple of minutes for the big Hawaiian to work his way through the arriving crowd. Introductions were made, and Grant and his friends settled down as the program started.

There were short speeches of welcome before Solomon Kama, President of the Royal Order, stood to introduce the speaker. "Mr. Charles Robinson is a noted journalist from Chicago, Illinois. He came to Hawaii over a year ago as the publisher and editor of the *Hinode Times*." Kama took his seat and Robinson strode to the center of the church. The pews were filled with Hawaiians and a mixture of other races, at least a hundred people had come to the talk.

Robinson stood to tepid applause. He studied the audience before he spoke. "Propaganda is the manipulation of news to deliver a one-sided message for a cause. What is said may or may not be true, for propagandists are trying to persuade people to adopt their message. The only way to counter propaganda is to present the other side of the story.

"After the missionaries produced the Hawaiian alphabet and the Bible in that language, Hawaiians became the most literate people in the world. Seventy-five percent could read and write in Hawaiian. Your people loved to print the news. For a time, the information on any subject or issue was balanced. But as the sugar planters gained power over the government, official news and information was printed only in English. When the monarchy was overthrown, the half-dozen Hawaiian newspapers that supported the queen and the kingdom were suppressed, editors and staff were jailed. Use of the Hawaiian language was made unlawful, and schools could not teach Hawaiian.

"The news became one-sided. Young people were not told of how a kingdom was stolen. And that brings me to my theme: Lost Land. The

Great Mahele, the land division law of 1848, provided for the establishment of private property. The four million acres of Hawaiian land would be divided three ways among the king, alii, and the common people of the islands.

"But greedy foreigners got nearly half of the land. That is why you see today massive sugar plantations, large estates owned by an elite few. But still there was a huge amount of land that belonged to the monarchy that should have been given to the people. Instead, after the overthrow, the new Republic of Hawaii ceded over to the United States close to two million acres of Hawaiian land. None of you knew of this I am sure, since pro-Hawaiian news had been suppressed.

"Today, Hawaiian people live in poverty. Yes, you can survive, but most live on charity for many do not have jobs. The plantations do not want you. They have imported cheap foreign labor and do not want to pay Hawaiians decent wages.

"Hawaii delegate to Congress, Prince Kuhio, caused to be passed a Hawaiian Homes bill setting aside 200,000 acres of ceded lands for poor Hawaiians. But this is a hollow promise for the homeless. No money has been attached to the bill to pay for infrastructure and to finance homes. The law only passed because the sugar people wanted to hold onto choice Hawaiian land for growing sugar cane.

"My newspaper will print the truth as it applies to native people and imported laborers. Because we will be telling the real story, we may face suppression, jail, and fines. We will also print news of the world. There is a revolution occurring. It started in Russia where the people overthrew imperialists and set up a Republic. This government promises equality for women and the worker. It believes that manual labor has more value than the machines of capitalism, that hard work, sweat, and the pain of the laborer must be rewarded.

"I'm sure you have heard of the massacre in Hanapepe. If you have not, read my paper. Filipino strikers were gunned down. Those still on strike were forced back to work at the point of a gun. Union leaders were prosecuted and jailed.

"The same thing happened to the Japanese. Why? Because these toilers of the soil demanded fair wages, fair working conditions, and the end of physical abuses. You need to join with these people to make change in the present system controlled by the imperialistic colonizers of these islands.

"My paper may be forced to close, but until then we will print true news and not the propaganda of the capitalists. If you want your lost land back, work with other suppressed people to change the existing government. Thank you for your time and attention."

The three friends applauded the speech vigorously. "That was great," Kamaka said. "I kind of knew about our past, but didn't know that America got almost half of Hawaiian land."

"Yeah, good story," Kawika agreed. "Eh, Grant, you see da guy gives da kine paper? He same one who pass out stuff in Kaneohe. Must be with Robinson."

Grant studied the man. He was of medium height and build. His skin appeared to be light brown. "The guy is either Filipino or Spanish. He doesn't look like the usual man from the Philippines, high forehead, nicely spaced eyes, slender nose, thin lips, strong chin. Let's go somewhere to talk. Maybe get some soup."

The three men wandered over to Queen Street and a Chinese noodle shop. After they ordered saimin Grant said, "I don't know if you guys got the same message, but I think he talked about ending the political control of the Big Five."

"Whatever gets da kine land back to us I'm for," Kawika said.

Grant's olohe uttered a sharp laugh. "No way will we ever get the land back. It belongs to the United States now. Take a bigger army than we have to beat them."

"But maybe Robinson is telling us to work within the system," Grant said. "Use the power to vote to change the local government and then influence America to give back. That part is a long shot, but it's something to consider. I know Robinson talked about Russia, but that's a different situation. There the people were starving. They were tired of fighting a war against the Germans. They wanted change and they got it by the poor battling against the rich with the army supporting them."

"What we going do?"

"Kawika, I think the first thing is to solve who are causing these explosions. I'm hoping it's not the Japanese. We tried to find out by dealing with yakuza. Something went wrong and we got into a big fight. At the moment we are at a stone wall."

"Let's talk about it tomorrow when we have a chance to meet with Asing," Kamaka said. "Tonight, Robinson gave us much to think about. Let's go sleep and tackle the problems in the morning."

# CHAPTER 44

Robinson stared at the five men sitting across from him in the conference room next to the church. "You will not help to stop the oppression of the sugar planters against the working people of Hawaii?"

"I have told you; we are not a political organization. We were created to preserve Hawaiian culture and our way of life," Alii Solomon Kama answered. "Overthrowing the sugar plantations is not our *kuleana*."

For many minutes, Miguel had sat patiently listening to the arguments made by Robinson for change and the negativism of the five officers of the Royal Society. Furious, he shouted, "Hawaiians have served the rulers as strike breakers! They have murdered Filipinos! And you will do nothing to stop this?"

"Eh, *manong*," Peter Maka, one of the five directors of the Royal Order, answered. "What you mean by this *kaka* we murdered Filipinos? Hawaiians did no such thing."

"Wait!" Robinson interjected. "My companion is upset. I made the mistake of telling him Hawaiians have been strikebreakers and that they may have been some of the men who shot Filipinos in Hanapepe. I apologize for his outburst. Please, let us move on."

"I don't know what the hell happened," Maka said. "But for sure the sheriff had a warrant for the two captured guys the strikers were holding prisoner. He got them away from the Hanapepe school house, and some angry Filipino strikers attacked with knives. If Hawaiian guys with the sheriff they only doing their duty helping him."

"My brother got killed!" Miguel shouted.

"Okay, okay everybody, slow down," Sol said. "Keep a cool head. I think, Mr. Robinson, our meeting is ended. The Royal Society will not help you. Good night."

With a shrug, the news editor took a struggling Miguel by the arm and marched out of the conference room. "You did a grand job of messing things up comrade."

Outside Miguel trembled with anger. "My brother got killed. Those guys don't care."

"Comrade, I know you are upset, but you can't get people to join us if you go around fighting them because of your brother's death."

"Why not? These alii do nothing to help make change. The Royal Order will not help us."

Robinson shrugged, "You are right about that. However, I ask you to concentrate on our mission. Too many deaths and conflicts will quickly end what we are trying to accomplish for the cause. If you don't agree to do this, I will be forced to withdraw my support."

Miguel groused, "Did you see how that Maka guy stood and wanted to beat me up? He outweighed me by a hundred pounds. The guy thought I'm only a scrawny Filipino that he could pound into the ground. *Gago pumatay!*"

"What do you mean by that?"

"He's a stupid man who deserves to be killed!"

"Stop that. Remember what I have said."

"Yes comrade, I obey your command," Miguel answered, sarcasm in his voice.

Hanapepe Massacre – 1924

by Judith Fernandez

# CHAPTER 45

When Grant got home, he met a jealous wife. Selena berated him. "You were gone all day and late into the night. Have you been seeing someone? You want to tell me about it?"

"No, I am not cheating on you. I did call and tell you I would be late, that I was working on my father's murder with Asing, and that I would be going to a talk about lost Hawaiian land. It proved to be very interesting. For the record, I love only you."

Selena smiled. "I'm sorry I met you with anger. Have you eaten? Can I get you something? Is the person a professor? What did he have to say?"

Grant laughed. "You are like a rapid-fire machine gun shooting out a list of questions. As to food, I am fine. Mr. Robinson is a journalist and the publisher of the *Hinode Times*. He first spoke of propaganda, which is news or information that is one-sided. It may not be factual and is meant to manipulate the listener to accept a particular cause or buy a certain product. It is not like a debate where you get both sides of an issue and can choose what side you agree with. His point appeared to be, those in power will manipulate the news to keep themselves in power and curtail any information that may cause them trouble."

"Sounds like Hawaii."

"I believe that was Robinson's point, feed the people manufactured news, suppress the native language of the different races, and thereby exploit them."

"He is spot on. Since Farrington became governor, the Department of Education is mandating Americanization. Permit only English to be taught, teach American values, and Democracy. The governor wants American language schools where those proficient in English can continue their education. Public schools will end at eighth grade."

"I'm afraid Mr. Robinson is going to get into trouble if he keeps talking like a 'Red.' I don't think there is a prayer in hell that he can overturn the control of the Big Five. The economy is in great shape and the military strength of America is increasing all the time. However, there is a lot of talk in the news about the 'Yellow Peril' and the 'Little brown men of Nippon' taking over the islands. Tomorrow there is a Japanese fleet due into Honolulu. News reports are that they are on a spying trip to gauge our strength. And there is Mr. Patterson wanting to imprison people for dynamiting the HSPA homes. This could all be propaganda to turn us against the Japanese and suppress them."

"How strange, the sugar plantations imported them by the thousands to work the fields and now they are turning on them. Why the sudden change?"

"It's the 1920 strike. It really has affected the labor dynamic in Hawaii. I think what the plantation people were worried about is that the Japanese union men were talking like Russian revolutionaries. Remember, there was a big scare going across America about a Soviet style upheaval set to occur with dynamite attacks on the East Coast. Then you had the trial of Sacco and Vanzetti, two emigre Italians who were believed to be anarchists espousing revolutionary violence and bombings. Add the Olaa Plantation dynamiting into all this national hysteria and you have a recipe for suppression of the Japanese."

"I get it. There is talk at the University about oppression in the islands. I mentioned the flyer that was passed around by someone about the imperialists and colonizers and calling for an end to the dictatorial rule of the Big Five. This is revolutionary stuff and I'm afraid to say there are intellectuals at the school who are debating whether the Communist belief in a classless society and their credo of 'from each according to his ability, to each according to his need' has merit as a governmental system."

"For some time, I have thought of these islands as the place for a Soviet style revolution. First the foreigners exploited the Hawaiians for their land, and then they exploited the workers they imported for their labor. Cheap land and cheap work force make for rich profits. We do have some multi-millionaires in Hawaii."

"It's late and time to go to bed. My father has the information you requested. See him first thing in the morning."

# CHAPTER 46

Robinson did not feel discouraged by the rejection of the Royal Society. His talk had gone well. The audience proved attentive and he received compliments and inquiries as to how to deal with the troubles plaguing Hawaiians. He had urged unity with the other races, cautioned against overt action at this time, and suggested that Hawaiians read his newspaper that he printed in English. He regretted doing this, but the island laws punished progressive news media that published in a foreign language, especially if printed in Hawaiian.

He was disturbed by what his Japanese contact confided to him. The bombings had accelerated the harshness that the HSPA inflicted on the Japanese. There had been a tearful plea that hostile actions come to an end. Robinson was surprised at this show of weakness by his latest convert to Communism. Japanese were known to be stoic and long-suffering. Crying did not fit the image that he had of the men of the Nipponese Empire.

Miguel sidled up to him. "You spoke well tonight, Master. I apologize for my wild words at the meeting with the alii. Don't you think it is time to start the revolution without the Hawaiians?"

Robinson was surprised by being called Master. Was his cohort sincere or sarcastic when he used the word? The man had been deferential since their first meeting. But tonight, his mood had changed. He had become surly. Did the order he gave to stop bombing, to stop killing, cause a separation between them? After his talk with his Japanese convert, he knew that he had been right to insist on ending the attacks. But was his comrade objecting to his claim of authority to run the Communist operations in Hawaii?

"It is too early to consider the overthrow of the existing order. It will take time and patience before we can develop the means to accomplish the task of Sovietizing these islands."

Miguel sneered. "I say we do not have the luxury of time. Already the capitalists are building forts here. They are increasing their military build-up. Soon there will be thousands of American soldiers camped in these islands. A Japanese fleet arrives in Honolulu tomorrow. We could enlist their sailors to seize Hawaii."

Robinson waited until his suddenly racing heartbeat slowed. "You must be insane to even consider such a suggestion. There are only six ships arriving tomorrow. It is a training flotilla for young Japanese sailors to learn their craft. They are not prepared for a war with America. There are many Japanese in these islands, at least a hundred thousand. They are not ready to take up arms against the imperialists. A revolt now would end in a horrible disaster."

Undeterred, the assassin answered, "I cannot wait forever to have my vengeance against the killers of Filipinos."

"You cannot rush into making change without knowing if you are able to accomplish your goal. It took many years and countless missteps before Russia could be freed of the Romanov Empire. Bear with me. Let us influence the masses by the truths we will tell them instead of the propaganda that is spewed out by the greedy capitalists."

Miguel shrugged. "I will wait as you caution me to, my Master."

Robinson heard the sarcasm in his comrade's voice. He realized there were limits to his control over the furious man. Would he turn against him in his pursuit of vengeance? He decided to buy a gun.

# CHAPTER 47

Grant walked along King Street shivering in the early morning breeze. The roadway was free of cars or trolleys at the moment. He enjoyed the quiet, but as he crossed the street to Maunakea he saw Chinese merchants already at work. Some filled outdoor bins with merchandise, others hung banners that advertised goods for sale.

Strings of hanging cooked red ducks filled many business windows. Grant caught the smell of sugary-sweet cha sui pork recently out of the oven. All around him, the air was laden with a cacophony of singsong chatter undecipherable to the occidental ear. It was wonderful to stroll in Chinatown in the morning, even though there were noxious smells from the alleyways. Grant realized that this part of Honolulu had rejected the Health Department's sewer system that took offal through pipes to a clearing station that dumped the waste into the deep sea. It is cheaper and easier to just throw junk onto the streets as in the old days and let it wash through open drains into the ocean.

He entered his father-in-law's office building, mounted the stairs, and rapped on the door. An eye looked through a peephole before the door opened. A burly Chinese guard stood aside and let Grant in. At a desk near the far wall Dan Choy worked. He motioned the servant away with a wave of his hand, stood, and approached Grant. The two men hugged, and Choy indicated a chair. "Sit, I think we may have much to talk about. Tea?"

Grant nodded, a bell rang, and a woman bustled in. She was Asian but dressed western style in a dark skirt, white blouse, and a string of pearls around her neck. "You have a very pretty helper," Grant commented.

"My secretary," Choy answered. "Come, pour the tea and leave."

The lady bowed, filled two cups and left. The two men sipped the steaming brew for a time before Grant broke the silence. "Selena enjoys her job at the university. Your daughter is a whiz in botany, in very high demand by the plantations for her knowledge of growing things. Your grandson is doing well. He has started day school. He loves it, but is still a little shy with other boys. We have decided to enroll him in martial arts class. It will give him a sense of worth and also provide him with the courage to deal with confrontation."

"At four do you not think him too young for such training?"

"No, at the start it will be mostly exercises, tumbling, and learning kicks and turns. Dan is already interested in these maneuvers which will make him easier to train. We will hold off until he is older before allowing him to learn the physical techniques."

"Very wise, bring him along slowly. Let him have success in each thing that he learns. Failures will come, for that is the pattern of life, but at the start he must know the joy of success before he receives the pain of defeat."

"You wanted to speak to me?"

"Yes, you had made a request because of my connections with the Immigration and Nationalization Service of the Territory. I think you pinpointed one man who appeared to enjoy a certain voyeuristic pleasure in embarrassing Oriental women when they arrived in Hawaii."

"He is a man sick in the head for ordering ladies to disrobe and be examined for bubonic plague. That disease is carried by rats and not secreted inside a woman's vagina or under her breasts."

"I do not know the truth of the man's claim, although, like you. I think it has been used as an excuse to discomfort Asian women. At any event, this miserable person is no more. He has committed suicide."

"Because of the unholy things he has done to Asian women?"

Choy frowned; his brow wrinkled as he considered his answer. "No, that would be considered a minor occurrence by the Immigration Service."

"Oh? Why is that? Isn't such conduct bordering on abuse of power?"

Choy sighed. "There is much you do not understand about men who control our lives. The wrongdoer did not subject white women to the indignity of being stripped naked and examined by a man. Asian women, like many women of color, are considered so inferior that they have no right to complain of male abuse."

"Like you were telling me to beat your daughter?" Grant said with disgust.

Choy looked sternly at his son-in-law. "I tested you at the time I said that. If you were an abuser I would have it out with you, even inflicted punishment. I loved both mother and daughter and would never hurt them, which unfortunately is not always the case in Chinese homes."

"I accept what you say that you were testing me. If it was not his treatment of Asian women, what caused the inspector to kill himself?"

Choy remained silent for many moments. When he spoke, he did not answer the question. "Let us just say he felt derelict in his duties to the service."

"Since we are not going to talk about it, can the Japanese consulate be assured that shameful practices involving women will no longer be tolerated?"

"An official complaint has been lodged. I have received word from the highest authority in the service that the utmost respect will be accorded to both men and women who immigrate to these islands. On to another matter, what progress have you made to find the killers of your father?"

Grant shrugged. "We have eliminated all the races except the Japanese as suspects. As to them, Asing hoped to come to an agreement with the yakuza to assist us in uncovering any plotters among their people or find leads to the killer. The detective tried to make a deal last night, but something went wrong. At this point I don't know why. I will find out later this morning."

Choy waved a dismissive finger. "You are not anywhere close to finding the wrongdoers. From what my sources have told me, whatever antics occurred last evening has raised a hornet's nest among the gangsters. I would be cautious, my son. There could be serious repercussions for the events of the last two nights. What about speaking to your old nemesis, Rudy Tang? He has much information as to what occurs in the underworld of Honolulu. I could arrange a meeting for you."

Grant sighed, "I hate to become involved with that man. I know he hasn't forgiven me for stealing your daughter from him."

Choy smiled. "Selena is an independent woman. As I told you in the past, she will choose her husband and nothing I can do or say would convince her to accept my recommendation. She chose you, a great choice. Please consider my suggestion."

"I will talk with Asing and let you know. I still think he wants me dead."

Choy's face and voice turned serious. "I caution you to be wary of the yakuza. They have corrupted many officials who are more interested in money than doing what is right. There are leaks in the detective department and your role in the counterfeiting operation will be revealed to them."

Grant's eyes narrowed, "How did you learn I was involved? Asing is the only one who knew what I would be doing to help him."

"As I said, there are many officials who will do evil things for money. You were very heroic last evening. You saved your friend from losing his head."

"Oh my God, the yakuza must know of my olohe's involvement in the battle. I need to warn him."

Grant rushed from Choy's office.

## CHAPTER 48

The morning sun finally thrust above the Koolau Mountains when Grant stepped onto Maunakea Street. *Although its warmth has swept away the coolness of the night, I still feel a chill in my heart. Had my desire to help the detective endangered my friend and his family?*

He felt uncertain as to what to do as he hurried along the street. People crowded into him. *Was there a killer lurking among them*? He had to pause in his rush to control his mounting fear. He did not worry about himself, but the others whom he had put in harm's way.

Grant began to run, jostling pedestrians on the sidewalk. He ignored the complaints hurled at him for his rudeness. The clang of trolley bells and the click of iron wheels on rails greeted his arrival on King Street. He continued his run to his office, entered, and seized the telephone. He stamped his feet when Selena did not answer his call. Lines of worry creased his forehead, where could she be? Then he realized she would be on her way to work at the university.

His fingers fumbled as he rang the operator and gave her the office number at Selena's school. When someone answered he asked for Selena. "Not in," he was told. He left a message to call.

He tried Kamaka's home. No one answered despite numerous rings. It took a few moments to still his anxiety and realize that they had made an appointment to meet Asing. His olohe must be at the police station. The first of his secretaries came through the door, and Grant asked her to call Asing.

When he left his office, Grant studied the street for hidden threats. *The yakuza know where I work, and I do not want a repeat of my last encounter. I must control the fear for my wife and friend – my heart beat is racing.* His eyes roved his surroundings as he walked, constantly searching for hidden threats. Grant sighed as he entered the station and saw the sergeant at his desk. His quickened pulse gradually slowed as he walked to the detective's office.

Kamaka was already there, chatting with Asing whose face twisted into one of his rare smiles as he said, "Good to see you. Come—"

"You have a terrible leak in your office that has endangered my family and my teacher. I thought I could trust you to keep our involvement in your capers secret!"

Asing's smile turned into a frown. "What are you saying? I revealed nothing!"

"Dan Choy knows of my help in the counterfeiting case. He knows of last evening's battle in the Park," Grant blurted out before he realized he should not name his source.

Asing winced. "I had to make a report as to why we had prisoners in our holding cell. There needed to be charges filed against them. I marked everything 'confidential'."

"It certainly isn't confidential if the news of those events is already known throughout the town!" Grant said.

"I am sorry for any distress I caused you. Other than my report I did not say anything to anyone about your involvement or Kamaka's help last night. You mentioned your family, what is your concern?"

"It should be obvious," Grant replied his voice shaking. "There will be reprisals against them."

"Calm yourself. The yakuza has a code of honor. They do not inflict punishment on wives or children because a husband has done them wrong. As to Kamaka I did not mention him in my report, only you for saving my life, for which I am grateful."

"I will accept what you say, but who would be the leak in your office?"

"There would be three in the chain of command and an interrogating officer who would have questioned the prisoners."

"Then one of them is corrupt and a paid spy for the gangsters. We need to find who it is and prosecute him!"

Asing shook his head, fingered his ear. "To do that we would have to reveal the source of your information. I think it might have dire consequences for Dan Choy. You are aware of the suicide of the Immigration Officer. The apparent reason for his death is he allowed illegal Chinese workers to enter Hawaii. He had been corrupted by somebody and he knew he would be found out for his wrongdoing. We both know from our experience in the *Cult* murders who is the prime labor contractor of Chinese workers."

Grant pursed his lips, stifling a bitter retort to this accusation. He had to blame himself for blurting out his informant. He realized that if he forced criminal charges for corruption it would have dire consequences for his father-in-law and seriously affect his relationship with Selena. *I must remember the admonition of my drill sergeant about unfairness: "Suck in your gut and shut up."*

"You have me between a rock and a hard place. I lose either way I turn, but if I accept your opinion that family is not hurt by yakuza and Kamaka is not named in your report then I will still my tongue. You will hear no more complaint from me, except I no longer trust your department. Kamaka, are you good with what I have said?"

"Do not worry about me. I can take care of myself. I got plenty friends, they not afraid of yakuza either."

"All right then, we agree. Asing, what happened last night when you made the proposal?"

"I didn't state it exactly as we had discussed. I told the boss man that I would have to prosecute the counterfeiters, but I would let the prostitution alone if his gang would help us find those who were behind the explosions.

"He laughed at me. He told me I offered him nothing. I couldn't prosecute the pimps and whores because there's a deal in place to permit the boogie houses. The American military demanded that Honolulu provide female services for the thousands of soldiers and sailors descending upon the town.

"When I said that I was just negotiating, he called me a stupid policeman and ordered his men to beat me. That is when you two intervened and saved my life."

"He must think that he can get all his goons out of jail without a problem."

"Either that or he is willing to sacrifice his counterfeiters since I'm convinced there is no agreement to allow that kind of crime to go unpunished. That makes me suspect the yakuza could be behind the bombings."

"How about questioning the hoodlums you have in custody?"

"Interesting you should say that; I think Lieutenant Hitchcock is doing exactly that right now. From your experience he knows how to beat information out of prisoners."

"It won't happen," Kamaka interjected. "To rat on his brothers would be a one-way ticket to hell."

"Then we are back to where we were before. No clues and no suspects," Grant said.

"There is still my friend Koichi."

"He's Japanese, wouldn't he face the same problem, a garrote around his throat if he talks?"

"I think we could keep our conversations with him secret, unless of course the detective has to make a report to his superiors."

"From what we have learned about leaks in my department, I will do no such thing. What makes you think he would be honest with us?"

"He and I worked in the same sugar fields a while ago. Big haole luna supervised us. One day, he started whipping Koichi. I pulled him off his horse. He turned on me, but I gave him a lua move and knocked him on his ass. When he got up and tried to fight me, I punched him out. The end result was Koichi and I got fired, but the good news is we became friends. I tell you it's hard for the first-generation Japanese to make friends with anybody but Japanese. They identify with their own for protection."

"That's why you think he will help us?"

"It isn't just that, my new friend had already decided to quit. He had brought over a picture bride and the two of them opened a store in the country. It was very dangerous to do so. The plantations were tough on those who left the sugar fields and went into business for themselves. They took a dim view of any Asians who competed with white merchants. Koichi asked me to work for him. I think he wanted protection. I was a young guy, had no one to care for and I accepted. Room and board, plus plenty of time off to work on my martial arts skills.

"My boss was a smart man. He had been in the merchandise business in Japan. But a recession struck, and the yen dropped in value. It turned out he could make more money coming to Hawaii and working in the fields than staying in Japan, at least four times as much. He came right after annexation. That is when most Japanese came to Hawaii. The yakuza arrived at the same time. These guys are not workers, they're predators, making money from prostitution and gambling."

"I remember those early days before the Great War," Asing interrupted. "It proved to be a wild time. We couldn't control those tattoo guys. They would come to labor camps with their girls and games of chance, dice, mah jong, you name it, they had it. The workers loved them and ganged up on the police if we tried to enforce the law. Finally, we had to make deals to confine them to one area, Iwilei, where the railroad has a terminal by Aala Park. Big barracks building was built by the gangsters. Housed two hundred women, seventy-five percent were Japanese. Picture brides, plantation wives, husbands sold them into sex slavery. But you know all this already."

"It never ceases to amaze me. I didn't know these things growing up," Grant said.

"That's because you were one of the wealthy few. Lived in Nuuanu, went to Punahou, and off to the East Coast for college. Are you finished with your story, Kamaka?"

"No, just a little more so you can see why he owes me and how well connected my friend is. Anyhow, Koichi is a very smart man, he not only knew how to make money, but he studied law on the side and began to help his Japanese neighbors get unionized to demand higher wages. Somebody in the plantations got angry, he was undercutting white merchants and also stirring up the workers with his union talk. That somebody decided to polish him off. One night, Koichi went to a union meeting. Within sight of home, four goons waylaid him and prepared to string him up, a real old-fashioned lynching. I was watching for him and laid into the guys. One of them was a Hawaiian I knew, he cut out right away. Two of the goons were hanging my friend and the third guy was watching. I smashed my *piikoi* across his skull and laid him out.

"The other two guys let Koichi go, which was a mistake since he promptly tripped one of them to the ground. The goon still standing tried to make a move, but I smashed him in the gut. His head came down and I threw an uppercut into his throat and jaw. He went down for the count. The man who got tripped got up, took one look at me, and took off. I took the rope off of Koichi's neck, tied the two knocked-out guys together. I put a note on them: 'Next time you die.'"

"So, Koichi was a union guy before the war?"

"Yes, and he kept gaining in power as time went on. Japanese looked to him for guidance. He had no more trouble from the plantations. When the war came, he kind of went underground and took on a low profile. I left him to make my own way. After the war when the big movement started for a strike, Koichi laid low because the workers weren't unified. Divide and rule worked. When 1920 came around, the Filipinos went on strike. The Japanese followed, but then within a week that coward Manlapit, who started the strike, sold out to the plantations, and the Filipinos went back to work. They say he got big money for what he did. The Japanese were left alone and suffered before they could make a deal to bring their strike to an end."

"I can see your friend was very smart," Asing commented. "When the conspiracy indictments were passed down, he was not on the list of twenty-one names accused of planning assassinations of sugar plantation executives."

"That is correct. The indictments wiped out the leadership of the Japanese unions. Koichi has been quietly rebuilding the labor movement ever since. I would say that he is one of the most important Japanese pro-union men in Hawaii right now."

"And you believe, because of your past services to him, he will help us?" Grant asked.

"More than that, he thinks the bombing attacks must stop or else the Japanese will be marked for severe reprisals by the HSPA."

"Which is already happening," Asing commented. "All we need to blow everything apart is another dynamiting. Then the governor might impose martial law. We have to catch the criminal or criminals soon."

"We still have the big problem of whether Koichi can be truly honest with us. To squeal on yakuza, or any other Japanese for that matter, could be a death sentence for him," Grant said.

"Let's cross that bridge when, or if, we ever come to it," Kamaka answered.

"I think we should use every source available since time may be running out for us. My father-in-law is urging me to see Rudy Tang."

"Superb idea," Asing clapped his hands. "Tang is Chinese, not bound by any honor rules like the Japanese. He is a long-time gangster and knows a lot about the underworld in Hawaii. I agree you should pay him a visit."

"I've resisted it. You know how he hates me. It's insane. But this is an emergency. Kamaka can speak with Koichi. Asing, back me up when I talk to Rudy. He's tried to kill me several times. Let me call Choy and set up a meeting under a flag of truce, for whatever that's worth. Before he lets me leave, I'm sure that snake will find a way to bite me."

# CHAPTER 49

Grant parked his Packard on a low rise a block from Rudy Tang's headquarters next to Nuuanu Stream and the ocean. He and Asing sat quietly for a moment. The detective broke the silence. "You say that when Choy spoke to Rudy, he gave him plenty of assurance that you would not be harmed."

"True, in fact he swore on a stack of Christian Bibles I would not be hurt by him."

"I thought he's a Buddhist?"

"No, not that either. I think his only religion is money and from what I can tell, in his church, he is its god."

Asing laughed. "Guy has a huge ego. He glorifies himself above all else. But I got to hand it to that Chinaman; he's a survivor in the criminal world. Chinese are going down in number since the Exclusion Act of 1882. Japanese have risen to the top, and the Filipinos are rapidly gaining ground on them. Between the two races they account for sixty percent of Hawaii's population."

"A formidable force if they could be united. I'll go first. Rudy's expecting me at noon. Wait ten minutes and then saunter over. There's a back door and front, you got to keep an eye on both. No way to tell what he will do."

Grant stepped from his car and worked his way over to Tang's building. At the door a young female answered his knock and advised him that Rudy waited upstairs. Grant noted that there was a new painting inside of a fat Chinese general with long, stringy hair commanding a host of mounted warriors waiting behind him. Grant had the impression that everyone in it would be charging into the room. It was uncanny to look at it. He stared at the picture from different angles. On each view he felt that he would be attacked.

Grant climbed to the second story, knocked, and heard a gruff sound. He entered and viewed Rudy's office. It had not changed in four years, the same deadly shark-toothed *leiomano* still fastened to the wall behind him. The sallow-faced Chinese, eyes beady like a small pig, waved a hand to a chair in front of him. The long, thin sideburns descending on each side of his face ended in a pointed goatee at his chin, creating a satanic look. Grant's heart beat rapidly, and his temples throbbed. *What am I doing here? he wondered.*

"So, you come seeking my help," Rudy smiled. "What do you offer in return?"

"Name a price."

"An evening alone with your sweet wife."

"Never," Grant rose to leave.

"Sit, sit, I was only testing you. In my business, men have traded wives for gain. You love her, as once I did. I envy you for what you have. We shall place her charms outside of our bargaining. Do you still have influence over Detective Asing?"

"I wouldn't call it influence. We are friends working on the same case."

"You are here about the untimely death of your father."

"Yes, and the explosions that have wracked the homes of members of the HSPA."

"Bah, I spit on them. Why do you think I would help those pigs?"

Grant thought for some moments, choosing his words carefully. "Whoever wants to kill them killed my father. The bad actors have riled up the HSPA who are promising to take vengeance on the Japanese. Asing needs to find the guilty parties before serious harm comes to them."

Rudy laughed, a deep-throated set of guffaws. When he finally got his mirth under control, he shouted, "You want a Chinese to help Japanese! That empire fought a war against China! They killed my people!"

Grant realized he had stepped into a quagmire. He had not expected that Rudy could be so emotional about a country he left a long time ago and had been ruled in a quixotic and cruel way by the Manchu dynasty. They had done nothing to make the life of the people they controlled better. But maybe Tang's vehemence was just an act to place himself in a superior bargaining position. "The Sino-Chinese war exposed the corruption of the Manchus. I cannot believe you aren't a supporter of Sun Yat Sen who, by his revolution, has ended that wicked dynasty and established a republic in China."

Rudy's cynical smile faded from his lips. "I see you know history."

"Yes, and I know you were one of Sun's supporters when he lived here in Hawaii."

"You are also well informed. You must have been coached before you got here. Might it be Dan Choy?"

Grant smiled. "You imply I do not have personal knowledge about many things of significance. However, I will admit to having excellent teachers."

"Who also may have knowledge of dark secrets involving me!"

"I did not come here to blackmail. I came seeking your help in solving a crime. Asing and I have been eliminating races who may want to seek revenge against the HSPA. We have eliminated all the races who could have a reason to attack the plantation people except the Japanese. They are under suspicion because of a dynamiting during the 1920 strike and the criminal convictions of fifteen labor leaders of conspiracy to assassinate members of the HSPA."

Tang fingered his chin and his long goatee. "You think I have knowledge that would assist you in your investigation. Let me ask, why did you go about your task by eliminating races?"

"Asing believes in motives for committing crime. The races in Hawaii have reasons for hating the sugar plantations, the Japanese for the horrors of the 1920 strike. The Filipinos are angered by the 1924 massacre. The Hawaiians weep over the stealing of their land and kingdom by the Big Five. These races have the greatest grudges. We considered the Chinese and Koreans as well. But we have narrowed the list to the Japanese."

"And if you eliminate them, then what?"

"We have no clues as to who it might be. We thought someone knowledgeable about crime in Hawaii could help us."

"That is why you seek my help, to find a killer. But you have not eliminated the Japanese."

"I don't think they are the guilty parties, but we have considered the yakuza. They are a gangster operation with the resources to commit the crimes."

"I think you are wrong. The yakuza are not interested in revenge. They want their business of prostitution and gambling to thrive. Why attack the HSPA and lose their protection?"

"You're suggesting that members of the business community engage in illicit acts?"

"I thought you were smart. Men want love. If they cannot get it by any other means they will pay for it whether it is quickie sex or the kind I provide, which is long, lingering, and unforgettable."

"Okay, we eliminate the yakuza, how about the other Japanese?"

Rudy's sinister face dawned into a smile. "I thought you were smart. Think about it. Any criminal can bash a head or shoot a gun. It takes planning, acquiring the means to accomplish the task, and great skill to avoid capture and not leave clues. That ability the ordinary Japanese does not have, he is more interested in existing and not wreaking vengeance."

"What you say is very reasonable. But who is the guilty party?"

"I am not a detective. I am a business man interested in making money. Would I be foolish enough to attack the people who make me rich? Never, only an idiot would do that. Whether you like or hate the plantations has nothing to do with accumulating money. Under the Hawaiian Kingdom the rulers did not know how to acquire wealth, the sugar people did. Look what we have in Honolulu, no longer a bunch of grass shacks, but big buildings, autos, thriving business people. It is plain stupidity to dynamite the hand that feeds you unless you are driven by hatred. That emotion is uncontrollable."

Grant palmed his hair and studied the floor for a moment. "Then what you are saying is to look for someone who hates and has no other motive than vengeance."

Rudy rang a bell and scowled. "You have taken my time. Acquired my knowledge and given me nothing in exchange."

Three burly Chinese entered the room.

"Take this lover boy outside, rough him up and throw him in the ocean. But don't kill him. That will be my payment, Mr. Kingsley, for all the knowledge I have given you."

Before he could rise, Grant's arms were pinned to his side. Two men lifted him and dragged him from the office. They headed for the rear door of the building.

# CHAPTER 50

Patience, that is the word he wanted. He would explain to Miguel that they must have patience in their efforts to Sovietize Hawaii. He, Robinson, had not given up on his mission to end the feudal empire that existed in the islands.

"Master," Miguel goaded him. "Your message is too weak. We must tell people to rebel against imperialism and end the dominance of the HSPA!"

Irritated by his sarcasm, Robinson responded with vehemence, "I am not your master and you are not my servant. Don't you recall Marx's basic instruction that true Communism calls for a classless society with no superiors or inferiors? I am comrade and you are my comrade I expect you will address me as such."

"But you are asking me to pass out these pamphlets which I disagree with. Are you not acting superior to me? Are you not exerting your power when you write what I cannot stomach? Everything you do screams of control over me. You abhor the basic tenet of achieving a classless society: conflict. Change occurs through a perpetual conflict of opposing forces and ultimate change can only occur by catastrophe or revolution. The struggle is filled with violence and hate. Destruction of the ruling class becomes a crusade for progress. Everything that resists Communism must be annihilated until a classless society is achieved!"

"I studied dialectical materialism which says that nothing is final, absolute, and sacred. Societal change is inevitable. But when you speak of catastrophe and revolution you are arguing an end game where you cannot persuade others to your goal of a classless society. I believe in a more moderate approach. The great Chinese strategist said: 'It is best to keep to the middle way.' That is what I intend to do. Unlike a debate, you identify the opposite of an issue and instead of one side winning and the other losing, you arrive at the middle way. Once you agree on this middle way, you provoke the opposite point of view. And by this continual dialectic form of argument you achieve your goal of a classless society."

Miguel shook his head. "You are talking compromise. Lenin said: 'The duty of a revolutionary is to put an end to compromise'. To end compromise means taking the path of socialist revolution."

"You do not understand what is needed for a successful revolution. You must have the people behind your cause. During the Great War the catastrophic military defeats drove the public against the Tsar. When he abdicated and the Kerensky government took over, their continued pursuit of war gave Lenin the opportunity to overthrow this ill-conceived republic. Russian people wanted an end to fighting the Germans.

"But when the call went out for worldwide revolution by the Comintern, that primal scream failed in America. The dynamite attacks and demands for social change ended with deportations, imprisonments, and a huge decline in the Communist party. America was not ready for a new ideology. There existed too much prosperity. All that resulted from this demand for change was the anti-syndicalism law of 1919, the Anarchistic Publication Law of 1921, and the Anti-Picketing law of 1923. Repression maintained the status quo."

Miguel protested, "Lenin said: 'We must stop at nothing to preserve the rule of the workers and peasants.'"

"But that was said in Russia during a time when the proletariat demanded change. You must set aside your desire to kill the people of the HSPA for what they did to your family. We must have patience in our efforts to bring people in Hawaii to accept Communism. Once we have tolerance, we can move to acceptance, and then adoption of our ideas."

"I will pause my hatred, but for how long I cannot say. The Third International taught me that a good Communist fight, with all available means, to overthrow the imperialistic bourgeoisie. I want to destroy these capitalists who suck wealth from the laboring man."

Robinson sighed; he had won momentary control over his restive comrade. He knew the man was impelled to kill by a hatred that transcended his zeal for Communism. How long it would be before the bombings would reoccur, he did not know. He fingered the revolver in his pocket, fearful that Miguel was not only a danger to the HSPA but could become a danger to him. He felt like a trainer dealing with a wild animal, at any moment the creature could lash out against the one who restrained him.

He rose from his chair standing to his full height to achieve a commanding posture. "All right then, here are the pamphlets to be handed out during the parade from the docks. I will be on the reviewing stand working on the Japanese consulate seeking to win him over to our cause."

# CHAPTER 51

Grant relaxed. He did not resist the two men pinning his arms and following a third Chinese downstairs. He sensed their grips ease, and he knew they did not expect him to escape. He weighed his chances to fight back while inside the building but decided to wait. *Outside, Asing could help him.*

The group reached the rear door. Grant was turned sideways as the two goons who held him twisted through the threshold. He watched the man in front, timing his actions to his movements. He suddenly sagged, bringing the two who held him down. He swung a foot into the crotch of the man in front, making him falter.

His downward movement unbalanced his captors and Grant broke free. "Ayah, Asing," he yelled as he hit the concrete floor of the seawall protecting the land from the ocean surges.

One of his captors swung a shoe into his side yelling, "White devil."

Grant felt a surge of pain and hoped no ribs were broken. He tried rolling away from the kicks, but the other Chinese stopped his movement with his legs and swung a fist at his face. He moved away from the strike, and felt a kick in the back. He swung his legs behind his head, placed his hands flat against the pavement, and thrust his feet high. He pushed off with his hands, and arched into an upright position.

A punch hit him in the kidneys and a karate chop glanced off his head. Though in pain, Grant smashed an elbow into one attacker and tried to head butt the other.

The piercing crack of a whip was followed by a scream. "You will back off from Mr. Kingsley now!" Asing shouted.

Two Chinese turned to meet the threat. Grant pulled away. The third Chinese, the one he kicked in the crotch, sat on the seawall. Asing stood with a whip in one hand and a club in another. "I am police," he said. "You will please move from Mr. Kingsley."

The thugs looked at each other and then at the man on the ground. Asing's whip whirled in the air and snapped with a sound sharp as a lightning bolt. "Move aside and let Mr. Kingsley through!"

A huge wave pounded into the breakwater, thrusting salt water above the stone restraining wall. Its spray doused the sitting man and flung water at the men standing nearby. "If you don't pick up your buddy and get out of here, I or the next wave will push him into the ocean," Grant said with all the menace he could muster.

The Chinese jabbered among themselves. Asing swung his whip from side to side, the sinuous rawhide leather snaking along the smooth stone. Grant took another step back before settling himself into a lua fighting position. He watched the feet of his opponents, ready for any aggressive move they made. With Asing's backing he could deal with the threats.

The ocean surged with a mighty thump into the wall. Water spewed over the concrete showering the Chinese struggling to rise. He yelled, his companions rushed to him and raised him up as the last of the lingering spray fell and rolled back into the sea.

As the three men went to the rear door, Grant called to them, "Tell Rudy I accept the bruising you gave me in payment for the information I received from him. Tell him he will not be trusted by me ever again. Should we meet at another time I will beat him until he screams for mercy."

The three men silently entered the building. Asing came to Grant and put an arm around his shoulder. "You looked like the cat who just lost his nine lives," the detective quipped.

"I'm glad you got here. The kicks and punches hurt. I don't know if I would have been much of a help if those goons decided to fight."

"Not to worry, I have faced many more belligerent men in the past and been able to handle them. But do you need to go to the hospital?"

"I think not, just need some time for the aching to ease off. Besides, we are due for the parade. The Japanese fleet should be arriving at any moment. In fact, I think I can hear the blaring from the tugboats."

"What did you find out from Rudy? From what you said a moment ago he gave you some insights toward solving the crimes."

"He said the yakuza is not involved. They have no reason to bite the hand that permits them to operate their whore houses. As for the Japanese, he says since the trial of the alleged assassination squad of union leaders, the rank and file are leaderless and without incentive to harm the HSPA. I think he would suggest that we look elsewhere than the races for our killer. Before I could get an answer to my question, he set his goons on me."

"We will have to evaluate where we are going with this investigation once we get a report from Kamaka on his interview with Koichi. But I fear that our inability to solve the crimes will go hard on the Japanese. Patterson is like a mad dog seeking revenge. I suspect it is not just the attack against him that drives his vengeance, but a desire to cow the Japanese into total submission to the plantations."

"I'm afraid you are right. The harsh treatment of the alleged conspirators of terrorism, the trial and imprisonment of their union leaders, the laws barring the Japanese language schools from operating, followed by the new school policy of Americanization makes it hard for the Japanese to maintain their ancestral identity."

"We can discuss this later. Let's hurry to greet the members of the Japanese fleet."

The two men strode toward a crowd roaring, "B*anzai*, *Banzai*, *Banzai*."

# CHAPTER 52

Grant and Asing stepped onto the reviewing stand erected on the ocean side of the Japanese consulate. On the wide green lawn of the building sat a huge white tent with many rows of chairs.

The Japanese Consul Sakamoto espied them and came over, bowing a greeting. "You have had success in stopping the dishonor?"

"Yes, I can assure you that the un-robing indignity has ended for all time."

"*So desu ka*," Sakamoto answered. "I thank you profusely. Come, watch the arrival of the officers and men of our glorious fleet. We have become a great naval power in the Pacific."

"But isn't the 5-5-3 battleship limitation going to hurt Japan?"

Sakamoto scowled. "That Washington Naval Treaty is a disgrace to my country. None of us feel we should have entered into such an agreement.

"Enough of politics, we will have dinner at your friend's restaurant. You might ask one of the officers who will be there how my country intends to cope with this insult to our proud navy. Come to the rail of the welcome stand and watch the arrival of our sailors. See this huge crowd waving their Rising Sun flags? This is a glorious day for Yamato," Sakamoto said, using the ancient name for Japan.

At the rail, Grant and Asing were introduced to Charles Robinson, publisher of the *Hinode Times*. Grant said, "We have met before. I also had the pleasure of hearing you speak at a meeting of the Royal Order. Your take on propaganda is most interesting."

"I'm glad you enjoyed the talk. Use of that one-sided media device is how the impoverished worker is controlled by the dominant power."

"Yes, I can see how it can be done by slanting the news so the truth can be distorted."

"Wonderful, you captured the essence of my talk. You also considered what I had to say about suppressing the native language newspapers in order to hide the Hawaiian side of events. As a publisher, I am hamstrung in my efforts to tell the real news by the Anti-Anarchistic Publication law that the legislature has passed."

"You seem to disagree with what our government does to stamp out sedition?"

"Ah, I am not that foolish as to oppose the decrees. I only suggest that America treasures the right of free speech and usually brooks no interference with it."

"I cannot disagree with that sentiment. The Japanese language schools have been suppressed by law. To the credit of their supporters they are appealing the judge's ruling upholding the law to the United States Supreme Court. Their basic argument is that the First Amendment of the Constitution guarantees the right of free speech."

"I applaud your thinking since you favor that freedom. Suppression of the schools means that the Japanese people do not get true information on the exploitation of the working man by the sugar plantations."

"You are very progressive, but we should not speak too loudly of exploitation, that is 'Red' talk and could lead to trouble."

Grant noticed a medium-sized man passing out papers to the flag-waving crowd. "Mr. Sakamoto, I see that someone is distributing information. Is that an announcement of the schedule of the Japanese fleet while it is here? I would appreciate having one."

The Japanese counsel frowned. "We did not prepare any such thing. I know nothing—"

"Let me explain," Robinson interrupted. "That is my fellow worker. He is passing out informative news that the Japanese should consider. I trust that we did not need your permission to hand out our bulletin? We did not mean to offend anyone."

"Hai, knowledge is very important, but hard times for the Japanese in Hawaii. We do not want to cause trouble."

"The truth is never trouble. I would love to talk to your staff about what is written and possibly some meetings may be arranged with influential Japanese to listen to what I have to say."

"I must know in advance your topic."

"Read the bulletin and it will explain my intentions in speaking to you."

"Your co-worker, he was passing out information at your talk to the Hawaiians?" Grant asked.

"Yes."

"And I was told he gave out pamphlets to Hawaiians in Kaneohe."

Robinson eyed Grant with suspicion. "I know nothing of it."

"My friend could have been mistaken."

"Listen," Sakamoto interrupted. "The crowd is roaring. The officers must have landed. Come, greet them."

Throughout the harbor, *banzais* were screamed by an aroused crowd. "What does the word mean?" Grant asked.

"It's a Japanese cheer meaning: 'May you live for 10,000 years.'" Sakamoto answered.

"May I invite my wife to this dinner tonight?"

"Hai."

# CHAPTER 53

Selena wore a smashing aqua green silk shantung dress to Ah Sam's Chinese restaurant. Grant nudged her neck. "You are especially beautiful tonight."

She pushed him away. "You men always want something when you want it, but are you ever home when I need you? No, you are too busy chasing after someone and visiting houses of prostitution."

"I've already explained I was on an investigation."

"Then you come home with bruises and complaints of pain and want sympathy and tender loving care."

"I am grateful for all you do. It's time to take our seat. We are with Captain Yamamoto. We met him four years ago. He is a very bright man who speaks excellent English."

Grant escorted Selena to their table, one of four in the blue room. At the back wall a long table was placed where the VIPs were seated, the assistant mayor of Honolulu, Sakamoto, the fleet admiral, and others.

"I recall you from our last meeting," Yamamoto said.

"Yes, I remember you well, Isoroku, fifty-six," Grant smiled.

"Hai, you recall the meaning of my name."

"Yes, you told me that your father was very proud he could produce a son at fifty-six."

"And he quit trying thereafter. At least no one came after me in our family."

The guests settled down for dinner. Yamamoto on Grant's right, Selena to his left. Next to her sat Matsu from the Japanese consulate and his wife, along with another member of the consulate and two naval officers.

Grant decided to pursue information that Trask wanted. "Isoroku, the last time we talked it was of air craft and the carriers of them. I have read that the British have commissioned one, how about your country?"

"It is the British who have taught us about air power. Because of them we are the first nation to complete an aircraft carrier. It is called the *Kaga*, a converted battleship."

"Is that because of the Washington treaty limiting the number of battleships the Japanese may build?"

"That is a factor, but your American General Billy Mitchell has been very persuasive. In his recent visit to Japan he spoke to our naval officers about the effects of air power. Did you know that in 1921 he sank a battleship, cruiser, and submarine by air bombardment?" Yamamoto took a deep breath before continuing. "There are still those who believe in the battleship. We have decided to build the biggest the world has ever known. The Yamato class is 73,000 tons with nine heavy guns hurling missiles at targets twenty-five miles away. We are planning to lay down three keels over the next few years."

"That is an answer to the treaty's limitation on the number you may have. But you also built a carrier upon a former battleship. Why sacrifice a battlewagon?"

Yamamoto munched on the excellent dim sum. He sipped tea and used his chopsticks to lift a morsel of sweet char sui pork. "When we last talked of airplanes you told me of how helpless you felt as an infantry man when attacked from the sky. There are some of us in the navy who believe that aircraft will be a key factor if war should break out again. As you point out, the British have built a carrier and they are planning more. We are also."

Yamamoto's candor surprised him. When they had chatted four years ago the captain had not been as forthcoming. Tonight, he spoke with great pride. Grant knew that the 5-5-3 treaty was perceived by the Japanese people as a dishonor to the Empire.

The rest of the evening consisted of small talk and welcoming speeches. Grant no longer pressed the captain for information. He had learned all he needed to know. Trask should be happy with the information he had received.

# CHAPTER 54

Trask sat hunched over a map when Grant entered his office. The Captain waved a hand to an empty chair and Grant sat. He wondered if the captain was more interested in his survey of the cartography in front of him than the tidings he bore of Japanese war plans.

Finally, Trask rose from his intense study, rubbed his eyes, and yawned. "Sorry to be inhospitable. The navy is so concerned about the Japanese menace, we are accelerating our proposed war plans for an invasion of these islands. I've been working for two days to get ready for the games. There are lots of things to consider when you're going to involve 45,000 men and 150 ships in a mock battle."

"How about airplanes? I understand General Mitchell believes they will become decisive in the next war and the battleship is obsolete."

Trask moved his chair back and stood. "That man is a thorn in the side of the Army and Navy. Just because he sunk ships that were stationary in the water doesn't mean his aircraft would be successful against moving vessels. The joint chiefs of staff have stated: 'The Battleship is the backbone of the fleet.' That is good enough for me. If the General keeps blabbering about the failures of the Army and Navy to defend this country he will be court-martialed."

"You are highly agitated on this subject of air power. You may not like what I have to tell you. From my visit with a Japanese captain I believe the Empire is following a two-pronged military strategy: build aircraft carriers and the largest battleships in the world."

Trask palmed his hair then said, "Tell me about this."

Grant related his conversation with Yamamoto the previous evening. He concluded by saying, "I think our military should listen to what Mitchell has to say. I served in the Great War. It wasn't until we gained air superiority that we were sure to win battles. If the conflict had continued into 1919 tanks and airplanes would have devastated the German army. Only the Armistice stopped the utter defeat of the Kaiser's military machine."

Trask shook his head. "Unfortunately, I did not see combat during the war. You were in the front lines and fought. You saw battle first hand. I think generals are always fighting the last war when they consider what the military should be like for the future.

"I think your analysis is right on. But conservatism and not forward thinking is the spider web which traps our military. It is easier to support what has worked in the past and ignore what developing technology might be able to do on the battlefield of the future.

"I for one am not going to buck the brass. My career in the service would end quickly."

"You will just follow orders and not make waves. In your war game planning are you including the Philippines?" Grant asked.

"No. Why would we do that?"

"Mitchell prophesies that Pearl Harbor will be hit at 7:30 in the morning and Clark Field at 10:30."

"That's a stretch. The General is just playing boogie man. No nation in the Pacific has the resources to do that."

"Right now, they may not, but given time who can tell? Let's move on to another subject, have you analyzed the metal I gave you?"

"I apologize. I haven't stayed on top of it, but I am sure I can have a written report for you tomorrow."

Grant sighed. "We are in a tough spot in our investigation. We are running out of suspects. What you are analyzing are the only concrete clues we have."

"I will attend to it immediately. Your country thanks you for all the information you have given us. The only other matter we need to know is the Japanese plan in case war breaks out."

"Let me hazard a guess, attack Pearl Harbor and the Philippines, then draw the surviving fleet deep into the Pacific fighting a war of attrition with submarines and air power. When our navy is near Japan, its ships will come out and crush what is left. It's an Armageddon-type scenario for the two nations."

"What you prophesize will never happen."

"Maybe not, but you recall that the Japanese took over all those German islands in the Pacific. They are building air and naval bases on them. That fits with an attrition strategy."

"And to counter it we would have to land on those islands and destroy the military forces on them. Waste our strength in numerous small battles."

"I believe that is the Japanese thinking at the moment. But to guarantee success with an attrition strategy, they should take Pearl Harbor and force America to fight to get it back."

"I think this is just academic and will never happen. Come back in the morning and I will have the information you need."

# CHAPTER 55

Grant headed for the Bethel Street police station. He felt elated, even though their investigation had gone stale. Soon they would have new clues to consider and possibly crack the case.

The desk sergeant waved him to Asing's office. He found the detective with his usual cigarette parked at the left edge of his lips. Smoke curled lazily toward the ceiling. Spread on his desk lay a leaflet. He lifted his eyes, smiled, and said, "Very interesting reading that we acquired yesterday. You have a chance to look at it?"

"Just a glance, hardly read it, seemed like it called for change."

"Right on, this memo urges Japanese to unite with the other races and vote to change the composition of the territorial legislature. It speaks of the exploitation of the working man by the profit seekers of the Big Five."

"That's pretty close to Communist thinking. Whoever wrote it is very smart. He doesn't preach revolution but urges democracy by people voting for change. Brilliant psychology, just point out how the poor are being used by the rich, and tell them how to make change, through the ballot box."

"It is a good strategy, but you and I know that the plantations spy on what goes on in the voting booth. Anyone who votes against the establishment loses his job or gets punished. The bulletin talks about this breach of democracy. It makes the claim 'there is a growing discontent in Hawaii due to a regime of repressive control' and states that 'The people have a right of self-determination guaranteed by the Constitution'."

"It is hard to argue against that claim. However, those words are very dangerous. The writer could find himself in serious trouble. There are no rights for the oppressed in a feudal society like ours."

"Aha, watch what you say. Enemy ears may be listening."

"You would turn me in as an anarchist! I thought we were friends!" Grant pounded his fist on the desk, then smiled. "By the way, I never thanked you for saving my life."

"I needed to pay you back for allowing me to keep my head. Those yakuza are mean guys, never thought they would stoop to decapitating me."

Kamaka knocked and entered the room.

"What news?" Grant asked.

"Aren't you going to say hello? How have you been? Maybe have some small talk before cutting to the chase."

"All right. Hello. How you been? Sunny day. Now that's done, what did you get out of Koichi?"

Kamaka laughed, looked over at Asing. "What's with this guy? He's Mr. Anxiety plus, got to talk serious right away."

The detective nodded, "I agree he is anxious. We got nothing concrete out of Tang except the yakuza is not involved in the bombings. The Japanese have lost their leadership and are either not smart enough to plan the explosions or not motivated to do so."

"That's what Koichi said. He mentioned the Filipinos who lost a lot of men, killed and wounded, in the massacre. But he didn't know of any conspiracy to strike back at the HSPA. Maybe it's one man doing the bombing."

"Possible," Asing answered. "When there is a conspiracy, one of members brags about what he did. Word gets around to people like Koichi and Tang. It spreads to others. It's hard for criminals to keep a secret."

"Hitchcock is interrogating Japanese. Anyone confess or implicate someone?" Grant asked.

"Simple answer is no. Everyone questioned knows nothing."

"If we threatened them with a severe beating or death do you think we would get some helpful information?"

"I'm surprised that you of all people would consider brutality as a method to solve the crimes."

Grant smacked his fist against an office wall. "Look Asing, I am desperate. Someone killed my father, a man I dearly loved. I have killed people in the past. I will do it again if I have to."

"But you were a soldier in wartime. You were supposed to kill the enemy."

"They were not always the enemy."

"Hey guys, we talk about tonight," Kamaka interrupted. "Koichi says there's a speech for select Japanese and Filipinos this evening that maybe you should come to. It's about exploitation of the worker and changing the government."

"Why should we be interested?" Asing asked.

"Koichi said that when the union leaders were talking about striking for higher wages in 1920 many of them were excited about what was going on in Russia and the communist idea that labor had a special value. Some felt to get what they wanted there had to be terroristic acts."

"I get the idea. When the dynamiters were tried for conspiracy there was mention made in the news of an assassination squad. There could be someone in the audience who was a member or maybe someone who believes that terrorism is the answer to getting higher pay. The topic of the talk is tailor made to get that kind of a person to attend."

"It would be a longshot," Asing commented. "But what have we got to lose? Right now, we do not have any suspects."

"You can arrange with Koichi to take us to the meeting?"

"He will, but I got to tell you the place is dangerous. The meeting is near the Palama Settlement - lots of thefts, beatings, murders in the neighborhood. Come prepared."

# CHAPTER 56

A mixed audience waited for Robinson to speak. Most of the crowd were Japanese. There were a few Filipinos, some Hawaiians, but no Chinese. As Grant surveyed the room, he thought that the races there had the most grudges against the HSPA. The three ethnic groups added up to more than seventy percent of the Hawaiian population.

Almost ninety people were squeezed into a classroom of the Japanese language school. A picture of Emperor Taisho stood in the center of the back wall. There were white flags with the red orb of the rising sun centered in them. The seating was laid out in auditorium fashion with a speaker's podium placed on a low stage just below the emperor's portrait.

"I believe that Japan is the only country in the world where the ruler is claimed to be descended from the gods," Grant whispered to his companions.

"The Hawaiian chiefs said they were descended from the gods Wakea and Papa," Kamaka answered. "In fact, every high *alii* had a scribe who could orally recite the descent of his chief. Genealogy was the big thing in the old days. If you didn't have a proven path to the two gods you were just a commoner."

"What's interesting about this emperor-divinity thing," Grant continued, "it was not a big deal for centuries. The man was just a puppet of the ruling lords of Japan. But when the Tokugawa Shogunate ended in 1868, the Meiji Emperor's divinity became a big deal. A god ruled Japan."

"So, is this Taisho guy all powerful?" Kamaka asked.

"I don't think it quite works that way. There is an elected body which actually makes the political decisions. What is decided is announced as the command of the Emperor which must be obeyed because he is divine. That's how the ancient Egyptian Pharaohs ruled and some Roman Emperors. There was a time when European kings claimed that they were 'anointed by God to rule.' The Great War ended the reign of the god-type rulers except for Japan, although the British still shout out, 'God save the King'."

Asing laughed. "Ha! The first democratic country in the world and they still worship the king. How do you figure that one out?"

The conversation in the room died out as Consul Sakamoto took the podium. He gave a background of the speaker and introduced Charles Robinson of the *Hinode Times*.

"Many of you in this room have suffered from the capitalistic government of Hawaii. There is a growing discontent in these islands because the feudal regime exploits the laborer. These elite few reap from your sweat and pain huge profits. They fail to give back to the working man any of their ill-gotten gains. You have a right under the Constitution to end this evil rule and vote for a new government."

Robinson went on to talk of the racial apartheid and exploitation that existed in Hawaii. He pointed out that these conditions only served the interests of the Big Five and allowed the companies to monopolize the economy. "They control everything," Robinson screamed at one point. He argued, "Monopolistic capitalism leads to a society of classes, an elite few, a group in the middle, and huge numbers of the working poor. Ownership of private property is the villain. A return to the old Hawaiian system of communal sharing of the land and its products means equality for all, and people will prosper equally."

Robinson concluded by saying, "The path to equality is not an easy one to follow. There are those who will make the movement to your goal difficult, but battles and conflict always occur when you seek freedom from the oppression of greedy capitalists. Use your right to vote to make change."

After the applause quieted Robinson invited questions. "My name is Grant Kingsley. You urge these people to make change by voting, but other than the Hawaiians none are American citizens. How do you expect them to make change? Is the only answer a revolution?"

Robinson smiled. "I expected someone from the ruling class to ask such a question. No, I am not proposing revolution. I am making Asian people aware of their rights in America to register and vote for candidates who will make change."

The detective stood. "My name is Chang Asing. Asians are prevented by law from voting. They are not allowed to be naturalized. Filipinos are here in Hawaii as nationals, but they are not citizens. How then do you expect them to vote? Isn't their only option to make change is to revolt as Mr. Kingsley says?"

Robinson scoffed. "You are a policeman. Like Mr. Kingsley you support the ruling elite. That is why you see no alternative to change but violence. I do not speak of immediate action; I speak long term. Everyone born on American soil is a citizen. The children of the people in this room have a right to vote when they come of age. That is what I am urging, that the *sakadas* and *issei* teach their children to exercise their elective power when they are old enough to do so."

The crowd applauded except for one person in the Filipino section who yelled, "Revolution Now!"

Grant swiveled, his eyes searching the room for the agitator. Despite his irritation with the theme of the lecturer he had to agree that his analysis of the Constitution was correct. Change could be made peacefully by the use of the ballot box. But could the disgruntled Filipino who had yelled be more than an overly excited listener, but someone involved in the bombings? He nudged Asing, "Did you see who called for revolution?"

"No, there were too many hands in the air applauding. Are you thinking that whoever screamed is a suspect in our investigation?"

Grant shook his head. "I am not sure. It did seem that as Robinson talked, I thought his bottom line would be a call for revolution and not to raise children to vote. That's a long-term proposition. The man who yelled may just have been excited by the speech and wanted immediate change."

"But you are thinking, where there is smoke there is fire, and we should investigate."

"If you noticed, no one in the room joined into the man's cry for revolution. We should find him."

But before they could act, the audience began to exit the room. They tried to push their way into the crowd but were slowed by the mass of people leaving. As they struggled to get by, Kingsley and Asing asked, "Did you see who yelled 'Revolution Now'?"

Their inquiry was met with stony looks. No one answered.

Kamaka had left early, before the question and answer period. He stood outside chatting with another Hawaiian when Grant and Asing exited. "Did you see where the Filipinos went?" the detective asked.

"Paid no attention. Did they cause trouble inside?"

"One of them did," Grant answered. "He made us suspicious by calling for a revolution right now."

"Suspicious of what, being a shit disturber?"

"No, of being the dynamiter," Grant answered.

Asing added, "We have eliminated races as being suspects in the crimes that have been committed. Our investigation has shifted to an individual or individuals who may have done the bombings. Your friend suggested we come tonight because we might learn something. We have learned of someone of interest who might be involved in this campaign of terror."

"What you going to do about it?" Kamaka asked.

"The call for revolution came from a section of Filipinos in the room. There were not that many who attended. We will get names from the organizers of this meeting and question each Filipino they identify," Asing answered.

"I agree," Grant said. "Whoever yelled 'revolution' left immediately. That makes me more suspicious that we may have a suspect in the killing of my father."

Hidden in the darkness, Miguel listened. He grimaced when he heard what the two men intended to do. "They must die," he muttered.

# CHAPTER 57

Miguel did not care if his comrade would be upset over what he intended to do. The man preached that revolution must be delayed while a whole generation grew up. "Never," he whispered into the wind that passed by him as he pedaled his bike. "I will have my revenge now. The explosion will be the greatest ever. No one can survive the bomb I have created."

He shifted his shoulders, moving the huge back pack more toward the middle of his spine. This caused a puff to blow from the burden he carried. The smell of ammonium nitrate stung his nose. He held his breath fearful that a sneeze would upset his overloaded bike. Despite his anxiety, he slowed to a stop.

An involuntary explosion exhaled from his nose, followed by another and another. Could he be allergic to the fertilizer? There would be no way to plant his bomb if his nose betrayed him. The lung spasms ceased. He breathed clear. He would go on.

At Patterson's home he searched in the dark for the opening in the iron barrier. He found it at the corner of the property where the fence ended at a stone wall. A narrow space allowed him to squeeze through. Clutching his knapsack close to his side, he moved onto the estate.

The saboteur had marked where the owners' bedroom must be on a previous visit. This time he promised himself there would be no failure. Ingredients for his homemade bomb had been carefully acquired. Even his comrade had been fooled when he told him, "This is fertilizer for the flowers". Very few knew of a guano bomb. The teachers at the CHEKA School of Terrorism knew and they had taught him.

Faster beat his heart as he came to the house. Panic, his nose twitched! What do? Sneeze and his surprise attack would be discovered. He never trained to control allergies. He placed a hand over his mouth and nose. The explosion came. He felt his ears throb as the force of the exhaled air became stifled by the cupped hand over his face. Another gasp occurred that he could not stop. He released his bag and forced both hands against his face. He thought his ear drums would break from the sudden pressure of air forced back into him by his hands against his nose and mouth.

Could he go on? He must. His time to act could be coming to an end. The detective and that miserable rat Kingsley made shrewd guesses. They would investigate and would find him. They must die before then. He had a plan to exterminate them. But if it failed...? He must destroy the architects of death who had killed his brother, before he was found out. He must be avenged.

Miguel reached for his pack breathing shallowly as he crept toward Patterson's home. At the spot below what he believed to be the master bedroom on the second floor, he stopped and listened.

Not a sound came from an upstairs window. He removed a trowel from his bag and began to dig. The house had been built off the ground, like so many homes in the islands, to increase air circulation and keep out vermin. White trellises were fastened to the posts holding up the house. It was under these that Miguel dug.

When he felt satisfied that he had gone deep enough, he shoved his sack under the home, the fuse of the stick of dynamite he used as a catalyst for the larger explosion trailed out from the hole. With a grim smile he lit it and scurried to his bike.

He did not have much time to escape before the blast. He ran, heedless of causing an alarm. Within seconds he reached the opening in the fence, squeezed through, and pedaled away.

Despite the urgency he slowed to be near Patterson's home to hear the powerful blast and the screams and moans of the dying. An explosion erupted. Disappointment pierced through his body as he pedaled away.

# CHAPTER 58

Grant woke with a feeling of contentment. They had narrowed the suspects significantly. Once they got the list of Filipino attendees, he felt encouraged that they might solve his father's murder before his sister arrived in the next four days. He did not dwell on the state of his dad's body. He could only hope that the embalming chemicals and refrigeration had preserved the corpse for the funeral.

Dan still slept. It was not a school day for him. Selena worked in the kitchen and had a cup of coffee ready as he entered. He inhaled the wonderful smell of frying bacon, his mouth watered in anticipation of the morning feast.

"You came in late last night. How did the meeting go?"

"It proved interesting. This man Robinson is a smooth talker. He speaks like a socialist. His words almost sound like he is a Communist, but he steers away from this label and enters into the safer harbor of democracy when he concludes his talk. Rather brilliant I would say."

"Good, then you will come with me to his lecture tonight at the University. Maybe he will steer his ship into turbulent waters. We have liberals on our faculty and conservatives. They will test him."

"From what I know of his style he will address the students who are there. He makes the point of encouraging the young to become voters for change."

"Where is he from?"

"He got his degree from the University of Chicago. Must have grown up in the Midwest."

"That's a left leaning school."

"You mean they are Bolsheviks?"

"From what I know, the University is not pinko. But they do provide students a liberal education. Some people might even call it socialistic."

"That's the way Robinson talks. I'll be curious to hear him a third time. He gave a different speech on each of the two occasions I listened to him.

"An interesting thing happened last night. Asing and I posed questions and someone from the audience yelled, 'Revolution Now!'. The detective and I think that person is involved with or knows something about the bombings. We are going to track him down."

"You've excluded the Japanese?"

Grant smiled. "Your old lover Rudy Tang thinks we should."

Anger spread over her face; Selena threw a wet towel at Grant. It struck on the side of his head. Water dripped to the floor. "He is not and never has been my lover. You know I don't like being near him. Tell me, under what circumstances did you see him? Went to visit one of his high-class prostitutes?"

"Darling, I love only you. Your father made a truce agreement with Rudy so I could question him about the explosions. Tang made it clear that the Japanese were not involved."

"When you came home last night you didn't tell me about your visit. But I did notice a severe bruise on your back and when we hugged each other, you winced in pain. Is that because of Rudy?"

"Yes, he broke the truce and ordered his thugs to beat me up and toss me in the ocean. Asing saved me." Grant paused for a moment. "I did give him a message that I would kill him the next time I saw him."

"Why would you want to waste your reputation and maybe your life on that scum?"

"Rudy has tried to eliminate me more than once. Maybe it's payback time."

"If I were you, I would just avoid him and never trust him again. I'll tell my father what he did to you."

"Please don't. They have a business relationship. I don't want to make waves. Got to leave. See you at dinner and then we will head off to the University for the lecture."

When Grant arrived at his office, his secretary greeted him with breathless excitement. "Detective Asing has called twice. Something terrible has happened at the Patterson home, another bombing. Call him ASAP."

When Grant connected with his friend, the detective said, "An explosion last night at Patterson's place. It wasn't as bad as it could have been. Seems like the makeshift bomb didn't totally blow up. But he is in an uproar, wants martial law declared and Japanese put into concentration camps. The governor has called a meeting at the government house early this afternoon to discuss the situation. We need to go to it and tell what we have learned."

"Okay, see you there."

At mid-morning another call came in. Grant's secretary took it and notified Grant, "Captain Trask is on the line."

"Kingsley, I have that report for you, all typed and ready to go."

"Can it keep for a while? I got an important meeting to attend within an hour."

"Sure, but I thought you might want to know that a foreign agency is involved in the attacks. It could be Russian."

"That is important. I'll be there right away to pick up the report."

"Call Asing," Grant said to his secretary. "Tell him I have some hot information that could blow this case wide open. He has to delay any decision by the governor until I get back from Pearl Harbor and can attend the meeting."

Grant rushed from his office.

When he forced his way past the guards who tried to stop him and entered the meeting room, he saw Patterson addressing five men seated at a table in front of him. Grant recognized the Governor, Mayor, Police Commissioner, Chief of Police, and the Commander in Chief of the National Guard. The room was full.

Patterson scowled at the disturbance at the entry doors. Two officers held Grant's arms, restraining his entry. Detective Asing rushed to them. The Governor looked over and said, "What is this disturbance?"

"I have important information to present to this tribunal," Grant shouted.

Asing added, "Mr. Kingsley is part of my investigating team into the murder of his father at the HSPA office. You will want to hear him."

"Governor, let me finish what I have to say before we listen to this Mikado lover," Patterson sneered.

Grant stifled a retort. He knew the HSPA chief was out of control, affected by the attack on his home. He sat down next to Asing.

The Governor said, "We will hear you out, Mr. Patterson, before we listen to whatever others may contribute on this subject."

"Thank you. I believe it is common knowledge that the HSPA has been attacked four times. Fortunately, only one life was lost, Mr. Kingsley's father. Last night there was an explosion at my home. The damage was minimal. I understand that the homemade bomb did not fully go off. What is clear from the evidence is that dynamite was involved in the explosion. That is the same deadly weapon used in the four previous attacks.

"This Territory knows that it is the Japanese who are the dynamiters. We proved a conspiracy by them to attack plantation supervisors by use of dynamite in 1922. We convicted fifteen members of the Japanese assassination squad. They conspired to terrorize the plantations and bring down the HSPA. The reign of Japanese terror is not over.

"What is the purpose of these attacks? Prince Kuhio, Hawaii's delegate to Congress, said it best when he testified to that body: 'The Japanese have plotted for many years to take over Hawaii'.

"We of the HSPA are dedicated to defeat this effort no matter what it costs. Dynamite terrorism must end. It will only end by taking the Japanese who are not working for the plantations into custody and shipping them back to Japan.

"I ask that martial law be declared and a roundup of Japanese occur as soon as possible. This will end the terrorism and halt the 'Yellow Peril' that threatens to take over these islands."

Patterson sat down to resounding applause. The governor gaveled for silence then called on Lieutenant Hitchcock to describe the latest attack and his efforts to solve the dynamiting.

"Gentlemen, I investigated Mr. Patterson's home this morning. I found minimal damage to the property. There was an abundance of fertilizer, ammonium nitrate, scattered around the area of the explosion. What its purpose was I do not know. There was evidence of dynamite in a small quantity at the scene.

"I have taken into custody twenty family members of the convicted conspirators. After intensive questioning I could not unearth any evidence that there is a conspiracy to dynamite the HSPA by the Japanese community. My colleague, Detective Asing, has more information that he may wish to pass on to this committee."

After his previous experiences with Hitchcock, Grant felt grateful for his honesty in this very serious matter. A man like the Lieutenant could tip the scales against the Japanese. He heard Asing's name called.

"I wish to defer my time to speak to my colleague, Grant Kingsley. He has important information to divulge in this hearing."

"Governor and members of this distinguished panel, we do not have a Japanese conspiracy to dynamite the HSPA, instead, we have a foreign saboteur bent on attacking the sugar industry."

There was an immediate babble of conversation in the chambers. "Preposterous," Patterson yelled. "What is your proof?" The gavel pounded several times with the Governor saying, "Order, order." The hubbub of excited voices subsided.

"A startling statement, Mr. Kingsley, what is your evidence to substantiate your claim?"

"He's a Japan lover," Patterson fumed. "Don't believe him."

"I am not any race's lover. I want the truth. My father was killed by the saboteur's attack. No racial group nor anyone else should pay for that crime. This is my proof. Detective Asing and I have investigated the bombings. We took from my father's body a piece of metal that came from the blast. There were other pieces of metal we gathered at the HSPA office. At Patterson's home following the first bombing we gathered up similar pieces of metal. We did the same at Masterson's home. I submitted this evidence to Captain Trask of the United States Navy Intelligence Service for analysis. I have a sworn affidavit by Captain Trask that the pieces of metal are from exploded rifle grenades of Eastern Europe manufacture, probably Russian in origin."

An uproar erupted; the word "Reds" resounded throughout the room. Grant stood patiently, waiting for the spontaneous noise to subside.

Once order was restored, Grant said, "In a second story office across the street from the HSPA conference room we found an expended cartridge. A search of the room, with Mr. Patterson present, uncovered a bullet that fitted the cartridge. These items were also analyzed by the navy. I have a second affidavit from Captain Trask that the cartridge is 7.62 millimeters from a rifle, probably of Russian manufacture. Trask and I believe that the killer of my father fired the bullet to break the glass window pane of the conference room and then shot the grenade through the opening. Incidentally, the same type of bullet was found in the wall of Masterson's dining room after the third grenade attack."

Grant paused to let this latest information sink in. He recognized that the original looks of incredulity on the faces of some members of the audience had disappeared. He knew that he had captured the attention of everyone in the room.

"Why do I use the term saboteur? During my service in the Great War, I learned about the weapons used by these undercover terrorists. The coal torpedo, an innocuous piece of metal filled with gunpowder that looks like a chunk of coal. Toss it into a furnace and it will explode, destroying a steam engine. Three of these weapons have been uncovered by Mr. Hamilton of the Oahu railroad. They were only found after a locomotive blew up.

"One of the simplest devices saboteurs use when they do not have TNT available is the fertilizer bomb. Acquire ammonia nitrate, infuse it with a little fuel oil, and light a fire to it. I think the mistake our saboteur made last night was using dynamite as a catalyst, not a fire. That is why the blast was weak, the nitrate did not explode.

"You are all aware of the Red scare in 1920. Dynamiting occurred on the East Coast. These acts of terrorism came as a response to a Communist call for worldwide revolution. From the evidence, the investigation of the bombings that Detective Asing and I have conducted, I believe we do not have a Japanese conspiracy. We have the act of a single Bolshevik to sow terror in the islands for whatever reasons he may have."

Grant's presentation and evidence caused the Governor to order that no action be taken on Patterson's demand. He urged the police to: "Marshal all resources to find the saboteur."

# CHAPTER 59

After the meeting, the two friends walked to the police department on Bethel Street. They did not speak to each other until they went into Asing's office.

"That presentation was brilliant. How did you narrow the suspects down to a single saboteur?"

Grant smiled, palmed his hair before answering, "We spent a lot of time eliminating races and were down to the Japanese. That looked like a dead end. Tang and Koichi began to steer us toward a single person. I had suspected it might be true ever since a coal torpedo blew up the Oahu Railway engine. It takes special knowledge to build one of those devices and fill them with gunpowder. When I saw Trask today and he disclosed the navy's findings, everything clicked into place.

"During the Great War it took a lot of skill and training to fire a rifle grenade. It takes expertise to put that missile on a target more than a hundred yards away. Soldiers during the war gave up on that weapon because they kept missing what they fired at, or worse, the grenade would explode near them.

"A lot of people don't know this, but the Russians are the ones who brought the rifle grenade into use. Before the Russo-Japanese war the concept of hurling a grenade with a rifle bullet was never considered. In that conflict you saw the first extensive use by armies of trenches for defense. How could an infantry man reach an enemy in a hole a hundred and fifty yards away? The Russian answer was the rifle grenade."

"That's why you thought the saboteur is Russian."

"Or Russian trained. The weapons used in the bombings required expertise that is far beyond the competency of the races that were brought here to work the sugar fields. Of equal importance is acquiring the grenades and the means to launch them. Those facts do not fit any of the imported races."

"Then your thinking is, we have a Communist killer in Hawaii."

"I believe so."

"We begin this phase of the investigation by finding out who yelled, 'Revolution Now!' It came from the Filipino section. I'll get a list of names from the organizers and start questioning each one."

"An excellent start. Selena and I are listening to Mr. Robinson tonight. Somehow I feel that man can lead us to a suspect."

"This tie is tighter than I want it to be. Do you have any objection if I loosen it and unbutton the top of my shirt?" Grant asked.

"Why would I mind?" Selena answered. "It is you who wanted to look fashionable this evening."

"I didn't want to shame you by appearing shabby in front of your colleagues."

"Look at the group that is here, most are college students wearing simple clothes. Even the faculty members are not dressed prim and proper."

"You are, however. Have you noticed the heads that turned to look at you when we came in? You are absolutely smashing in that pants suit, both professional and glamorous."

"Mr. Kingsley, are you making moves on me? Words won't work, but maybe a diamond will." Selena smiled coyly.

"My, my, there is a price for everything. I'll put my libido on hold while we enjoy the evening. I think we are about to start."

After the introduction, Robinson gave a talk that was similar to what Grant had heard before but with several changes. "There is a growing discontent in Hawaii due to profit taking at the expense of the working man. Labor has value and there is a huge surplus of this value beyond the costs of production. The greedy capitalists get very rich from this. It is time that the impoverished laborer is recognized for this increased value and permitted to share it."

Grant whispered to Selena, "That is right out of Karl Marx's *Manifesto*. This guy is talking like a Red."

"Don't you think what he says makes sense?" Selena asked.

Someone behind them said, "Shush." They fell quiet and listened.

"There will come a time when the working man throws off the chains that repress him and demands change. He may do this by strikes or other means."

Heavy applause broke out in one section of the room. During this noise, Grant whispered, "That's right out of the Communist book on revolution: 'Workers of the world unite. You have nothing to lose but your chains.' This guy is a Red."

Robinson took no questions and disappeared after his talk. Selena and Grant walked out with the crowd. Someone gasped, "Knife." He felt a sudden pain at his side and shoved Selena away from the attack. Fortunately, the coat he wore blunted the force of the strike.

His attacker released the weapon and fled. Grant caught a fleeting glimpse of him. "Selena, can I leave you to care for yourself?"

"Go after him," she answered.

Grant forced his way through the crowd. His six-foot-two-inch height helped, he thought, until he realized his assailant might have shrunk into the people leaving. He searched for some sideways movement against the current of the exiting audience. Then he saw it, a slouched hat over a man's ears moving into the parking lot. People insulted and threatened him as he shoved between them.

The hat left the crowd. Grant saw the figure of a man running in the darkness. "Stop!" he yelled.

Grant's quarry moved faster. When the man came to a rack of bicycles, he pulled one out. His momentary pause to retrieve the bike gave Grant the chance to get close. He reached to grab a dark shirt, his quarry rose up and pushed down on the pedal, darting away.

Grant watched the bike speed through the parking lot. He calculated his chances quickly and ran to a low hill. At the top he saw the two-wheeler racing toward him. Without hesitation he launched himself from the hill into the path of the bicycle. The front tire hit him. He lost his balance. The bike and its rider also fell to the ground.

Grant rose and saw his attacker extricate himself from under the bike. The man got his machine upright. Grant grasped the front wheel. His opponent shoved the vehicle into him, turned, and ran into a nearby copse.

He paused at the edge of the trees to listen. He heard movement and followed the sounds. A branch slammed into his body. It made him falter. The stick struck again, barely missing his head and striking his shoulder. He grabbed it and pulled. Grant fell backward as his assailant released the limb. The man turned and fled into the trees, slid down a rise and into a creek.

He searched the dark, but could not find his attacker. He moved to the water. Listened and heard nothing. Disgusted by his failure he returned to Selena.

"You are back and didn't catch him."

"He got away. We have his bicycle. Most important I suspect there is a connection between him and Robinson."

"We had better tend to your wounds. I see blood on your shirt."

# CHAPTER 60

Grim faced, Robinson eased himself into an overstuffed maroon chair. The soft cushions gave him little comfort as he considered the disaster that had befallen his mission. He picked up the glass of whiskey at his side and swirled the amber liquid. The aroma of the intoxicating beverage made him suddenly thirsty, and he drank the strong liquor in eager gulps.

He rose to fill his glass from the sidebar in the dining room. At the decanter he pounded his fist on the table. "Damn," Robinson swore, his powerful hit on the finely polished furniture rattling the glasses on a solid pewter tray. His movements and expressions betrayed anger. He poured his glass full, and contemplated his face in the mirror above the bar.

The door into the house creaked open. Robinson knew it would be his comrade. He scowled when he saw Miguel silhouetted within the framework of the entrance. "You look like you were in a fight and lost, comrade."

"I was fighting for our cause," Miguel whispered as he straightened his slumping shoulders and stepped into the room.

"How were you fighting, by setting off bombs that blew up in your face? You broke your promise to me, and our crusade in Hawaii has been found out. Our time here is now measured by hours because of your stupidity."

"You insult me, but call me comrade. Why do you utter this blasphemy?" The saboteur's posture changed as he stood tall with his fists clenched.

"Bah, you don't understand the turmoil you have caused for the movement. The story is laid out in the evening paper that I read before the lecture. Your homemade bomb fizzled and led to a high-level meeting to discuss jailing the Japanese. This interfering man, Kingsley, convinced everyone that it was not the Japanese who did the bombings, but a Russian saboteur! You have aroused a 'Red' scare and our cause here is compromised."

"Kingsley! I tried to kill him tonight, but my knife failed me. But his life will be short if my other plan succeeds."

"What are you saying? Another murder, how will we convince people if all you do is kill?"

"You say that we may be finished. Then I will move faster and kill the HSPA members for the evil they have done to the last member of my family!"

"I finally see your game. You were not interested in promoting Communism when you came here under the guise of helping me Sovietize this land. You arrived with one purpose in mind, revenge. You have ruined our chance of being successful by your vendetta."

"You treat the horrible death of my brother as if it were nothing? All he sought was equal pay for equal work. Instead, he was shot in the back for striking. That is what imperialists do. What do you think happened to my parents and my other brothers and sisters in the Philippines? They were butchered before my eyes by American conquerors seeking to suppress my people and steal our land. Let me ask you, how would you feel if mercenaries of the capitalists gunned down the last member of your blood?" The saboteur's cheeks became wet as tears welled in his eyes and slowly dripped to the floor.

Robinson sighed, shook his head and haltingly answered, "I-I-I did not realize the pain you have within you for the evil that the imperialists have done. Despite the sad feelings I have, killing people will not advance our cause.

"I came here to end this feudal society. To my way of thinking the repressions of the many imported races is fertile ground for change. It cries out for reform. Land was taken from the natives to lay the foundation for large plantations. These Hawaiians were pushed aside because the planters could not dictate to these citizens of the islands. They had legal rights. Instead, they imported slaves on indentured contracts who were forced to work ungodly hours at minimal pay to ensure huge profits for the few elite rulers.

"I saw the grip on the working man that exists here. The military is powerful and getting stronger each day. You must know from history that revolutions in the Philippines against the Spanish were put down by huge massacres. The same occurred when Americans took over. This place cannot foster a successful revolt as occurred in Russia in 1917. To accomplish my purpose, I have taken the only course that I felt could work, education of the masses."

"Bah, you sound like a *poputchik*, an intellectual who has not dedicated himself to the cause. I want Revolution Now!"

"You are blinded by your hatred, Miguel. It is an insult to call me a 'fellow traveler'. I worked for the cause when I lived in Chicago. I have used my wealth to spread Communism to the masses in America and intend to do the same in Hawaii."

"Bah, you were not trained in freedom for the proletariat like I have been. I studied at the feet of Lenin and Trotsky. They taught me that the shedding of blood is the only way to achieve the goal of a classless society. To accomplish the purpose of our movement, there can be no middle ground. There is no room for compromise. Those who do not support us are marked for destruction."

"What I am trying to say is that your understanding of the teaching you received is warped by your hatred. Lenin was a pragmatist. He knew before the Great War that his agitation of the masses would not succeed. He was aware of the failure of the mutineers of the Battleship Potemkin during the revolution of 1905. Those sailors, angered by the brutality of their officers, revolted and tried to get the citizens of Odessa to join them against the oppression of the Tsar. The Cossacks descended on the city and slaughtered the militants by the thousands. Twelve years later, when conditions were ripe, the Germans returned the master to Russia. Lenin orchestrated the October Revolution successfully because the army and police supported him. That is why I have counseled patience and to work slowly to achieve our goal. Your desire for revenge has ended our chance to achieve this goal."

Miguel palmed his hair as he thought over what his comrade said. "You spew out words like an older uncle cautioning delay in seeking fulfilment of my vengeance. You also have said our cause may be lost. I battled tonight with the scum who revealed us. He will die. The HSPA poltroons will die." Miguel stamped his feet then stormed from the house.

Robinson shook his head, clutched his glass, and slumped into his soft chair. He knew his comrade was beyond reason. As he drank, he mulled over what he should do.

# CHAPTER 61

Grant woke with a sharp pain on his side. The knife had sliced into his skin. It had taken ten stitches to close the wound. The doctor said he was lucky it had not penetrated into his stomach. In a few days he would be fine. The sedative for pain knocked him out so he had slept for some time. Dan and Selena were gone to their schools.

When he got up, he winced from the soreness. His assailant had proved very capable in dealing with him despite all of his martial arts training. Could it be the saboteur who had done this? It must have been. Who else would try to kill him? His revelations at the hearing must have motivated the man to seek revenge.

The telephone rang. "Where have you been, you lazy Hawaiian?" Asing scolded.

"In bed wounded. I endure all the pain and do all the work to solve these crimes, while you sit in your office blowing smoke rings into the ceiling."

"I'm sorry to hear that you have been injured," Asing's voice became serious. "You must tell me all about it when I see you. I have been working. Found out from the promoters of the lecture the names and contact information of five Filipinos. A sixth was there, but there is nothing about him. Since it is late, you take two names and I'll take three and we will discuss what we have found this afternoon."

Grant did not unearth any helpful information from the first Filipino he visited. He went to the address given for the second man. It was near the Palama Settlement close to the Japanese hall where the lecture occurred.

After he parked, he walked east on North King Street, searching for the address. Tinkling music drew him to a one-story building. Through the open windows he saw couples gyrating across its floor stepping in time to the music of a three-piece band. He walked to the entry where a burly Hawaiian held up a hand. "You want to dance? Tickets are ten cents. Buy 'em over there." The big man nodded his head in the direction of a sales table.

"I'm a police officer." Grant showed a badge that Asing had given him. "Is Pedro Sanchez here?"

"You don't look like a cop."

"Undercover policeman, where is Sanchez? I know he is here," Grant blustered, challenging the bouncer to lie. They both knew obstructing justice is a crime.

"Okay, don't want trouble. He is in the back office, over there." The bouncer pointed to a door. "Buy a couple of tickets. That way I can tell him you're a patron and didn't know you were a cop."

"Or maybe you want to take a picture of me buying them so you can blackmail me."

"Never crossed my mind," the bouncer laughed. "Go and knock on the door."

Grant worked his way through the dancers. Most were Filipino men dressed in colorful clothes. The pants they wore did not match their shirts. The outfits were bizarre. Some men wore suits with wide shoulders and coats that tapered down to the waist with the bottom hem spilling over pants that were choked at the shoes.

The women were slender and a mix of races. Most were white with a smattering of Filipinos, Hawaiians, and Chinese. Grant wondered if they were willing dancers or forced by a husband or boyfriend to work in the business.

He got to the door and knocked. A gruff voice answered and Grant entered. The room was sparsely furnished, but there were pictures of scantily-dressed women on each wall. A Filipino sat at a desk across from him. "Aloha, my name is Grant Kingsley."

Before he could continue, the man said. "I remember you. At the meeting, you asked hard questions."

"Yes, and you are Pedro Sanchez?"

The man nodded. "What you want?"

"Lecture was very provocative. Someone near you yelled 'Revolution Now!' I'd like to find that man, talk to him."

"You want join him, start a revolt? Get rid of the plantation bosses?"

"At the moment neither one, I'd like to learn more. That's why I want to talk to him."

"I don't want trouble."

"I'm willing to pay for information."

Santos eyes narrowed; his face took on a cunning aspect. "How much?"

"Will ten bucks jog your memory?"

"Make it twenty."

"Fifteen dollars if the information is useful."

"I don't know what you mean by 'useful'."

"Something that will help me find him."

"Let's see the money."

"Ten now and the other five when you tell me."

Sanchez lips curved in a wide smile. "I think I can give you what you want. Ten now and ten after I tell you."

Grant shook his head. "This is an elevator-type negotiation. Right now, the cab is going down. Five now and fifteen if you give me something useful." He slapped a five-dollar bill on the desk.

Sanchez chewed his lower lip. "Okay, I was testing the waters. The guy sitting next to me yelled 'Revolution Now!' I don't know him, but he said he worked with Robinson. Does that get me the fifteen?"

Grant took back the five and tossed the club owner a twenty-dollar bill. Sanchez loosened a smile. "You're a fair man. Want a girl? Dances are on the house."

Grant shook his head. "Where do you find these women?"

"Broken homes, divorce, runaways, girls work here for a variety of reasons. If you talk to them, they will tell you they love to dance. It's easy money, more than they can make somewhere other than a whorehouse. We treat them good. The men you see outside we call monkey chasers; they are guys interested in nabbing a girl. But we don't allow that. No sex permitted. That way you keep things clean, no fights."

"Police raid you?"

"They snoop around, try to find some crime to charge me with and then ask money for their silence. But I'm clean and I don't pay except for a little protection from harassment. Enough talk. You got what you want. Goodbye."

The bouncer stood at the door watching the action in the dancing arena. The three-piece band began a waltz. The floor, which had been empty, filled with a dozen couples stepping to the rhythm of the tune. Grant stopped abreast of the big Hawaiian. "Any trouble keeping this place under control?"

"What you think 'brah, I no can handle da job?"

"Sorry, I meant no offence. I just know some places where there is a lot of male-female action there's up to half-a-dozen guards."

"You mean da kine whore houses. We no allow dat kine action. Filipino guys wear colorful clothes just like da rooster to attract the woman. They on the make, but good guys, no trouble.

"Da bad guys? Them sailors. Some no like see white gal dance with Filipino. Say bad words. Good thing this place, lot of locals. Keep most navy guys away."

Grant shook his head. "I hope you can keep things under control, but more navy guys are coming every day. I know the whore houses are gearing up for a lot of action. Maybe Pedro has got to do the same and get you more help. I've heard that taxi dance halls have been closed in California because of race riots."

The bouncer shrugged. "Not my problem."

Grant left to report to Asing.

# CHAPTER 62

When Grant entered his office, his receptionist looked at him, her eyes wide. "Detective Asing called for you, it's an emergency. He wants you to get in touch with him right away. Something about a white powder that kills!"

"Detective Asing!" Grant shouted into the receiver.

The desk sergeant said, "This Mr. Kingsley?"

He continued when Grant identified himself. "The detective is out getting something analyzed at the laboratory. A letter came in today addressed to Asing. Our custom at the desk is to open the mail for the officers. The man on station slits the envelope. A white vapor came out. He must have breathed it in and immediately keeled over. He is at the hospital right now, near death.

"Asing believes you have gotten a similar white envelope. Do not open it!"

Panic jolted him. Grant felt a sinking in his heart. "Any white envelopes in the mail today?"

His secretary shook her head.

"If one comes in don't open it, deadly poison. Call my wife. Tell her what I just told you. I'm going home."

His head pounded with worry. He geared his Packard and raced for Nuuanu Street. He skidded the car into his driveway. Its tires screeched from the sudden braking. He rushed to the post office box. Nothing. He ran into the house, and yelled, "Selena did you pick up a white envelope in the mail?"

"Whatever possesses you to make this racket?"

"White envelope did you see one in the mail?"

"Dis what you want?" Daniel answered waving a white envelope. "Catch me!"

Daniel raced for the kitchen, clutching the paper in his fist.

"Daniel, stop! Danger! Give daddy the envelope."

"What's going on?" Selena asked.

"There's poison powder inside. Sudden death."

Selena gasped. "Daniel, give Daddy the envelope, please."

"Catch me, catch me," the little boy shouted as he slid through chairs and got under the kitchen table.

Grant slowed to a stop. His thoughts were jumbled, unsure what to do. If he tried to snatch the envelope it could break and everyone in the kitchen might die. He had known of poison like this during the war. Saboteurs killed using various devices. Pens, umbrellas, canes, darts - the sharp metal tips of each weapon laced with a deadly substance. He suspected that the powder in the envelope was ricin. It looked like ordinary table salt. Ingestion by smell or injection of a few grains would kill an adult.

Selena came to his side, her hands shaking. "What shall we do?"

"The envelope must not break. If the powder escapes, we could all die or become seriously ill." Grant felt Selena's body convulse, and for some moments she shivered uncontrollably.

"Keep calm," Grant whispered. "I think we need to negotiate."

Kneeling at the table Grant said in a voice as calm as he could muster, "Daniel you know that trike you wanted?"

Daniel's eyes that had been watching his parents through the kitchen chair grew wide, "Yes."

"Can we make a deal, the trike for the envelope?"

Daniel paused for many moments.

"I'll teach you to ride it," Selena said. "Take you to the park and you can race after the birds. Won't that be fun?"

"Yes."

"Give daddy the envelope."

"Trike first," Daniel answered, a belligerent tone in his voice.

"This is not working," Grant whispered.

Selena ignored him. "Daniel, we need to go to the store. But mommy can't go without you. You'll have to pick out the color, what bells you want, all kinds of things. Will you come out now so we can go?"

"Okay." Daniel scooted out and gave his mother the envelope. She handed it to Grant who took it carefully and secreted it.

"You will have to head to the bike store before it closes. I'm going to check in with Asing. This devil has gone too far. We've got to catch him before he does more damage."

Grant called the detective, "We have to stop this saboteur before he kills more people. Robinson is the key. I'm picking you up, let's go question him."

# CHAPTER 63

Grant drove to the offices of the *Hinode Times*. Asing said, "Your four-year old boy held you hostage awhile. How did he accomplish such a feat?"

Grant grimaced with the memory. "He held an unbeatable card, the white envelope. It is the same one I gave you in your office. I'm sure if the laboratory tests it, they will find it's ricin."

"How would you know such a thing?"

"I was in the intelligence service for a time during the war. I learned a lot in a short period. The Germans were the first to use gas in 1915 against the French. Thousands died. Gas attacks became very common. When you were in the trenches and heard the rattle squeal, you dove for your gas mask and put it on. Poisons were used by both sides. Close to 100,000 died from inhaling and many more were injured. It is dirty stuff and a horrible way for your life to end. Before the Great War the Hague Conventions banned the use of poisons, but that didn't stop the Germans from breaking the rules."

"And our saboteur is not bound by any norms of civilized warfare. It appears that he will do anything to kill those he hates. Why are you thinking Robinson is a key suspect?"

"I've listened to him three times. Each time he has sounded more and more like a Communist. Someone connected to him yelled, 'Revolution Now'. I was attacked at the University the same night he lectured. His follower has been passing out revolutionary literature. Robinson will lead us to the saboteur."

At the *Hinode Times* news office, they were told that Robinson had left for his home in Manoa so they drove to the valley. Dusk had come, but Grant refused to turn on his car lights. "We want to take him by surprise. Maybe his stooge will be with him and we can interrogate both." They parked a block from Robinsons' home and approached the residence.

"Lights are on, someone is there. Shall we storm in?" Grant asked.

"Let's do a little scouting first. A door could be unlocked. That's the way it is in Hawaii."

"You're right, we never lock our homes. No thefts. Neighbors are honest."

The two men peered through the windows. They saw no one. Grant tried the front door. "It's unlocked," he whispered. "Just walk in?"

Asing nodded.

They pushed the door open and entered. Robinson sat in high-cushioned maroon chair a glass filled with an amber liquid in his hand. He reared up when he saw the two men. "Don't you knock before coming into someone's home?"

"Police," Asing answered. "Where is your companion?"

"Who the devil are you talking about?"

"You know who, the same Filipino who has been to all your lectures. He passes out your printed materials."

"Preposterous, whomever are you seeking?"

"The man who killed my father, nearly caused the death of a number of HSPA people. He poisoned a police officer, and almost wiped out my family. He tried to kill me last night."

Robinson began to shake. Amber liquid spilled from his glass. He fell back into his chair. His voice quavered when he spoke. "I don't know what you are talking about."

Grant knew he was a guilty man. He saw Robison put down his glass and reach for his pocket. He grabbed Robinson's arm with his left hand and pinned it to his side. His right elbow smashed into the publisher's jaw. Robinson sagged back into his chair, dazed. Grant wrested a gun from his pocket.

Eyes glassy, Robinson complained. "You're a police officer, do something."

"I think you are a Communist spy. A saboteur who has killed many people. It is time to confess."

"What...what are you saying? I...I have done nothing wrong."

An image of Daniel clutching a white envelope flashed through his mind. Grant felt a surge of anger spread through his body. Grant smashed his palm into Robinson's face then struck again. "Talk now, you scum, or I swear I will kill you like I have killed other men. It will not be pretty."

Robinson winced; tears welled in his eyes.

"Crying will not save you," Grant spoke harshly.

"My tears were not because of fear. I cry because of what I have lost."

"What in hell are you talking about? Tell us what we need to know, or I will start the torture by breaking your fingers one at a time. Then I will do worse."

"No more threats. It was never my intent when I came here from Chicago to kill people. I meant only to persuade folks to accept Communism. After I got here, I was joined by a Filipino, Miguel Santiago. He had excellent credentials because he trained in Moscow.

"I did not know much about his past when I accepted him as a comrade. Together I thought we could make governmental change in Hawaii. But he has an agenda different from mine. His family was slaughtered by American soldiers in the Philippines. His surviving brother was shot to death in the Hanapepe massacre. He came here with revenge in his heart.

"I did not know he attacked the HSPA office and killed your father until recently. I learned of the bombings from the news. I confronted him, reasoned with him, spoke of our mission. I thought he had agreed with me to stop his attacks. But now I see he did not."

"Where is he?" Grant asked his voice harsh but no longer belligerent.

"I don't know."

Grant drew his arm back.

"Don't hit me. I don't know where he is. We had an argument about what he has done and how he compromised my mission to Hawaii. He left in anger. I haven't seen him since. Most of his things are still here. My guess is he will return."

"You were not involved in the death of my father, the bombings, and the ricin attack on Asing and my family?"

Robinson cried. His body shook with his sobbing. "I swear to you I was not. Despite my socialism I am not a murderer. I believe in peaceful change, not killing."

"That is hard to accept if you are a true Communist," Grant said.

"I understand your cynicism. Miguel accused me of being a *poputchik.*"

"What is a poputchik?" Asing asked.

"It means a fellow traveler," Grant answered. "Leon Trotsky coined the word. It describes an intellectual who sympathizes with Communism, but does not accept all of its tenants including violence to achieve change."

"You state it correctly. I think the ideals are great, but I prefer to persuade, not foster revolution."

Grant nodded. "I understand what you are saying. You may follow the path that Lenin has created, but refuse to take it to its end. When I remained in Europe after the war, people struggled with ideology. Four empires had been crushed and new isms had risen to replace them. Several countries drifted toward Communism, but soon people moved away from the bloody path that would need to be taken to achieve a classless society."

"It is all very interesting, but enough of these academic discussions," Asing groused. "Call me when he returns."

Grant brought over two towels, one wet and the other dry. "You may want to wash up. Your face is bloody. I'm sorry that I had to rough you up."

"You are a strange man. One minute you beat me and threaten more harm and the next minute you apologize for your brutality."

"Mr. Robinson, your comrade has caused me great stress. He killed my father and attempted to kill my family. As insane as it may seem to you, I would beat and even kill if that would end the threats to the people I love."

"Do you have a picture of Miguel?" Asing asked.

"In the drawer by the sidebar, you may take them."

"I will leave your gun there. Do not get it until after we are gone. We expect to hear from you soon."

As they walked from the house, Asing asked, "Do you believe his sincerity?"

"I do. After the Russian revolution people embraced Communism thinking it would solve their problems. But the idea of everybody possessing the property of the nation equally does not have lasting appeal. Capitalism rewards the owner of private property for his industry, initiative, and intelligence. I call it the three I's. Communism does not reward those traits. The credo 'From each according to his ability, to each according to his need.' only favors the lazy.

"I can understand the barriers that ownership of private property places upon the poor. In the Philippines the land is owned by a few favored people, especially the Catholic Church. The bulk of the population are tenant farmers and must pay fifty percent or more of what they produce to the owners by way of rent. It is easy to see that under such a monopolistic system the only escape from poverty is revolution. That is the Communist appeal.

"The Big Five monopolizes our economy. An intellectual like Robinson would want change. His comrade had other plans, vengeance for the death of his brother. I cannot say he did not have cause for hate. But he killed my father, and in my mind, there is no forgiveness for that."

"Here is our car, let's go."

In the shadows, Miguel watched the two men drive away. He heard what they said. Robinson must be confronted for his betrayal.

## CHAPTER 64

Robinson sat in a semi-stupor when Miguel entered. Traces of blood had soaked into his shirt. A glass of whiskey sat on the small table to his right. His hands lay to his sides. His eyes fluttered as his comrade walked in.

"You had visitors."

Robinson blinked as he came awake. "What?"

"Kingsley and Asing were just here. What did they want to know?"

"What are you talking about?"

"The police detective and his sidekick were just here. What you tell them?"

Robinson yawned, his eyes slitting as he focused on Miguel.

"Looks like you got beat up. One of them hit you?"

"Big guy."

"Did you talk? Say things about me?"

"No…no, I'd never do that."

"You lie. Kingsley knew my brother was killed and I wanted vengeance."

"He must have guessed that."

"After he beat you and you confessed? He knows about me and you told him."

"Listen to me, he saw you at my lectures. He investigated. You were foolish enough to attack him last night. He's a smart man, He put two and two together, and bingo, concluded you were the killer of his father."

"I don't know if I can believe you."

"Why not? I have never given you cause to doubt my loyalty to the cause."

"Damn it, you are a bull shitter. You are a poputchik. You spin a good line, but have never fully embraced Communism. If you were a true believer you would never betray. You would endure punishment all the way to your death before you revealed what these capitalist dogs must not know. You are a betrayer!"

"You are not only ungrateful for the welcome I have given you, but you are false to the cause. You were sent here to help me convert people to Communism. This is a place fertile for governmental change. Instead, you flew false colors before me. Talked about how you would Sovietize the people. Hidden inside you was only hatred. You were only interested in revenge and not helping the working man. You are the liar in this room."

Miguel raised himself to his full height and flung his fist into Robinson's cheek. "Drunken swine, how dare you accuse me of being unfaithful to the cause! I who have screamed for revolution! I who have fought the imperialists in battle! You are nothing but milk toast wanting only compromise. You are not worthy enough to criticize me."

Robinson fell back in his sofa. He felt dizzy. The blows to his face ached. Fear swept over him. Miguel was mad. He stifled caustic words that were on the tip of tongue. He must think carefully. He would get his gun at the sidebar and end this charade. "I'm sorry. I misspoke. You are correct. You have always been loyal to the cause. Forgive me, it was the liquor that twisted my tongue." Robinson wobbled up from his chair.

"That is better. You can make amends by helping me. My time here in Hawaii is over. I will destroy those pigs from the HSPA, kill the detective and his stooge. Then go."

"What is your plan?" Robinson asked as he edged toward the sidebar.

"I have used up the weapons I brought except for the bullets for my rifle. I will lay in wait for each of the five and shoot them."

"How do I help you?" Robinson edged closer to the pistol on the sidebar.

"I will need your car. With your position as newspaper publisher…wait. What are you doing?" Miguel screamed as Robinson reached for the gun. He grasped the weapon, but Miguel lunged into him and locked a hand on his arm. The two men wrestled in the room. Robinson tried to bring the barrel of the pistol into Miguel's body. His former comrade forced it away.

With his free hand Robinson struck Miguel's face. The killer shrugged off the blow, seized the hand. For a moment both men faced each other, their arms locked together and spread wide in V fashion. Each man struggled to gain the upper hand.

Miguel thrust his head into Robinson's chin. Dazed, he fell backward into the sidebar drawing the Filipino with him. Their combined weight knocked tumblers and whisky onto the floor, glass shattered, alcohol spread over the wood surface.

"You are going to die for your treachery," Miguel taunted as he shoved Robinson's gun hand into the wall. An explosion echoed in the room. The sound and smell of ignited powder dizzied the news editor. Unfazed, Miguel smashed the gun hand a second time into the wall. The weapon fell to the floor.

Glass broke underfoot as their shoes milled the broken pieces. Both men scrambled for the pistol. Miguel found it and turned into Robinson who caught his arm and tried to push the weapon away. Miguel's other hand smashed into the news editor's face. The force of the blow caused him to blink, but he did not release his grip on the gun. Miguel proved to be stronger than Robinson. Slowly, his hand moved into Robinson's body.

A second explosion rocked the room. Robinson felt sudden pain in his stomach. He screamed. He slumped to the floor as everything went dark.

## CHAPTER 65

His eyes opened. Robinson realized death had not taken him. Blood drenched his clothes; he could feel it pulsing out from the wound in his stomach. All house lights were on, only his labored breathing broke the silence of the room. Miguel was gone. Robinson crawled toward the telephone on the wall. Broken glass tore into his shirt, penetrating his skin. He ignored these new wounds, fighting instead the dizziness that threated to engulf him and bring an end to his misery.

He reached the wall. The telephone hung in the box just above him. Weakness swarmed over him as he tried to raise himself. He grasped a nearby chair and levered himself up to the speaker. With a hand slimy with blood, he cranked the handle with the hearing piece next to his ear.

"Number please," A female's voice asked.

"POLICE 777."

"Officer Naupaka, how may I help you?"

"Detective Asing, Robinson..."

"Sorry, he has gone home for the evening. Call tomorrow. Any message?"

Robinson felt his strength ebbing. He began a slow slide down the wall.

"Hello you still there?"

"Death is coming to..." Sudden pain shot through his head.

"What idiot could be calling at 4:00 in the morning," Grant grumbled as he forced himself from sleep and staggered downstairs to the telephone. Selena stood holding the receiver out to him. "Detective Asing, urgent."

"Kingsley. Why the early call? Oh, I'll be right there."

"What's going on?" Selena asked

"Robinson's in trouble. Something about death is coming. Asing wants me to pick him up and get out to his home now."

Grant dressed and drove to the Bethel Street police station.

Asing waited on the sidewalk and jumped into the car. "Let's get cracking for Manoa. Don't know what we will find, but whatever happened this evening can't be good."

"Tell me what you know."

"Duty sergeant took a call around midnight. A weak voice said, 'Detective Asing, Robinson'. The officer said something, and the caller whispered, 'Death is coming to' then silence and no further response to the officer's inquiries. He finally realized the line had gone dead."

"The call came in four hours ago, what did the sergeant do?"

"He waited for his supervisor to show up and tell him what to do. The connection was gone. Something had happened on the other end to kill the call. He didn't know who Robinson was and didn't want to wake me until he got instructions from higher up. When the supervisor finally showed up just before four, he called me right away. That's when I called you."

"Your desk sergeant deserves a demotion. If Robinson's a victim then whoever did him in is long gone and the bad guy has had plenty of time to cover up the evidence of the crime."

"Let's be optimistic about what we will find. Maybe the editor is still alive and can tell us what happened."

"I'm thinking worst case scenario," Grant answered as he swerved off the main highway and headed up Manoa Valley.

"This area is becoming a favorite spot for military officers to rent homes," Asing said as he glanced out the car's windows searching the unlighted houses. "Nuuanu is too expensive for them, but there are many nice houses in this valley with decent people living here. Most are retired folk or have businesses in town. This is a good place to raise a family."

"We're getting close to Robinson's home. I'll slow down, cut the headlights, and coast to a stop a block away. We will approach on foot."

"You brought your pistol?" Asing asked.

"I am always prepared for the worst. Did you bring a gun?"

Asing shook his head. "I have my trusty whip. It has served me well in the past."

"Don't you think for a change you could give up on that relic and use a real weapon? We are not on the Parker Ranch chasing cattle. What we are dealing with is a homicidal maniac who wants to wipe out the HSPA and, for all I know, the rest of the Big Five. He might also want to give you and me a one-way ticket to hell. Don't forget the poison envelopes."

Grant parked. Asing got out, uncoiling his whip. "This little snake has never failed me. Remember how it saved you from Rudy's goons."

"I do recall that, but your whip has never fought a rifle grenade nor dealt with a sniper's rifle. You got to get out of the 19th century and learn to handle and fire modern weapons. Let's cut the argument and deal with the present situation. Everyone in the neighborhood appears to be asleep. Robinson's digs are just ahead. Lights are on. Best to check things out before we go bursting in. I'll pull out my revolver and cover you. Creep up to the windows and peer in, stay low at all times."

"You certainly know how to give orders," Asing complained.

"Listen up, I went on dozens of nighttime patrols during the war. We were always afraid of being ambushed or picked off by some boogie man. This guy we are dealing with has a lot of military training. He's a killer and we can't take chances."

"I'll head to the nearest window and look in while you watch my back," Asing said, and hurried to the house, weaving in a zig zag pattern and running low. Grant followed, standing upright and sweeping his pistol left and right. His eyes searched their surroundings for any changes from their last visit five hours ago. The garage door lay open, otherwise all appeared the same as before.

Asing crept to a window, looked in. He signaled, no danger inside. He went to another window, made a long search, then shook his head. Grant advanced to the door and tested the handle. "Unlocked, I'll go in fast and to the left. You follow and head right. On my signal 1, 2, 3, go!"

Grant opened the door and dashed in, his pistol sweeping the room. Asing followed and moved rapidly to the right. "No one alive in this room.

Looks like a big fight. Robinson is lying by the telephone. Blood all over. I'll check him. Then we search the rest of the house." Asing hustled over to the body lying in a pool of red on the floor. The telephone receiver dangled from a broken box; its handle slimed with blood that also splattered the wall where the telephone had once hung.

"Robinson is gone. A crushed skull. Let's secure the house."

The two men searched together, opening bedroom doors by throwing them wide, darting glances into the rooms, before moving in. Two bedrooms were empty. They entered the third at the back of the house.

"Miguel's room."

"How so?"

"Picture on the dresser, he and another young man. I'd bet it's his brother. Both boys smiling. Looks like normal young kids."

"Yeah, with one mind warped by too many deaths to his family."

"War and killing changes people. I saw it first-hand. Normal guys would go nuts with all the mayhem falling on them night and day. When your best buddy got killed you either went to pieces or became berserk and wanted to kill the other guy. I can just imagine what Miguel went through with his family massacred in the Philippines and his brother shot in Hanapepe. It's not an excuse for killing my father, but I can see why he wanted revenge against the American Capitalists."

"You're talking like a Red."

"What if I am? You can only take abuse for so long before you change and strike out at your oppressors. That's what I learned after the Great War; Russians destroyed their former masters. Empires fell and revolt swept throughout Europe by people who had been suppressed by Emperors, Kings, and Tsars."

"Are you thinking like Robinson, that revolt could happen in Hawaii?"

"Lots of ingredients for brewing up a mess of trouble here. Only problem for revolutionaries is the number of American soldiers and the disunity among the races. It won't happen."

"Agreed, but it is time to end philosophy and search the room for clues."

"Okay, boss man." Grant moved to a desk in the corner of the room. Asing opened a closet and then dresser drawers, searching.

"I think I'm onto something," Grant said. "Three drawings of houses and sight lines from the right border of each to a front door."

Asing came over to study the penciled pictures. "Each looks like the home of an HSPA executive. What do you make of the straight lines crossing the pages with numbers above them?"

"They have some meaning and why are there lines on each of the drawings?"

"Last thing Robinson said is: 'Death is coming to…'. Did he mean 'coming to me'?"

"If he knew he is about to be killed he would say, 'Miguel is going to kill me.'"

"Logical, but still, he could be explaining to the sergeant that his killer was after him."

"But we also know that Miguel wanted to wipe out the HSPA and the two of us. Maybe that is what Robinson tried to say before he died. These drawings of the homes indicate that the man was planning something at each house. The car is gone from the garage. He's got a rifle, that we know of from the expended bullets. He is planning an ambush this morning. Quick, back to the station. We have to stop him."

# CHAPTER 66

Grant let Asing off at Bethel Street. "Sun's not up yet, but soon. Alert Doolittle, Marston, Patterson of what we fear. Send officers out to each house. I'm going to Patterson's home. As chairman, I believe he will be the first target."

Grant tore away from the curb and headed for Nuuanu Street. He raced the Packard up the empty roadways of the valley. As he made a fast halt at Patterson's home, gold colored the horizon. A slight drizzle patterned the ground. Lights shone from a few houses. But the HSPA chief's place lay dark.

He found the wrought iron gate locked. He rattled it, hoping to draw attention from the home, but then thought better of it. Miguel might be close, lying in wait, biding his time until Patterson stepped from the house.

Grant studied the parked cars on the street. They were empty. He ran by each, checking the interiors. Nothing. Maybe he was wrong? Still, he had to be sure. Grant glanced across the street where two one-story bungalows stood, one painted dark brown and the other green. A copse of pine trees grew to the left of them. Along the woods, a dirt road sliced uphill. Through the limbs he made out a dark car parked on the path. In the back of the bungalows, the ground sloped up to a hill crest covered with brush.

Puzzled, Grant checked everything around him once more. His eyes fell onto the wrought iron fence. A thought struck him, and he went over to the dark rails. They were about the same height as his six-foot-two inches. He returned to his car and removed a drawing. A vertical line was drawn adjacent to the fence with the inscription: "2M." The horizontal line from the right border to Patterson's front door read: "800M." Grant did the math, a meter, thirty-eight inches, is just over a yard long. The height of the fence was the same as his. What could be eight hundred yards away, to the right of the Patterson home?

Grant looked. His eyes fell on the hillcrest covered with brush. A perfect hiding spot, but a massive distance from the door, almost a half-mile. He remembered that snipers with telescopic scopes could pick off targets further away than that. He studied the high ground searching for any sign of a hidden gunman. Nothing.

The morning sun began to push above the horizon. Lights had gone on in homes up and down the street, including Patterson's. He had to decide soon. Would the sniper be lying in wait at the hill's crest or somewhere else? He looked at the drawing and spied a vertical line where the bungalows would be. The number "800M" had been scratched in beside it.

Grant ran across the street, hopped over a low fence, and sped across the green lawn of the brown bungalow. He moved as far to the right as possible. If a sniper lay above him, he did not want to alert him of his rush to the hill.

A dog barked inside the home. He regretted disturbing the occupants, but he had no time to ask permission. He leaped over a rear fence and began to climb. Stones and low shrubs slowed his movement. Though he felt anxious, he needed to be careful. This would not be the time to fall and sprain an ankle.

He stopped his climb and studied the crest. Again, he saw nothing, but somehow, he felt he would find someone above him. The black car parked on the path within the copse of trees meant a person was out early, and on the hill above.

He kept moving up, anxiety adding to the strain of climbing. The sun had escaped above the horizon. People below him would be preparing to go to work. Maybe Patterson might be later than most, but he couldn't risk being slow to the top.

Within a hundred feet of the crest, he stopped and studied the bushes above. Still nothing. Could he be on a wild goose chase and the attack would come from another, or even against another member of the HSPA? Maybe Asing's calls had alerted the three men and this effort was for nothing. He couldn't stop now. He had to climb on and investigate the brush.

A chip shot from the hilltop, he saw a flash of metal. The barrel of a rifle poked through the shrubs. He pulled his revolver, yelled, and fired a round into the bushes. Almost at the same time, the gun above him spoke. A thin curl of smoke escaped the front of the weapon.

Grant went to ground as he saw the rifle's muzzle tilting in his direction. A bullet creased the earth beyond his head. Grant realized the man would have to move up from his prone position to secure a better angle of fire. He fired blind into the bush. A sharp cry from above confirmed he had hit someone.

He listened to twigs and leaves being crushed as the attacker moved away from the crest. He went along the side of the hill following the sounds made by a running man. He kept low to avoid a lucky shot. Ahead he saw a figure in the copse of wood. He chanced another shot, but knew he missed when the shadow of the man moved into a dark car.

He fired again without any luck in scoring a hit. He headed back to the street. An auto engine came alive. He jumped over a fence and rushed across a green lawn. A dog charged him, slowing his pace. He had no intention of harming it, but he had to get to the road. Would the creature get him before he made it across the yard? He waved his weapon, hoping to frighten the animal as he stepped to the front yard fence.

A car's gears engaged. He heard a vehicle moving. He must get to the road and stop the killer before he got away. The dog barked furiously moving at him, then fell back when he growled at it.

A front door opened. A man came out. "Who are you?" he yelled. "What are you doing in my yard?"

"Sorry, I'm a police officer trying to catch a killer. Please call off your dog."

"How do I know that? Maybe you're a thief."

Out of the corner of his eye, Grant saw a black car moving down the earth path and onto the highway. "I'm not a thief. The murderer is getting away. Please call off your dog so I can stop his escape."

The homeowner glanced right. The car entered Nuuanu. "Rex," he called. "Come here now."

When Grant moved forward, the dog charged. He holstered his pistol and grasped the collar of the animal, holding him back. The black car picked up speed.

"Rex, heel, heel."

Grant's stomach churned as he saw people on Patterson's porch, and he caught a glimpse of Miguel as he drove by. Had he failed? Is the HSPA chairman dead?

Rex's owner grasped the struggling dog. Grant whispered, "Thank you," jumped the low fence, got into his Packard, and raced after Miguel.

# CHAPTER 67

Asing's office door flew open. Lieutenant Hitchcock stalked in. "What in tarnation are you doing with my officers sending them off on assignments that I haven't authorized?"

Startled, the detective stammered, "It's an emergency, couldn't find you."

"What's so urgent that it couldn't wait for me to okay it?" Hitchcock scowled, pointing an accusatory finger at Asing. "You know the rules. Explain yourself."

"Robinson of the *Hinode Times* called about midnight. Duty sergeant put him off. Before he died, the publisher said: 'Death is coming to…' When I was notified this morning, I got ahold of Kingsley. We rushed to Robinson's home. The man was dead, next to a broken telephone. From evidence we found the killer is a Filipino Communist named Miguel. He plans to ambush members of the HSPA. I sent out officers to protect them. I made calls. Couldn't reach Patterson. Kingsley is on his way to his house. He thinks the HSPA chairman is the first to be murdered."

"Kingsley! Patterson hates him. Why would he protect that man?"

"He believes the killing must stop. Miguel has already murdered three. The man is out for vengeance against the HSPA and plans to wipe them out."

"We never should have let those danged Malays into this country. The number one criminal in prison are Filipinos, it used to be Hawaiians. They are a travesty, parading around in zany outfits like a bunch of peacocks. Then there are the dance halls where they love to cozy up to white women.

Don't seem to like their own kind. Pretty soon they are going to try to marry these gals and contaminate the great Nordic race."

"It's not their fault they search for love. Plantations didn't allow them to bring families or Filipino ladies. The sugar people just wanted to bring in uneducated men who wouldn't give them any trouble."

"Didn't do the HSPA any good. They went on strike twice. Once in 1920 and again this year. Only way the present walkout ended was by gunfire. That's what you need to do, use force to put fear into their hearts."

"I can't believe that is the only answer to labor unrest. How about equal pay for equal work regardless of color? How about reasonable working hours, like forty a week instead of sixty? The HSPA created this serial killer by violence to end a strike. In a way, this vendetta of Miguel is justified by this repressive society we have in Hawaii."

"Whoa there, you are talking like a radical, even like a pinko Communist. Watch your language."

"I'm not saying anything that is untrue. Any person who looks at this one-sided situation we have in the islands would realize we are ripe for revolt. Plantations bring in all these different races to pit one against the other to somehow buy labor peace. This has backfired at least in this instance. What's that old Biblical phrase: 'As ye sow so shall ye reap'? If all you do is plant discord, what do you expect to grow?"

A rapid knock interrupted the conversation. An officer looked in, "Reports of gunfire in upper Nuuanu, in the vicinity of Patterson's home."

"Got to go. You, grab a gun and come with me." Asing and the officer rushed out of the station, into a waiting police car and throttled fast toward Nuuanu.

A warm sun bathed the island on a crystal-clear tropical day. Asing worried about his friend, wondering if somehow Kingsley had been killed by the assassin. He saw traffic ahead and turned on his siren and warning light. He crossed Vineyard and headed onto Nuuanu Street. A black Ford going south attempting to pass another vehicle nearly smashed into the police car. Only by swerving hard right and driving into the grass border was Asing able to avoid a collision.

"Damn fool," Asing yelled. "Didn't you see the red light and hear the siren?"

The Ford passed by. Asing couldn't see the driver. He thought to go after him, but decided his mission to Patterson's home was more important. He drove off the grass onto the roadway and headed north on Nuuanu.

# CHAPTER 68

Southbound, Grant saw that traffic was sparse. Two blocks ahead, he spied the black Ford cutting around a slower vehicle and nearly colliding with another one. "Police car, stop that vehicle," he shouted. But no one heard him, and the Ford kept going south.

Grant stepped on the gas but slowed when he saw the red light and siren blaring on the auto ahead. He recognized the driver. "Asing, Miguel in black Ford, follow me." He didn't wait for confirmation of his demand but continued after the pursuit.

He wondered if Miguel intended to get to Ala Moana and head toward Waikiki, but he caught a glimpse of a black car turning left onto King Street. Traffic was heavier on this roadway. Despite this, Grant got closer to the fleeing Ford. He was unsure how he would stop the car. He didn't dare fire his pistol. There were too many vehicles and pedestrians. Puzzled, he continued his pursuit. The black car would have to stop sometime.

Once they passed Iolani Palace, the Ford sped up. Grant throttled his car faster. The gap between the vehicles narrowed. But he was forced to slow down by an intervening vehicle. The three cars raced up a hill, the Ford in the lead. Grant had to slow as the middle car reduced speed to make a left turn. He watched the black car crest the hill and disappear.

Once the roadway cleared, Grant accelerated then slowed, approaching the top of the rise. A trap could lie below.

He rolled over the crest. Death stared at him. The Ford lay athwart the lane, Miguel rested his elbow on its hood with a sniper's rifle aimed at Grant's car. If he swerved left, he would drive into oncoming traffic or right he would enter the shoulder of the road with his entire body exposed to a shot.

Grant pulled the wheel right then sprawled onto the passenger's seat and grasped the parking brake as he moved down. A bullet shattered side window glass. Another shot thudded into the metal door frame. The driverless vehicle bumped over a rock and hit a stone wall with a loud crunching of metal. The hood popped open and steaming water boiled out of the radiator.

Shaken but uninjured, Grant forced open the passenger door. Miguel had stopped firing. Probably waiting to see if I emerge, Grant thought. He rolled out of the car. It lay wedged into a concrete enclosure. To his left, the roadway was clear of autos. He crawled to that side of his vehicle, peering below the body of the car as he went. He reasoned his attacker still waited below, refusing to run if he could still kill him.

Far behind, Grant heard an approaching siren. Asing sped into an ambush. He had to expose himself to save his friend.

In a crouch, Grant scrambled up the slope, weaving as he ran. A bullet plowed into the roadway to his right. "Miguel thinks I'll act like a frightened deer and go left," he muttered as he ran onto the roadway before darting in the other direction. A bullet plowed into the highway where he had been.

The sound of the siren neared the crest of the hill. With a supreme effort, he bolted to the top, waving his hands, headless of the danger. A death shot did not come. Asing's police car slowed to a stop below the top of the hill. Grant rushed to the detective, "Miguel, ambush below."

Asing nodded, "This is officer Maka, Grant Kingsley. You two work your way up the hill and check things out. I'll keep the car ready to go if we need to move fast."

Grant heard screeching tires. "I think our quarry is leaving."

"Get in," Asing yelled.

The detective gunned the engine. Over the crest they bounced and spotted the Ford racing on the roadway ahead of them. "Siren and red light on. We will catch him."

The distance between the cars rapidly closed. "Get your pistols out," Asing ordered. "Lean out the windows and shoot the tires."

Almost within range, a green pickup driven by an old papa-san turned onto the highway. A large pig tethered to the bed of the vehicle stared at the rapidly approaching police car and squealed as if anticipating a collision.

Asing swerved left, his car skidding along the pavement. An approaching car cut to the right flinging up dirt and debris from the side of the road. The heavy braking caused the police car to tip up on its two right wheels before it came to a sudden stop then settled back to the pavement.

"I okay, how about you guys?" Asing asked.

"Good," both men answered.

The driver of the car that had swerved onto the shoulder got out of his vehicle and shook his fist, "You crazy. You almost killed me," he yelled.

"Hey, 'brah, wats a matter you, wats a matter me? You no see da kine red light and siren? You got to pull over. We chasing criminal, got to go," Asing answered. He turned the police car back into its lane and sped on in pursuit.

The green truck lay ahead, the pig, now quiet, its wide eyes staring at the approaching police car. Despite the siren and red light, the old driver did not pull over.

"This guy is deaf," Asing complained.

"Hey, what you going to do? An old man, probably senile," Maka answered.

"Senile enough to almost get us killed. He's letting Miguel get away."

"I don't think we have too much to worry about. This is a country road. It leads up to Hanauma Bay and Koko Head Crater. I can't figure out why he is heading that way, unless he is planning another ambush, which is a possibility," Grant said.

The green truck turned off the highway. Asing blared his horn, the pig oinked back, and the vehicle it rode in bumped over the humps of a dirt road, unsettling the animal, rousing his squeals to a higher pitch. Its cries, the blaring horn, and the siren made a rising cacophony of sound which did not cause the old man to slow his truck and investigate. He simply drove on, heedless of the medley of bizarre noises that pierced the air.

Grant laughed. "If we weren't trying to catch a killer, I'd visit that old guy, tell him about this adventure, and find out if he heard anything. My guess is he missed what happened."

"Man should lose his driver's license," Asing groused. "We almost had Miguel. Now he is far ahead, on his way up the hill that overlooks Hanauma Bay."

"Be careful, he could be waiting in ambush when we reach the top."

"I hear you, but I got a plan."

"Okay, you're the driver. Tell us what to do."

"Get out your guns. Be ready if there's a sudden stop. I'm turning right near the crest. Head for the ocean then turn left. Road is straight for a hundred yards or more. That's the place to ambush us. Here we go up the hill, right, then left again."

Grant saw the Ford blocking the lane. Miguel braced himself with his rifle on the hood of his car. "Incoming," Grant shouted.

"Duck," Asing answered. "Ramming speed."

A bullet shattered the windshield. Another shot plowed into the engine. The police vehicle headed dead center for the Ford and the sniper. Another shot struck the car, then the siren squealed to a halt as the police vehicle smashed into Miguel's car.

# CHAPTER 69

Braced for impact, Grant felt his body slam forward into the seat ahead and then back into the rear cushions. He sensed the force of the collision pushed both vehicles to the right. He did not know if the ground they slid over sloped to the sea. If it did, they faced a greater calamity then the initial crash. He had to get out.

Grant pushed out of the police vehicle before it came to a stop. He stumbled on rocks that littered the shoulder of road. He saved himself from falling over an incline by dropping to the ground.

On his buttocks, Grant swerved his eyes right and left. The Ford lay stopped and partially tilted toward the sea, the police car nestled into the middle of it. He could see the blow hole in the distance. Waves crashed into its protective rocks and then flew foam high into the air. He did not see Miguel. He called, "Asing, Maka, you guys okay?"

"I'm dizzy," Maka answered. "Asing is out, breathing. No blood."

"Can you leave the car?"

"I think door jammed."

"Climb over. Rear door opens. I'm going to find Miguel."

Grant dashed to a large boulder to the left of the smashed cars. Koko Head Crater sloped upward toward the round crest of the dormant volcano. Rocks and shrubs pocked the hill side. Excellent high ground for a sniper, Grant thought. He could see the roadway ahead, winding in hairpin curves toward Waimanalo. He wondered if Miguel had purposely chosen this wild and beautiful spot for a final showdown. It seemed foolish for him to do so. He could not escape.

Should he just wait here, sheltered by the huge rock, Grant thought? Miguel had a rifle that outranged his pistol by hundreds of yards. It would be safer to remain hidden, staying put he would not be shot.

Worry nagged Grant. Did Asing need medical help? The coastline roadway led to Honolulu. What if Miguel commandeered a passing car and killed its occupants? He just couldn't take the chance of this deranged killer being on the loose and a threat to people. He must flush the man out and end his terror trip forever.

Grant crouched and carefully edged to the right. He focused on the ground, studying the roadway, its edge, and the descending rocks beyond. Waves crashed on the shoreline, their incessant pounding and the wind the only noise. Maka lay outside the police car, sheltering in the protection of the two joined vehicles. He gave thumbs up. The policeman nodded, shaking his head from side to side. Grant realized that for the moment, he would be on his own.

He moved to the left, peering out from the edge of a boulder at the rugged land on the ocean side of the crater. Bushes, grass, jutting rocks covered the ground. No human shapes were visible. He judged from the slope that a sniper might find it difficult to secure level ground to accurately fire his weapon. Grant also suspected Miguel did not have enough time after the crash to find a convenient spot to use his long-range weapon.

He crouched and stumbled uphill, keeping low. His eyes focused on the terrain around him. Grant looked for bushes high enough to conceal a man, but on ground flat enough to allow a gunman to kneel or lie prone to fire a killing shot.

Grant's breath came quickly as the climb became steeper. He held rocks in his hand, ready to use them. He judged it time to make something happen. He bent back as he had been taught to throw a grenade, and flung a stone into brush below him.

The ruse worked. Miguel rose and fired. He was below Grant, not more than fifty feet away. In pistol range. He triggered his weapon and got off a snap shot. The Filipino shrieked and fell back into the brush.

Elated but cautious, Grant stumbled down the crater side, loose rocks starting a small avalanche which almost unsettled his plunge. He kept his pistol cocked. Ready for anything. Brush moved, he judged it to be Miguel. His heart pounded with the excitement of the chase, and he fired again.

Only the noises of nature and the crack of the escaping bullet buffeted his ears. No one screamed. Amid all the sounds, he heard something thrashing in the shrubs. Without hesitating Grant plunged into the scrub, heading in the direction that he heard telltale signs of movement.

He had an adrenalin rush of energy as he forced his way through the spiky grass that grew in clumps on the hillside. He did not worry about the rifle. He realized it would be unwieldy in the natural growth about him. His pistol was a perfect short-range weapon in these shrubs. He hadn't counted on another weapon just as deadly in close quarters.

A long knife thrust at him through the brush. Grant barely had time to hit the hand away with his pistol. He felt sharp metal slash his skin, followed by a backward slice of the object across his arm. His pistol fell to the ground as Miguel's body barreled into him, forcing Grant backward onto his buttocks.

He realized that all his martial arts training would be useless in such rugged terrain. It would be strength against strength, and right now a berserk man lay on top of him with a knife plunging toward his chest.

He grabbed the descending arm, stopping the killing strike for a moment. With his free hand, he sought Miguel's throat. The Filipino pushed it away, but the momentum of his movement and the slope of the hill tipped both men sideways, and they slid out of the brush.

The struggle became fierce as Miguel tried to free himself from Grant's grasp and plunge his knife into his heart. With a cry the Filipino yelled, "Die capitalist dog!" And with an insane frenzy, he forced the point of the weapon to Grant's chest.

Death only a shirt's width away, Grant thrust the fingers of his hand into Miguel's eyes.

The saboteur emitted a wild shriek, dropped the knife, rose, and staggered away with his hands to his face. Grant stood, seized the fallen knife, and went after the agonized Filipino. The imminence of his near death and the killing of his father released an anger within him that he could no longer control.

The two men stumbled onto the roadway. Though in agony, Miguel seemed to sense Grant's attack. He raised a hand to fend his opponent off. But Grant ignored the restraint and plunged the knife into Miguel's side.

The deadly thrust brought the two men together. Miguel wrapped his arms around Grant, falling backwards over the edge of the road. The ground sloped and Miguel struggled to pull his opponent toward a cliff's edge.

Surprised by the strength of the wounded man and realizing his intent to bring both of them to the brink of death, Grant thrust the knife into Miguel's chest. He felt rewarded for his final effort by convulsions in the Filipino's body and an end to his efforts to reach the edge of the cliff.

Grant pulled himself away from the dead man.

*What a waste of lives, all caused by plantation greed.*

# CHAPTER 70

Flowers filled the altar and spilled over the railing onto the main floor of the church. Mourners sat in the pews and temporary chairs lined the sides and rear of the place of worship.

David, Dorothy, and Grant gave moving eulogies of their dead father. None of them mentioned the reason he had been struck down or the confrontation with the HSPA. They paid respect to the wonderful father he had been and his special love for each of his children. There were tears shed as they spoke, especially Grant who eulogized the humanity of his father when he returned to Hawaii after the Great War.

Not to be outdone by the children of the deceased, Reverend Rollins gave a rousing recounting of James Kingsley's life in the islands. "He came as a financier from New York at a time when the plantations were growing in number after the Civil War. It would be his money which allowed entrepreneurs to begin new mills and with the coming of reciprocity his efforts fueled the economic boom that saw the number of plantations quadruple and the imported workers multiply in number by the thousands.

"He was a great supporter of the business community during the difficult times of the dying monarchy. Along with his father-in-law he held together the new government that replaced the queen and financed the administration of the Republic.

"A believer in the importance of the HSPA he helped that organization weather the many labor storms of the first decade of this new century. The presence of so many business and community leaders here today are evidence of the great role that James Kingsley played in turning Hawaii into an economic sugar giant."

At the reception following the funeral, David approached Grant. "Dorothy and I have been discussing the future. I know you don't have any great love for the plantations with all the strife it has caused you. For me, I'm tired of trying to run the operations. We believe that it is time to sell what we have. From past conversations I sense you have no objections to doing that. Your law practice has been profitable and will get better with the peace you have made with the HSPA."

"There is no peace if Patterson believes I am a Mikado Lover."

David laughed. "I didn't think you could be so pessimistic. Whether you believe it or not you've become a folk hero like Saint George who slayed the dragon. This saboteur had become a major boogie man, with all the bizarre devices he used to kill people. You can't believe how frightened he made the folks at the Big Five."

"I hope it proves to be a wake-up call for them to treat workers fairly."

David laughed so hard, people around the two men stopped talking and stared at them. With a Cheshire cat smile on his face David whispered, "You know what they say about legends, once the dragon is slain everybody lives happily ever after. No, my optimistic brother, nothing will change. You got rid of a troublesome pest and the crisis is over. It's 'Go forward and make more profits'."

Grant's brow wrinkled. "What you're saying is we should be thankful if we can sell out and you can get out of town with a whole skin."

"Exactly. I'm getting good comments from the board. I don't think we will be hurt too bad when we put our property on the line. I know Patterson is eager to talk to you. He sent me over to make sure you're okay. Please be nice to him and not grouchy. Dorothy and I need to make good deals for our property in Hawaii, especially since I can use the money to have a new beginning in Los Angeles."

"So that's what this chumminess is all about. Okay, I won't be the one to make waves that unsettle your plans."

"Good. I think Patterson's coming over to talk to you now." David left.

Grant waited for the rich plantation man to work his way through the reception crowd and walk to him. With a crescent moon smile on his face Patterson reached out his hand, "I want to thank you for saving my life.

From what I have been told, you put yourself in danger to ensure that the rotten scoundrel who haunted us missed his shot. As it was, he came dangerously close, his bullet hit the door frame above my head. An unbelievable shot from eight hundred yards away."

"I'm happy I spoiled his aim. From his scream I think I nicked him."

"The report said he turned his gun on you. How did you escape?"

"Went to the ground like I had been taught during the war. Show only a low profile. His bullet passed over my head."

"Then I understand you got involved in a dangerous high-speed chase. Why didn't you let the police handle it?"

"From what I knew I believed he intended to kill all three of you. If he got away then Marston and Doolittle might be his next victims and, who knows, maybe he would try to get you again."

Patterson frowned. "That is what my fellow board members believe. He would try to kill us all, and with that rifle he might have succeeded. That's why we of the HSPA are grateful to you for risking your life and hunting him down. I know I have insulted you in the past for being Japanese friendly. I apologize for my intemperate remarks. You must understand how hard this is for me to do. I firmly believe, from all my dealings with the Japanese, that they intend to seize control of these islands for the emperor."

Grant stifled a caustic response, mindful of his brother's request. "No apologies necessary. I had to find my father's murderer and bring him to justice."

"And you wound up killing him."

"I had no choice. He had a knife to my heart. I did what I had to do to survive."

"Yes, I can appreciate that, but I would love to have seen him squirm as he swung back and forth at the end of a rope."

Grant bit his tongue. He wanted to yell, 'None of this would have happened if you treated men fairly instead of fostering a massacre'. Instead, he controlled the anger that welled up inside him and said, "My brother wants to sell what we have. He believes you won't oppose us."

Patterson smiled. "He reads our intentions exactly. At the moment it is a good market. The economy is booming. There is an unparalleled rise in the stock market. People are making fortunes. We will not impede your sales and possibly even acquire what you have at the market price. This is to show our appreciation for what you have done."

"Thank you for your cooperation. I'll let David know what you have said."

"Be assured I am grateful for saving my life and uncovering the truth behind the killing of your father and the attacks on the HSPA." Patterson grasped Grant and drew him in. "You are a hero," he said, then released him from his grasp.

Grant sighed, "All I can say is 'All's well that ends well'."

"With that I can agree. I'm glad that there are no hard feelings between us."

Grant nodded.

Patterson left.

Grant decided to search for Selena and seek comfort in her undivided love.

# Epilogue

When fifteen Japanese labor leaders were convicted and imprisoned in 1922, followed by the Hanapepe massacre in 1924, and the subsequent conviction and imprisonment of Filipino strike leaders, the sugar plantations in Hawaii acquired an uneasy labor peace for a few years.

On the West Coast of America in the mid-1930s, the longshoremen of the ILWU flexed their muscle. Waterfront work stoppages in San Francisco would be joined in by harbor workers in Hawaii. Since eighty-five percent of all goods consumed in Hawaii are imported, and sugar and pineapple depend on shipping for export, labor strikes at the seaports meant economic disaster for the islands. Financial concessions to stevedores were made by the Big Five companies to ensure a constant flow of products and produce in and out of the islands.

The use of deadly force to suppress unionism did not end. In August of 1938 in Hilo, Hawaii, fifty unarmed union supporters of striking longshoremen were shot and bayoneted by policemen. In the aftermath of the bloody event, the authorities whitewashed the force used as necessary to end turmoil on the waterfront.

For the next three years unionism in Hawaii flourished. Serious labor unrest was halted by the attack on Pearl Harbor in 1941 and the resulting declaration of martial law. Strikes were suppressed as unpatriotic. Despite this, a working relationship developed between the military and labor groups.

With peace, union organizers went to work to encourage all workers to unite as one to seek fair wages and working conditions. Led by the ILWU and its chief, Harry Bridges, more than 28,000 plantation workers went out on strike in 1946. Unlike previous times, the union people stuck together. This unified approach allowed the strikers to achieve a successful conclusion to their walkout. Harry Bridges would announce: "Hawaii is no longer a feudal colony, and the Hawaiian agricultural worker is the highest paid in the world."

It would take another eight years before this labor success finally concluded in a social revolution in Hawaii with the sweeping legislative victories by the Democrats in the 1954 elections. The absolute political power of the Big Five companies came to an end.

Great wealth had been acquired by the plantation owners through importing poorly paid foreign workers to labor in the sugar fields. Once agricultural wages and benefits soared, the mill owners could no longer compete with foreign growers.

At the start of the 20th century there were one hundred sugar plantations. By 1980 there were fewer than a handful struggling to survive. The pineapple canneries that had at one time flourished in the islands were closed. The economy of Hawaii shifted to tourism, the military, and construction.

Radical economic and political change came to the islands, not by a bloody revolution or the beheading of an aristocracy, but through democratic means. Unified protests by the laborer and the use of the election process brought better living and working conditions for the masses of immigrants brought to work on the plantations and for their children.

After completing this novel, the Kaua'i *Garden Island News* featured the *Hanapepe Massacre Mystery* in articles in Sept. 27 – October 1, 2019, papers. An award-winning documentary film maker raised on Kaua'i, Stephanie J. Castillo, brought a film crew for a future PBS documentary. The local chapter of the Filipino American National Historical Society members assisted her.

# ABOUT THE AUTHOR

Bill Fernandez, half native Hawaiian, was born in Kapaa, on the island of Kauai in the state of Hawaii, and is a graduate of Kamehameha Schools, Stanford University, and its Law School. He practiced law in Sunnyvale, California, the future home of Silicon Valley, served as its mayor, and was appointed to the Santa Clara County Courts. Married and retired, he and his wife returned home to Kauai where he began his writing career. He served on the board and as president of the Kauai Historical Society, is on the boards of Hale Opio, a social service agency on Kauai, and the Kauai Native Hawaiian Chamber of Commerce. The governor appointed him to the Juvenile Justice State Advisory Commission.

To learn more about Bill and his books, visit his web site and fcb page at www.kauaibillfernandez.com.

fcb: Bill Fernandez Hawaiian Author

Books available at the Kauai Museum, Hanapepe Bookstore, the Kauai Store in Kapaa, other local Hawaii stores, and on Amazon.

## Bibliography:

Alcantara, R. *Filipino History in Hawaii Before 1946; The Sakada Years of Filipinos in Hawaii: Lorton, VA 1988.*

*Plaque Remembers Hanapepe Massacre*, Associated Press. Sept.10, 2006.

Tiffany Hill. *A Massacre Forgotten*. Honolulu Magazine. Dec. 30, 2009.

*Hanapepe Massacre*. Wikipedia.

Burley, Stewart. *Hanapape Massacre: 9 September 1924*. Private term paper; author now deceased. December 2019.

*Hanapepe Massacre: 9 September 1924*

Was it a strike or incident?

By

Stewart Burley
For HST 496H
December 2006

They came from the cities, suburbs and fields of different islands in the Philippines. They spoke three dialects. They wanted a better life. They heard about high pay. They heard that they could go to Hawaii, make big money and return home to the Philippines. They heard how they could help their families. They received a prize or a reward of ten dollars to go. [1]

Then…They signed up and said good-bye to their families. They boarded ships like the SS. General W.H. Gordon and sailed to Honolulu.

They were the last immigrant group to arrive on Hawaii's sugar plantations. Approximately 48,000 Filipinos, more than four-fifths of whom were men, were brought to Hawaii between 1906 and 1924. [1]

These were Filipinos. Some were educated, some were field laborers Those who were educated usually started a business. Many of the laborers sailed on to Kauai on interisland ships like the S.S.Kilauea. They started work at the Kapaa, Kolea, Olokele, Makee, Lihue and Kekaha Plantations.

Then...They found out the pay was the lowest on the plantations, living conditions were poor, the hours were long and most of the haole luna (white bosses) were mean. They were given the least desirable jobs. A 12-hour day in the hot sun was normal. Sickness was not tolerated. It was not an excuse to stay home sick. The company store took much of their meager wages. They watched the Japanese laborers. The Japanese were organized. They had one language and a newspaper. The Filipinos had problems organizing. They were divided by background, culture and three dialects. The Visayan from the central and southern islands of the Philippines stayed together. The Ilocano from the main island seaports of Manila, Davao, Cebu and Zamboanga of the Philippines stayed together. The Tagalog from the main islands stayed together.

Pablo Manlapit emerged as a leader among the Visayans. He organized the first Filipino newspaper in Hawaii and became a labor organizer. He urged the Filipino laborers to join the Hawaiian Sugar Planters Association (HSPA) and then asked the plantations for a double wage increase. He worked for equal wages for both men and women and tried to set an eight-hour day. [2]

Cayetano Ligot convinced the Ilocano population not to join. He claimed the working conditions were better in Hawaii than the Philippines. He asked Hawaii Ilocano Filipinos to be content and work hard for their wages. [2]

An overwhelming proportion of single men compared to women, scant education, a general lack of community roots, and the lowest status jobs became part of the problem which helped fuel the 1924 strike on Kauai sugar plantations. Pablo Manlapit called a strike on 21 July at the

Lihue and Koloa Sugar Plantations. Only the Visayan went on strike. The Ilocano followed the words of Cayetano Ligot and tried to remain on the job. By 5 August there were over 300 Filipino strikers housed in Kapaa and Hanapepe. On 12 August the Visayan Filipinos of Makee Sugar Plantation and Kapaa Sugar Plantation went on strike The Ilocano still refused to strike. [3]

On Tuesday, 12 August 1924, a strike was also called at the Hawaiian Sugar Company plantation at Makaweli – a small community about 5 miles west of Hanapepe. Again, only Visayan took part in the walkout. The Ilocano remained at work. The strikers from Makaweli were quartered at the old Japanese School in Hanapepe which was right next to the Brodie banana patch. [3]

The first incident happened that very same day, 12 August. Two Ilocano tried to leave and the strikers held them. Sheriff Rice, in Lihue about 17 miles east of Hanapepe. Two Ilocano tried to leave and the strikers held them. Sheriff Rice, in Lihue about 17 miles east of Hanapepe, was called to take care of the incident. When the Sheriff arrived in Hanapepe at the old Japanese School, he asked the Ilocano Filipino to come out, but the Filipino was scared due to possible later retaliation. Sheriff Rice, with the help of the Deputy Sheriff Crowell, took care of the incident. However, this was just the spark that set off the incident four weeks later on 9 September which resulted in a massacre of 16 Filipinos and 4 law enforcement officers. [3]

On the infamous day of 9 September, two Ilocano Filipinos went into Hanapepe to purchase goods at the store. As they returned back home, the Visayan strikers near the banana patch captured them and would not let them go. The banana patch was on the main road into Hanapepe next to the old Japanese Language School. The banana patch was owned by Brodie. [3]

Sheriff Rice was called again about this incident, so Sheriff Rice sent Deputy Sheriff Crowell to get the two Ilocano and take them to Lihue where they could press charges. Deputy Sheriff Crowell took some back-up help with him. When they arrived, the strikers with the two captured

Ilocano were at the old Japanese School which was on the Waimea side of the Hanapepe River near the Brodie banana patch.[3]

Deputy Sheriff Crowell asked the strike leaders to allow the two Ilocano to come to his office as he was under the impression that they were being intimidated. The strike leader refused to give the two Ilocano over to Deputy Sheriff Crowell. In order to better speak with the strike leaders, Deputy Sheriff Crowell took a Filipino with him to explain what was wanted. The two Ilocano were eventually turned over to Deputy Sheriff Crowell, but in the meantime, the strikers started to gather around the law enforcement officers. Deputy Sheriff Crowell started to back away from the gathering Visayans. He saw that they were armed with cane knives, guns, hoes and rakes. [3]

Deputy Sheriff Crowell cautioned his men not to shoot unless he gave the order. The Visayans kept pressing the police against the police cars and trucks and then someone fired a gun. No one remembers who that set off a chain reaction with bullets flying both ways. The police had rifles and Filipinos had hand guns with two bullets. [1] The majority of the Visayans who were in the rear of the group broke and ran when the gunfire started. Those in the front row were shot down like fish in a barrel. A Filipino jumped at Deputy Sheriff Crowell with a cane knife and cut him on the head and arm before the Deputy shot him. If it had not been for some sharpshooters stationed on a knoll nearby, Deputy Sheriff Crowell would have been killed. The massacre became a bloodbath of Filipino and Hawaiian blood. [3]

The wounded and bodies were later taken to the Makaweli Hospital until it overflowed. The rest were taken to the Waimea Hospital. All of the deceased Filipinos were identified, but to this day the actual names are not known. Some had only one name. [3]

No one won this confrontation. Both sides lost. The greatest loss was lives. The names of the Filipinos are unknown. The names of the deceased police are:

Ah Boo – stabbed in abdomen

Moke Kua – shot over the heart
Kailuaaiai – shot in the abdomen
Kipe Naumu – shot in the abdomen
The two police officers who were wounded are:
Henry Naumu – stabbed in the neck and back
Deputy Sheriff Crowell – cut on the head and arm

The people of Hanapepe, the striking Filipino laborers and police were shocked. The next thing they watched was the digging for a mass grave and the bodies being placed in the mass grave. The earth was shoveled over the bodies in the mass grave. No marker was made – no grave stones carved – no cross driven over the mass grave. Only three wives attended the mass burial because of possible retaliation.

Some of the present stories of where the mass grave is tell of it being under the Banana Patch store. This store was once the Hanapepe Pool Hall and is now on the National Historical Buildings list. Another story has the grave in Glass Beach in Port Allen. Another story has the grave on Puolo Road on the Hanapepe River side.

It is now 2006 and a show of respect was performed in Hanapepe. A small monument was placed in Hanapepe Park where the present-day Farmer's Market is held every Thursday. The words on the monument are:

*"Hanapepe Massacre: On September 9, 1924, at the height of the Filipino sugar plantation strike in Kauai, sixteen (16) Filipino Plantation workers of Visayan ancestry and four (4) local policemen died during a violent confrontation along Hanapepe Road. This incident has come to be known as the "Hanapepe Massacre".*

*The lapse of time and the loss of records have obscured the identities of several of those who died. Out of respect for those whose names are not known, none shall be listed here. They shall remain nameless, known only to themselves, to their families, and to God, until time shall have discovered their complete identities.*

*This marker honors the memory of all those who died in this incident, and commemorates an event that symbolizes the significant role played by Filipino workers in the long and bitter history of the labor movement in Hawaii.*

*Acknowledgements – This memorial was made possible through the efforts of the Filipino Centennial Celebration Commission, The County of Kauai, the Kauai Filipino Centennial Committee, The Congress of Visayan Organizations, the Kauai Visayan Club, ILWU Local 142 and HERE Local 5 AFL-CIO.*

*Hanapepe, Kauai – September 9, 2006*

The Filipino mass grave is the area between the two trash cans on the right and the freshly dug grave on the left. This is located in the Filipino graveyard in Hanapepe.

[Author Bill Fernandez note: Mr. Burley then interviewed several people to track down the site of the mass grave. Since I do not personally have their permission to use their names, I will not include these conversations.]

Bibliography:

[1] University of Hawaii Center for Oral History, Historical Events: The 1924 Filipino Strike on Kauai.

[2] John E. Reinecke, "*The Filipino Piecemeal Sugar Strike of 1924-25*", Honolulu, Hawaii, p. 1.

[3] The Garden Island Newspaper, September 9, 1924.

[4-9] Notes from personal interviews (not included).

# MAP OF HANAPEPE IN 1924

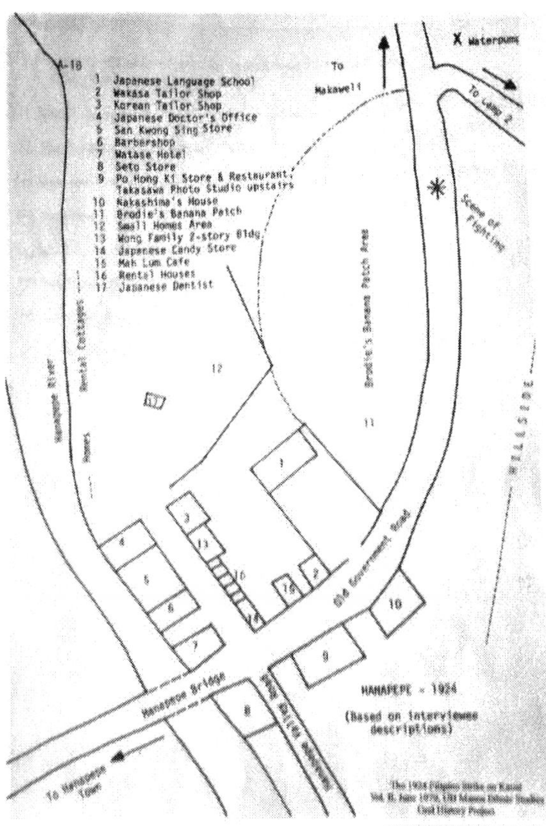

Author Bill Fernandez at Hanapepe Massacre Plaque
2019